Tempting TAYLOR

Books by Joan Elizabeth Ward

THE PRICE OF PLEASURE

NEVER ENOUGH

CLUB FANTASY

NIGHT AFTER NIGHT

THE SECRET LIVES OF HOUSEWIVES

NAUGHTIER BEDTIME STORIES

HOT SUMMER NIGHTS

MADE FOR SEX

THE MADAM OF MAPLE COURT

TAKE ME TO BED

TEMPTING TAYLOR

Published by Kensington Publishing Corporation

Tempting TAYLOR

JOAN ELIZABETH LLOYD

KENSINGTON BOOKS
http://www.kensingtonbooks.com

KENSINGTON BOOKS are published by

Kensington Publishing Corp.
119 West 40th Street
New York, NY 10018

All Kensington titles, imprints, and distributed lines are available at special quantity discounts for bulk purchases for sales promotion, premiums, fund-raising, educational, or institutional use.

Special book excerpts or customized printings can also be created to fit specific needs. For details, write or phone the office of the Kensington Special Sales Manager: Kensington Publishing Corp., 119 West 40th Street, New York, NY 10018. Attn. Special Sales Department. Phone: 1-800-221-2647.

ISBN-13: 978-0-7582-2373-9
ISBN-10: 0-7582-2373-0

First Kensington Trade Paperback Printing: June 2009
10 9 8 7 6 5 4 3 2 1

Printed in the United States of America

Prologue

Logan Cortez had paid quite a tidy sum to have this fantasy of his fulfilled, and as he stepped into the backyard of the magnificent house on Maple Court, in Westchester County, New York, he had high hopes. He'd been warned to let go of his preconceived notions, but it would seem that he'd really lucked out, at least with the weather. It was midafternoon on a Tuesday, and although it was early April, the weather was unseasonably warm, the sky crystal clear and the sun bright, heating his skin. Had the people he'd paid all that money to been able to order such a perfect day? He almost believed so. He grinned. Yes, his fantasy was about to become reality. Could reality possibly live up to his dreams?

He'd been interviewed by a woman named Marcy at a coffee shop near Club Fantasy's Manhattan location. "She won't be the woman of your dreams," she had said. "We can try to match height, weight, and hair and eye color, but even if we're totally successful she won't be the person you've fantasized about for all these years. Please understand that."

He'd considered and nodded. It was sad that this wouldn't be his ideal woman but, of course, she couldn't be. His ideal woman lived only in his dreams. "I'll be content with whomever you come up with," he'd said. "I do want her to be very petite, however. That's a must."

"No problem," the woman had replied, smiling. "I've got the perfect woman in mind. You said on the phone that you want everything to happen outdoors and I have just the place. I know you'll be pleased, but, of course, your satisfaction is guaranteed."

He knew he could demand a refund if things didn't work out. "Your service comes very highly recommended, so I'm sure there will be no problems on that score." At three thousand dollars for the afternoon, there better not be. So many of his friends had told him about their fabulous experiences with Club Fantasy that he'd finally decided to give it a try. He and Marcy spent half an hour more in an extensive conversation about his desires, then he'd been given an address in Westchester, on a cul-de-sac called Maple Court. He arrived right on time.

He'd been told to walk around the garage. His dream woman would be waiting on the rear lawn of the large house. He barely noticed the house as he arrived in the yard, and then he'd seen her. She looked almost exactly as he pictured her every night. How they had managed to find his fantasy woman he neither knew nor cared.

Now he gazed at her as she extended her tiny hand to welcome him. She was exotic looking with stick-straight coal-black hair that hung almost to her waist and eyes that were almost as black, accented by long, black lashes and perfectly arching brows. Her complexion was dark, as if she'd spent time in the sun, and, in contrast, her lips were full and brilliant scarlet. All exactly as he'd wished. Beneath the soft robe she wore he could tell that she had a lush figure. Her breasts were obviously unfettered and they swayed as she moved, making his palms itch to feel the weight of them. And he would. In due time, but not just yet. He wanted to live this out to its fullest.

He felt a tingling in his groin and smiled his approval. No, she wasn't his fantasy woman—she was better because she was real, breathing and smiling at him. Without a word, she guided him toward a bright plaid woolen blanket that had been spread on the deep green lawn, among baskets and pots of brightly colored flowers. Splashes of the early afternoon sun illuminated her filmy gold caftan, gold bracelets and large, dangling gold earrings. She was barefoot and as she walked her full-length gown swayed just enough for him to see that her toes were polished bright red and she had an ankle bracelet joined to a ring on her center toe by a slender chain. She even smelled exotic, spicy and foreign.

"You look like some Middle Eastern princess from an *Arabian Nights* tale," he said, unable to believe his good fortune.

"Isn't that what you wanted?" she said softly, her voice a melody to his ears.

"Oh yes," he said, sighing at how right she was for him. "You're exactly what I ordered."

"Then let's have some wine."

A large hamper had been placed on the edge of the blanket and now Aisha—that was the name he'd given her years ago when his fantasy first materialized in his mind—settled gracefully beside it. From the basket she withdrew a bottle of red wine, two glasses and an opener. "Shall I serve you?" she asked with proper deference.

"Please," he said, settling beside her, stretching out and leaning on one elbow. She showed him the label and he saw that it was an exceptionally fine vintage from a grand cru vineyard he knew well. "A very good selection," he said, nodding for her to open it.

She was quick and deft, opening the bottle with smooth, sure movements, then pouring a small amount into a glass that she passed to him. He sipped, filling his senses with the rich, full flavor, and again nodded. He held out his glass and she filled it, then her own. "Would you care for something to eat?" she asked, her voice soft and sultry.

"Let's make this last," he said, nodding.

From the hamper she took a plate of hors d'oeuvres. "I have prepared a few delicacies I think you will like." He saw small slices of pâté on tiny crackers, surrounded by several kinds of black olives and cornichons, small sour pickles. She also had a fine triple crème blue cheese, neatly arranged toast points, intermingled with small green and red grapes. Marcy had obviously heard every word he'd said. "I hope this pleases you."

He loved the deference with which she spoke to him. It fit right into his fantasy: his power and her subservience. Add this wonderfully manicured lawn surrounded by already-blooming forsythia and early azalea, and air filled with the sounds of calling songbirds, and it couldn't have been planned better. He wanted to calm his delight. It just couldn't continue to be this wonderful. *Hell, relax and enjoy it, however it turns out,* he told himself. So far Club Fantasy really was living up to its reputation.

And Aisha. Ah yes, Aisha. Her attitude conveyed the essence of his fantasy without being overdone. Her head wasn't bowed, merely slightly lowered. Her hands moved gracefully, handing him tidbits from the platter, feeding him grapes. She refilled his glass often, with sure, easy movements.

They talked softly, with her asking him about the things that interested him, never injecting her views or opinions. *Perfect,* he thought again.

"I would like to see you now," he said when he could wait no longer.

She rose easily from the blanket, no awkwardness in her movements. Her gold robe fastened down the front with several dozen golden buttons which she opened one by one. She seemed to be moving quickly, but the robe parted exquisitely slowly. When it was open all the way down the front he realized that beneath it she wore only a slender gold chain around her waist. As he gazed at her, he saw that there was a second thin chain attached to the center of the first one which then pulled backward until it disappeared between the lush lips of her shaved cunt. God, she was more perfect than he could have imagined. He felt like a fool, thinking *perfect* with every gesture, every new revelation, but there was no other word for all of this.

She allowed the fabric to slide from her shoulders until she was naked.

"Would you like me to undress you?" Although she did not use the word *sir*, the deference was there in every line of her body. *Not too fast*, he thought and when he hesitated, she continued, "Perhaps you would care for a massage. I have very talented hands and I would love to touch you."

Massage? This wasn't part of his fantasy as he'd explained it to the woman named Marcy but what a wonderful idea. "I think I'd like that. Can it be done out here?" Being out of doors had always been part of his dreams.

"Of course. First, let me make you more comfortable."

She stood and guided him to a standing position. Her bracelets clinked together as she slowly unbuttoned his shirt, hands stroking his chest, fingers threading through his chest hair. As she moved around him he was surrounded by her exotic, spicy scent. Her nipples brushed his skin as if by accident. He was sure, however, that nothing this woman did was by accident.

She unfastened his belt and unzipped his slacks. He was hard and needy but he didn't want this to end too quickly. She brushed her palm lightly over his tented shorts, then slowly lowered his slacks and urged him to step out of them and his loafers. She knelt at his feet and carefully removed his socks, holding each foot in her hand and rubbing the arch as he kept his balance by leaning one hand on her naked shoulder. Then she removed his briefs, pausing only a moment to look at his raging erection.

"We're not nearly there yet," she said softly as she led him to a hot tub almost invisible among leafy green plants at the back of the property. She guided him to a padded bench beside it. As his legs brushed it he discovered that it was heated to counter any chill in the air. She took several towels from a compartment beside the spa and spread one on the bench, stacking the rest on the sun-warmed flagstones surrounding the water. Then she asked him to lie on his stomach on the heated surface. It took a moment for him to adjust his position so that his hard-on was comfortable.

He felt heated oil being poured into a pool on the small of his back and then Aisha's knowledgeable fingers went to work on his muscles. She spent long minutes on his shoulders, then slowly slid her oily fingers down one arm. More oil and his hand was slippery, allowing her to make love to each finger as if it were a cock. Yes, he thought with the small, coherent part of his brain, she was fucking his hand. It made his cock still harder, but somehow he was also relaxed. Eventually she moved to his other arm and repeated her ministrations with the fingers of his other hand.

It was amazing. He never would have imagined that, although his cock was rock hard beneath him, he would have the patience to let her work her magic on his body. Next time he pictured this scene as he masturbated in bed late at night he'd have new wrinkles to add to his long-honed fantasy.

His legs were next and he became aware that his toes were as sensitive as his fingers had been. When she dug her thumb into the arch of each foot it felt both relaxing and arousing. How that was he didn't know, but his body did. She inserted one finger between two of his toes and it was as though she fucked him there. He had thought he'd be too ticklish to deal with what she was doing, but squirming or laughing were the furthest things from his mind.

Her clever fingers then moved to his buttocks, kneading each cheek, pulling them apart, rubbing her slick fingers through the crack between, playing with his nether hole. He had never tried anal sex but now he realized there were so many nerves in that part of his body that his cock twitched as she touched him. One finger penetrated slightly, then she stopped.

He quickly realized that she was asking a question with her movements and when he slowly shook his head no she wiped her hands. "As you wish," she said softly.

She helped him over onto his back next and smiled as she ran an index finger slowly along the length of his raging hardness. "Mmm," she purred. "This will be mine soon." Then she spent a long time on his chest, playing with his nipples. Were men's nipples as sensitive as a woman's? He'd never thought about it, but his became erect as she lightly pinched and squeezed. She pressed her finger into his belly button and it was an additional intimacy. Finally she moved to his face and neck, moving to kneel behind his head to massage his scalp. As she worked, her breasts brushed against the sides of his head. Never had he been so relaxed and so aroused, both at the same time.

Finally she moved to his cock and balls, rubbing still more oil onto his sac, making him need to come, yet able to wait just a few minutes more. He realized that he was harder and hotter than he thought he'd ever been.

"How do you want me?" she asked softly. "My hands, my pussy?"

"I want it all," he moaned, "but I'd like your mouth this time. Next time I will want your cunt, or maybe your magnificent tits."

She wrapped the fingers of one hand around his thick staff

while cupping his balls with the other. Her scent almost overwhelmed him as she leaned over until her swollen nipples brushed his thighs and took his stiff cock into her mouth, swirling her tongue over the tip, then sucking the length into the hot wet cavern. "Shit," he hissed. "Too fast."

"Do you want me to stop?"

"Hell, no," he growled, knowing that stopping was out of the question now. "Do it."

She scratched her nails lightly over his testicles while she fucked his cock with her tongue. He felt climax boil in his belly and then semen spurt from him, filling her mouth. She swallowed most of his come, but a few drops dribbled from her lips, falling onto his belly. His climax seemed to last forever. God, she was worth every penny he'd paid and more. He lay on the bench for several minutes, trying to catch his breath. *If I die now,* he thought as his pulse finally slowed, *I die in ecstasy.*

There was an outdoor shower at the side of the house and later, beneath the warm water, she used her hands and the valley between her breasts to again bring him to climax. Two violent, gut-wrenching climaxes in under an hour. Amazing.

Finally, weak-kneed and totally sated, he dressed and left, knowing that all he had to do was call up Club Fantasy to arrange to meet her again. And he would, soon.

Pam DePalma wandered to the blanket and poured herself another glass of wine. As she sipped she heard his car back down her driveway, then she pulled off her wig and ran her fingers through her short, dark curls. As soon as she could wash the makeup off her face more thoroughly, she'd remove the hated colored contact lenses so her hazel eyes could stop itching, then shower off the exotic scent and tanning cream she'd found to wear today. It would take a week or so for her skin to return to its light tone but it had been well worth it.

She loved what she did and enjoyed the men in her life in whatever capacity. As she walked into her house, glass in hand, she smiled and thought of the twenty-five hundred dollars the afternoon had added to her bank account. And she was sure Logan would be back. She laughed out loud. The Madam of Maple Court had done it again.

Chapter 1

"He's going to take me. I'm really going along. It's going to be so great. My first real field trip."

Melissa Bonner's squealing voice was so loud that Taylor Barwick had to hold her cell phone inches from her ear. "Slow down, Lissa, and tell me how you finally got him to agree," she said, her voice pitched to its usually low, husky timbre.

"This trip's a six-month photo shoot in China somewhere. He's doing a spread for *National Geographic* and he's going to take me along. He's really going to take me." Tay knew all about the trip since Lissa had been talking about it for a month. However, she let her best friend prattle on. "We leave somewhere during the first week of April. I'm going. Come what may, I'm going."

"Okay, I get it. You're going. He's going to take you along." Her slight sarcasm was lost on her friend. Tay had known for several weeks that Dave Bonner, a world-renowned photojournalist and animal-rights activist, was going to spend from six months to a year in God-Knows-Where, China, photographing some endangered species or other. With a deep desire to follow in her famous father's footsteps, and a talented photographer in her own right, Lissa had been telling

Tay how she'd been deviling her dad to let her accompany him. Tay had seen a lot of her friend's work and she had to admit that Lissa knew how to tell an entire story with one photo or brief video clip. Her father had won numerous awards and his guidance would be of great help to his daughter.

Lissa had explained the art behind great photography several times. "Anyone who's ever written a short story thinks he or she is a great author and the only thing keeping them off the best-seller list is the time to actually sit down and write the great American novel. We all know that's not true at all.

"Well, it's the same with photography. Anyone with a digital camera thinks that taking really great pictures is just a matter of point-and-shoot. Dad learned, and has taught me, that great pictures take time, effort and patience."

The voice in Tay's cell phone continued. "Begging, whining and wheedling seems to finally have worked. I'm so excited." Her voice hadn't dropped from its original squeal and Tay flipped her cell phone to speaker and held it at arm's length.

"I'm delighted for you," she said, trying to sound overjoyed. She'd miss Lissa, the rock that had held her together since Steve's defection three months before.

Tay and Lissa had met in their freshman year at the Manhattan Art and Technology Institute. Over the seventy-five years since its founding as the Manhattan Art Institute it had added various aspects of computer graphics to its program so that, ten years before, the word *Technology* had been added to its original name. Lissa majored in photography, both still and movies, studying everything from composition and dark-room work to software and digital editing. Tay had gotten a small scholarship to study Web-page design and programming and from her first class had found that she loved the challenge of combining the artistic and practical.

The girls had met at freshman orientation and had almost

immediately become friends. Tay commuted from her family's home in New Jersey and Lissa took the train each day from Westchester County. Eventually, by taking on various part-time jobs, they'd been able to afford to move into a small loft in SoHo together, which they filled with furniture that they referred to as either Modern Salvation Army or Contemporary Castoff.

In her senior year Tay took advantage of a work-study program to intern with a small graphic-design firm that hired her immediately upon graduation. Tay had worked for them for a few years, then had been wooed away by the large multinational firm she still worked for.

After trying unsuccessfully to get freelance work, Lissa had taken a job with a small magazine, specializing in fabulous photographs of wildlife around the world. Although Lissa knew she had talent, she had confided to Tay that her father's name had opened doors for her. She'd always wondered whether her talent would have been enough on its own.

Once they were both working, they were delighted that they could finally afford to join the local health club and began to indulge one of their mutual interests, swimming. For years, since her dad had moved to their current house, Lissa had been able to swim several times a week in the Bonner pool. Tay had been on the swim team in high school and lamented that she was going to get flabby if she didn't get regular exercise.

They swam laps several times a week, keeping their bodies trim, enjoying the rhythmic strokes and racing toward the end to see who could complete fifty laps fastest. Then they'd lounge in the sauna while they unwound and shared the events of their respective days. The talk was usually about the guys they dated and their sex lives. Both women were open about their love of good, hot, steamy sex. It was gradually becoming awkward to combine a good love life with sharing an apartment, but they put up with it, inventing a series of signals to alert each other to the need for the other to "get a cup of coffee" at the local Starbucks.

The two women managed to continue to room together until a year after graduation, when they both were making enough so that Lissa could afford to move into her own place and Tay could pay the rent herself and keep the loft. Tay had continued to live there until she'd moved to Brooklyn Heights with Steve seven months before.

"So begging finally payed off," she said now into the phone's speaker.

Tay could hear Lissa's chuckle. "Yeah, that and persistence, moaning and the occasional tear. I pulled out all the stops. Oh, Tay, I wore him down and he's really agreed."

Tay huffed out a breath, genuinely delighted for her friend. "Lissa, I'm thrilled for you. I know you've wanted this for a long time."

She stopped pacing, dropped onto the bed and put her feet up. Now that Lissa had calmed a bit and her voice had gone back to its normal level, Tay flipped the speaker on the phone off and propped the instrument back against her ear. She looked around the small rented apartment, three months later still scattered with bits of her now-ex-boyfriend's stuff, detritus from their suddenly aborted love affair.

Love affair? Not! Certainly not on his part. It had taken longer than it should have for her to realize that she'd been a meal ticket, a sex partner and little else. Steve had been a taker and she, to her eternal shame, had done the giving until she began to wise up. That had been after a dinner just before Christmas, when they'd been living together for almost four months. They were sitting at the little kitchen table sipping glasses of Burgundy. As she thought back she remembered that as a special treat for him she'd bought a new, more expensive vintage.

"I'm sorry, Steve, but a two-thousand-dollar sound board

is out of the question," she said after he explained the intricacies and importance of a new piece of sound electronics.

"Listen, baby, you can afford it. I really need it and it could be my Christmas present. Without really top-of-the-line equipment the band's music sounds awful. Think of it as an investment in our future."

"How is my buying you a new sound board an investment in *our* future?"

"The band is a business. The new stuff that I'm writing is going to take Steak and Potatoes to the top of the charts. We might even let you do a vocal or two." Let her?

Dumb name, Steak and Potatoes. She'd been singing along with the band from time to time and had gotten a pretty good reception wherever they'd performed. Steve never said what kind of reaction they'd gotten without her. "You've posted a music video on YouTube and very few people have watched it," Tay said. "You thought that would be your big chance, but it hasn't turned out as well as you'd thought. Why don't we just wait until you've had a little more success?"

His face darkened. "No one's interested in it because I don't have the electronics to make it really great. I need a sound board and some really fine video equipment. But it's okay. You don't have any interest in my career. I can see that now."

"Career?" Her voice rose. "I talked Lissa into letting you use her digital camera and editing software to make that two-minute thing you call a music video and I provided some cash for God knows what. 'I'll get it back to you when this video makes us famous,' you said. Well, Steve, you still haven't made a dime and I've invested *mucho* bucks already."

"Okay, okay," Steve said, his attitude softening. "Let's just let this drop." He walked behind her chair and began to rub her neck to relieve the day's tension. Slowly his hands slipped down the front of her blouse, sliding beneath to find her nipples. Pulling and pinching, his fingers immediately caused the flesh between her legs to swell and moisten. "Oh baby," Steve said, "your body makes me hot."

Tay let her head fall back against his groin and she could feel his hard erection beneath his jeans. His hands were magical, playing her body as if it were one of his instruments. He leaned over and bit the tendon at the side of her neck, while he efficiently unbuttoned her blouse and rubbed her belly. The zipper of her slacks came next and all thought became impossible.

He walked around her chair and parted her knees so he could stand between them. She quickly freed his rampant cock from his slacks. Since he usually wore no underwear she could easily lick precome from the tip. She marveled that she could so easily excite him.

She sucked and listened to his moans. Then they were naked, stretched out on the bed in the tiny bedroom. He quickly covered his cock with a condom, his only accommodation to her needs, and, draping her legs over his shoulders, rammed his swollen erection deep inside her.

As always she was more than ready for him, and as one of his hands played with her nipple and the other rubbed her clit, she came. He continued to ride her while she rose again and her second climax was matched with his.

The following evening he brought up the subject of the sound board again, and when she again told him she wouldn't pay for it, he again made love to her. Later that night she told him that despite the sex she wasn't going to spend that kind of money on new equipment, Christmas gift or no Christmas gift.

"You're really serious," he said, incredulous.

"Totally." She was replete, happy after good lovemaking, but she was slowly smarting up, too. Any time she turned him down he fucked her brains out. As she thought back she realized that, up to now, it had always worked. Not anymore, she thought.

"I don't get your total disinterest in what I want."

"It's not what *I* want and not what I intend to do." She sighed. Sadly, it was time they had it out. Steve was going to have to decide whether he was in their relationship for her or her credit card. She was very afraid she knew the answer, but she hoped she was wrong. She had to be wrong.

She wasn't, and Steve moved out the following day. It had been a Saturday, and after a morning spent in bed, he'd asked again and again she'd turned him down. Furious now, finally realizing that she wasn't going to change her mind, he climbed out of bed and threw on his jeans and a T-shirt. He flung a few things into his backpack and said, "You're a selfish cunt. I don't understand why I'm not worth a measly few thousand dollars. Selfish, selfish, selfish. Well, so be it. I don't want anything more to do with you." He turned to her and said, "And your voice isn't that much, either. I'll be great without you. I don't need you."

Now that a decision had been made, Tay found herself surprisingly calm. She watched from bed as he pulled on his sneakers and stuffed his canvas bag with his precious DVDs and an assortment of video games she'd bought him. Grabbing both bags, he tucked his guitar under his arm and stormed out, slamming the door behind him and making the wood rattle.

The following day while she was at work he'd picked up his keyboard and amplifier and the pair of five-hundred-dollar speakers she'd gotten him for his birthday. For good measure, he also took the two hundred and fifty dollars she thought she'd secreted in her underwear drawer. That had been three months before and Tay was still smarting, not so much about Steve's leaving, but about her stupidity in letting him string her along for so long. Steve had manipulated her with sweet words, promises of making a life together once his career began to take off, and lots of really active sex. She'd had relationships before but never one like him, sex at least once a day, and she'd gotten used to it. Now she'd been without it for months and missed it. Her vibrator just wasn't enough. She'd gone to clubs and out with folks from her office but no one had clicked with her. The drought was beginning to get to her.

Tay tried to jam an errant strand of baby-fine deep blond hair back into the French braid that hung partway down her back, but when it flopped over her ear again, she merely tucked it behind.

Lissa squealed again, bringing Tay back to the present. Again she had to hold the phone at arm's length. "Calm down, Lissa. You're going to burst a gut and ruin my hearing."

"Sorry. Sorry. Okay, yeah, right." The tone of her friend's voice had changed slightly and slowly Tay sensed that something was up.

"I hear something in your tone. There's more, isn't there?" Tay said when Lissa became silent.

"Well, there is one thing. There's still one obstacle and I need your help."

What in the world could *she* do? "Okay, I'm listening."

Chapter 2

Tay could hear Lissa let out a long breath. "It's the animals." Lissa had three cats and two dogs, all adopted in one place or another, along with a snake, a rabbit and two ferrets.

The collection had begun when the girls first moved into their SoHo loft. "I'm a wildlife photographer so I have to have a good subject for my photos," Lissa had said, trying to justify bring home the largest, hairiest dog Tay had ever seen. Shades of white, gray and brown, the dog constantly had his tongue hanging out and seemed to pant even when sleeping, which he did most of the time.

"That," Tay had said, pointing to the hairy beast, "isn't wildlife."

"I know that, but he's going to teach me a lot about photographing animals."

"Animals. Is that what he is? He looks like Chewbacca from *Star Wars*. Remember that someone called him a walking carpet? Well, this guy doesn't walk upright, but the carpet part fits."

"Don't be like that," Lissa pouted. "I'll do all the walking and cleaning up, I promise. You won't even know he's around." She gazed at the dog. "I got him at the pound. They think he's mostly sheepdog, with a little other stuff thrown in. I call him Mopp. With two *p*'s."

Tay looked around the small apartment, shaking her head. "Lissa, we can't have a dog." She sounded less than convincing.

"Why not? There's nothing about dogs in the lease and he'll be a great guard dog."

"Sure," Tay said, looking into Mopp's sad eyes and wet mouth, "but only if a burglar was allergic to saliva." Tay gazed at the animal, thinking about the problems of dog hair on everything, but when Mopp stood, padded over and licked her hand she was hooked.

Tay, Lissa and Mopp made a workable threesome, with Lissa truly doing most of the doggie chores. Then, in the year before the two girls moved into their apartments, Lissa had added Precious, a tiny, homeless black and white kitten who'd grown into a cat with a remarkably miserable disposition, and Honey, a sweet Persian whose hair was almost as long as Mopp's. Each girl had adapted her wardrobe so that fur brushed off most things easily. Clothes brushes could be found everywhere in the apartment.

After she moved out, Lissa had added a homeless, mostly beagle puppy named Fred and a third cat, a gold and red tabby named Ginger, who had adopted Tay and curled in her lap any time she visited. Tay, on the other hand, was delighted to finally not have any animals in the house. It wasn't that she didn't like them, but it was a relief not to have to turn her clothing inside out as soon as she got home, and keep a lint roller in her purse.

True to her original purpose, Lissa photographed her menagerie constantly and used those photos to improve her technique. Pictures of the animals in every type of setting covered almost all the walls in Lissa's apartment and Lissa's animals had learned as much as animals could about photography. They seemed to enjoy posing in every nook and corner of each room, in every kind of lighting, alone and in every combination possible. When she went to Yellowstone Park on her first assignment, Lissa came back with fabulous photos, at least to Tay's eyes. "Photographing your critters seems to have paid off. These are wonderful."

"Yeah. I e-mailed them to my dad—he's in Borneo right now—and even he said some good things. We both agree though that I still have a lot to learn."

Living in Westchester, Lissa had the opportunity to do a lot of outdoor photography, catching the local wildlife in pictures both ordinary and wonderful. Birds at feeders, raccoons, skunks and squirrels in the yard and even a few of Honey attempting to befriend a woodchuck and Precious chasing butterflies. Since her father was gone most of the time she had the house to herself and had made liberal use of the elaborate darkroom and computer facilities there.

"I can't take the critters with me to China," Lissa said into the phone, interrupting Tay's reverie, "and I really can't board them for six months or even longer, so, well, I thought of you."

"Me? You're in Westchester and I'm in Brooklyn Heights. I certainly can't walk your dogs and feed your zoo from here."

"You're right, of course, and that's my point," Lissa said, her voice calming. "There's nothing in Brooklyn Heights for you anymore. Just the leftovers from a relationship I think you'd rather forget. You don't have a lease, do you?"

"No, I'm on a month to month." Tay quickly caught her friend's drift. "I've been thinking of finding a new place. This apartment was Steve's idea and it doesn't feel right to me anymore." She looked around again. She hadn't said it out loud but now that she'd admitted it, she realized that she'd have to find someplace else. Shit. Part of her still missed him, and she hated herself for it. She'd be better off getting out of an apartment that still even smelled of him.

"Fabulous. Serendipity. It all works out. You don't have anyplace else lined up yet, do you?"

"No, but . . ."

"Perfect. Drop that place like a hot potato and move up here. Bring what you think you'll need and put everything else in storage. There's everything here you might want, including high-speed Internet, so you can work from home when you don't want to commute." Lissa was talking at a mile a minute. "You can even borrow all the clothes I'm going to have to leave here." The two girls had always worn the same size and when they'd lived together had made liberal use of each other's wardrobe.

Tay heard her friend take a long, calming breath. "God, clothes," Lissa said, still talking quickly. "I can't believe it. I mean, really. Can you picture me wearing sweat-stained khaki shirts and cargo pants every day, crawling through the bushes or whatever they have in China, to get that perfect shot?" She made a rude noise that made Tay giggle.

Lissa had always been a clotheshorse, with a wardrobe that filled most of their closets. In college she'd never worn the same outfit more than a few times and when she thought everyone had seen it, she and Tay had gone shopping. Again. Lissa had a flair for the outrageous and Tay had an eye for what items would fit together, so with judicious shakes or nods of her head, Tay had managed to keep her friend from looking like too much of a weirdo. Actually Lissa usually looked stunning. The rat.

Tay had always envied her friend's looks. Tall, slender—stacked, the guys said, when they thought she couldn't hear—with baby blue eyes and soft reddish hair, Lissa had spent much of her time in college fending off the latest crop of drooling guys. Tay was also tall, though where she thought of Lissa as slender she'd always thought of herself as skinny. Zaftig was a word that could never be used to describe her.

Tay had had her share of dates, of course, one-night stands

and short-term relationships that usually ended in bed, but none of the guys had knocked her socks off enough to become semi-permanent, until she'd met Steve at an after-work watering hole in Manhattan. Of medium height, with puppy-dog brown eyes and great hands with long, artistic fingers, he'd caught her attention immediately. When he wandered over and they'd struck up a conversation, they'd found that they had a lot in common. He told her that he played several instruments, primarily the guitar, and she could easily picture those fingers on the strings. He told her that she had a sexy voice, and as they sat, he draped his arm over the back of her barstool. She didn't quite remember when he'd started stroking her shoulder, but the intimacy increased and later that evening they'd ended up in her apartment. The sex had been great and they quickly settled into a relationship.

They both loved old movies, but while Tay watched the actors, Steve studied the score. They went to a couple of small, out-of-the-way clubs regularly and Steve often sat in with the group performing. He worked at a menial job in music publishing, earning just enough to pay for his basic needs. Tay found herself paying for more and more of their evenings together. He and a few friends sometimes took over for bands at a club while the group being paid took a break. He, however, never made a cent.

After a month he'd told her that a friend of his was vacating an apartment in Brooklyn Heights and he urged her to pick up the payments so they could move in together. "What's wrong with living together here?" she'd asked.

"It's a nice place, but it's too girly."

"Girly? We can redecorate, add guy stuff. It's got plenty of room for us."

"I understand, but Donny's place is where it's at. There's a club around the corner that might have a job for me and the band, so it would be really convenient." Of course the job at the club had fallen through, but they'd moved anyway.

"I've got a job," Tay said to Lissa, considering moving to Westchester to care for her friend's animals. "I can't just drop it, and although telecommuting part time might work, I have to be in the city several times a week."

"You work near Grand Central and this house is five minutes from the train station. Or you can drive into the city." Lissa was talking even faster now. "I'm leaving my car, so you can use it while I'm gone. We need someone to watch the house, see that the cleaning folks don't slack off and, of course, take care of my animals. I talked it over with Daddy and he agreed that you'd be a great solution." Lissa's voice dropped. "He even agreed to cover any extra expenses you'd have and it's a great opportunity for you to get a new start over in a new place. No lingering Steve anywhere."

Lissa sounded like she was dishing out a sales pitch, but Tay cut her some slack. She knew how much this meant to her friend. "Tell me this. Can you go on this safari if you don't find someone to take over the house and your animals?"

She could hear a long sigh and Lissa's speech pattern slowed. "Frankly, no. It's one of Daddy's conditions and I think he hopes you won't be willing to do it."

"Doesn't he want you to go along?"

"Oh, he knows I'm talented with a camera, all right, and he really could use the extra hands on this one, but he's always been a loner." She chuckled. "Having his kid along might cramp his style with the ladies, too. Please, Tay, do this for me. It fits all the parameters for both of us."

Tay hesitated. "I don't know."

"Think about it. Please," Lissa wheedled. "We'll be leaving in three weeks and I'd need to show you everything around here before I go, so there's not a lot of time. Get back to me soonest. Please! Do this for me!"

Before she could offer another protest, Tay heard the phone click off, leaving her to realize just how Lissa got her father to agree to this adventure.

As she thought more about Lissa's offer she wandered into the tiny kitchen and grabbed a box of trash bags. She'd let things go for too long. She opened the top drawer of what had become Steve's dresser and began to stuff items he obviously no longer wanted into one of the trash bags. She held up the deep burgundy cashmere sweater she'd bought him. He'd looked so great in it, but she guessed it didn't fit his grunge image. It was a great sweater and she might just wear it herself, she thought, tossing it onto the bed. Slowly she pulled out a pair of Steve's torn jeans and stuffed them into the bag. "Bastard," she muttered. "Smart up, Tay," she told herself, "and get over him. You were a shmuck and he took advantage. Whose fault was that?"

She picked up her pace, rapidly slamming items into the trash bag, and when it was full, she grabbed a second one. Grab and stuff, grab and stuff. She found herself getting madder and madder. Then, when she finally deflated, she dropped onto the bed and wept. She'd loved him . . . or maybe she'd just loved the sex. Whatever, that phase of her life was gone, so she'd just have to get over it. Finally drained, she carted all the stuff down to the building's Dumpster, dropped the bags inside and slammed the lid. Done! Over! Why did it still hurt? Who was she mad at?

As the late afternoon sun set, she realized that she felt better having exorcized the evil spirits, as it were. She collapsed onto the bed, eyes crispy, shirt now sweaty, and thought about Lissa. What was wrong with spending six months in swanky-ville? Lissa and her father lived in a custom-built house in the middle of Westchester. Somewhere near the Clintons, she thought. She'd been there several times and been overwhelmed by the opulence of the place. Olympic-sized, heated pool, a sauna, a spa on the deck outside the master bedroom and another one in the yard by the pool. There were a zillion bedrooms and baths, framed copies of Dave Bonner's award-winning photographs all over the walls of everything, shelves of trophies along with figurines, statuettes and plaques. The furniture always looked like no one ever sat on anything. Actually, as she thought about it, most of the time the entire house looked like nobody lived there, and the cleaning staff kept it that way. It would be like living in a museum, but maybe she could bunk in the little guesthouse for the duration.

However . . . It would solve lots of problems. She pulled the scrunchy off the bottom of her braid, finger-combed her hair and rubbed her scalp. She would have to leave this place anyway. It was lonely.

Living at Lissa's would give her a whole new start and she did want to help her friend out. The commute wouldn't be bad at all, really, and she'd have six months or more to enjoy the luxury of it all. She'd also have no rent, no health-club fees, so she could bank a good part of her salary to replace the money she'd spent on Steve. She took a deep breath and flipped her cell phone open.

When Lissa answered, Tay said, "Why the hell not?"

"Oh my God, you'll do it?" Lissa shrieked. "Of course you will. Oh God. You're a lifesaver. I'll tell my dad he's stuck with me." She paused. "Oh, Tay, I'll learn so much. I want this so much. I'm even going to use my mom's maiden name so no one will think I'm just Dad's kid."

Lissa's mother had died of breast cancer several years before, as had Tay's mother, and Tay and Lissa had participated in several "walks for a cure." As Tay listened to Lissa ramble on, she wished she could be like her friend, so dedicated, so involved, so sure of what she wanted out of life.

At twenty-nine, Tay hadn't a clue. Sure, she liked her job, but that wasn't life. Lissa droned on about her trip, then finally wound down. "How soon can you make it up here?"

"I need to give notice here and I'll have to pay April's rent since I can't give them thirty days. It will take me a week or so to get organized, but then I'm yours. How about you come down weekend after next and we can pack up your car? I don't have much. Just my clothes and books and a couple of things from around here." She gazed at a small painting of a cat sunning itself in a sunny window. "I'll spend evenings packing a few boxes, but that will be about it. And my books, of course."

"Do you want to bring any of your furniture? We've got plenty of room in the garage. Or we'll rent you one of those storage units nearby. Whatever works."

"I might decide to rent one of those storage places." She paused, looked around, then continued, "On second thought, no. I don't think I want to keep anything." Now determined to get rid of everything from this life, she said, "I'll have an apartment sale and ditch all of it." She was amazed at how quickly she'd jumped into the whole idea, but suddenly it seemed the absolutely right thing to do. Looking around again, she said, "With no rent to pay, by the time you guys get back I'll have enough money saved to buy whatever I need fresh."

"You're my goddess, Tay, and I'll worship at your shrine all over Asia."

With a deep laugh from both women, they disconnected.

Chapter 3

The next two weeks were given over to moving. It took Tay a while to go through all her stuff. As she told Lissa during one of their long phone calls, she had both an apartment sale and a throwing-away party and she'd gotten rid of tons of junk. At last her hoard was whittled down to just a few things, and eventually the final boxes were stowed, filling the backseat and trunk of Lissa's Toyota, the one that Tay would be using while she was living on Maple Court. Tay was behind the wheel so she could get her driving legs, as Lissa had put it. Living in New York City, Tay had had little need for a car, so although she'd driven in high school and early in college, she'd done little since.

As they drove up the Saw Mill River Parkway, Tay inhaled deeply. Yes, spring was imminent and she became aware of it more here than she had ever been in the city. It was the beginning of April, and although the forsythia was a little behind that in Brooklyn Heights, what bright yellow there was stood out among the still-bare trees. "I love this time of year," Tay said, cracking open the driver's side window so she could try to smell the country. Although she thought of herself as a city girl, having grown up in Jersey she found that she really missed the open spaces, too.

"Me too," Lissa said. "The forsythia is almost there. Three-cythia, my dad calls it. You'll love watching things bloom. The backyard will delight you with something different every day."

"You can stop selling now," Tay said with a chuckle. "I'm here, with all my stuff in the car. I'm not going to go back on you now."

Lissa grinned. "I'm just so happy the way this has all worked out that I'm afraid something will go wrong."

"Nothing can go wrong."

"Can go wrong, can go wrong, can go wrong," Lissa said, chuckling at the punch line of the old joke.

"So has your dad set the date for the embarkation?"

"Next Tuesday."

Tay felt herself start to panic. "So soon? I have so much to learn about taking care of your house."

"Nonsense. Marta will come in every Tuesday and clean. She'll even change the sheets and do your laundry."

Tay didn't like the thought of someone going through her dirty clothes. "Not my laundry, she won't."

"Okay, we'll tell her to leave your stuff alone. The pool guy comes on Wednesday and he'll take care of both the pool and the spas. The garden guys come every Thursday to do the lawn and they know what's to be done with the flowers and all that. Payments have already been arranged, but if you have any trouble or questions you can always e-mail."

"Sounds like it takes an army to keep the house running."

"I guess it does." Lissa sat back in the passenger seat and let out a long breath. "I couldn't have done this without you, Tay, and it means everything to me."

Tay reached out and patted her friend's thigh. "No sweat, hon. It will be my pleasure."

"I know it will, but sometimes I think it's a big imposition."

Tay glanced over and raised an eyebrow. "Now she tells me." Then she burst out laughing, soon joined by Lissa.

They turned off the Parkway and made the few turns onto Maple Court. The first time Tay had visited she'd been awed by the affluence of the neighborhood, and she found that now that she was going to be living there, she was even more overwhelmed. What would a girl from a middle-class neighborhood in New Jersey do every weekend in this palatial house?

The cul-de-sac contained six houses, although most could not be seen from the road. Tay knew that the builder had had to create some oddly shaped parcels to conform to the local zoning laws and wetlands ordinances, so although each house had a narrow frontage on the court, the driveways were long and the houses sat far back among the carefully arranged landscaping.

The Bonner house was the second on the right. Tay drove up the long driveway and pulled to a stop in front of the doors to the four-car garage. "We're leaving the Mercedes and Daddy's Corvette. You can keep the Toyota on this side," Lissa said, using the remote button to open the leftmost of the two double doors.

Tay gazed again at the huge house. She was going to be house-sitting in this mansion, she thought. Amazing. The grass in the front yard was as slick as a putting green and several flowering trees were getting ready to bloom. The foundation of the house was concealed with azaleas, rhododendrons and mountain laurels, with several trellises covered with vining roses, none of it yet blooming. Tay knew that the backyard was as carefully manicured as the front and the area around the pool would be a riot of color from now until late into the fall, with flowers blooming everywhere.

"You might not meet any of the neighbors," Lissa said, pulling Tay back to reality. "Everyone around here pretty much sticks to his or her own business, but as the weather gets warmer and dogs need to be walked, occasionally you'll see some of the folks."

Tay climbed out of the car and stared down the long driveway, then back at the house.

"You're getting that deer-in-the-headlights look," Lissa said.

Tay did feel like someone totally out of her element. Was she really sure she wanted to do this? *Yes*, she told herself. *Lissa needs me and it's only for six months. And there's always the pool.*

She'd arranged to telecommute every Tuesday and Thursday, starting in a week or two when she could get organized, but the other three days, and when her job needed her, she'd take the train into Grand Central. But what was she going to do on the weekends? Well, she'd have a train ticket and a car and she could go into the city on Saturday or Sunday and do what she always had. Movies, museums, visits with her few friends; she'd find things. And the Internet got her anywhere and everywhere.

She stared up at the three-story, white clapboard house with black shutters. "I guess I had forgotten how big this thing is."

"It's nothing so special," Lissa said lightly, gazing at her friend.

"You've lived here since your dad bought this thing in 2004. I can remember back that far and I seem to recall you being very impressed at the time."

Lissa smiled ruefully. "I guess you're right. I had forgotten." She took Tay's hand and squeezed. "It really is just a house." She giggled. "A big motherfucker, but a house nonetheless."

Tension broken, the two women laughed easily as they began to lift cardboard boxes from the trunk. "That's Pam DePalma," Lissa said as a Lexus pulled into the cul-de-sac.

"She lives in that one." Lissa pointed to the driveway at the end of the circle. From her vantage point, Tay could just make out a cream-colored convertible as it pulled into the driveway. "She's a delightful woman who throws parties for a living. I've seen a few famous faces coming and going, and when she's entertaining, the street is full of limos. My father went to a few of her galas. A good-looking man with a worldwide reputation like Daddy is always welcome at any function."

Dave Bonner certainly would be an asset to any gathering, Tay realized—broad shouldered, rugged looking, with bedroom eyes and the perpetual five o'clock shadow that seemed so in fashion. Sexy, actually. She'd never discuss this with Lissa, of course. Finding a friend's father sexy was just too weird. "Is your dad around?"

"Nope. He's in the city meeting with his agent. They're going to some gallery opening. He'll pick up some lovely woman, go to dinner and stuff, then adjourn to her place for 'a nightcap.'" Lissa make quote marks in the air. "Ahh, the life. 'I'm going to be on location in Africa for six to nine months,' he'll say. 'Just me, my daughter and the wild animals.' The women melt, thinking they'll be the last sex he'll have for all that time." She giggled. "So he probably won't be home until tomorrow, or maybe Monday."

"You seem to know his routine pretty well."

"Oh, I've watched him operate for many years, so I'm used to it. That was why I was so sure he'd never take me along. Now I guess he thinks I'm old enough not to cramp his style. Well, Daddy, I'm old enough to develop my own 'style.'"

"It's more difficult for us girls," Tay said. "Guys have it pretty good. They can pick up women whenever they want." She thought about Steve. "And toss them when they're done."

Catching the edge in Tay's voice, Lissa said, "You're sounding very jaundiced."

"Sorry. A little of my ex-boyfriend crept into my thinking."

"Well, toss him," Lissa said, opening the front door and punching the security code into the keypad. "You're starting all over."

"True enough." She put down the box she'd been carrying. "Okay, show me the security stuff I need to know."

As Lissa showed her the code for the alarm system and told her the password for the alarm company, two cats, Ginger and Honey, arrived to spec out the visitor. Once they sniffed and ascertained that they knew Tay, they rubbed against her legs and snaked around her ankles. Precious stood in the doorway. If a cat could glare at an intruder, Precious was doing just that. However, she couldn't be bothered enough to take any overt action.

"The dogs are in their area in the side yard," Lissa said. "I'll show you where everything is, including the vet's number just in case. Come on out back."

Tay knew that the dogs were perfectly happy in their partially covered enclosure with executive doghouses, but they did like to get walked and have a ball thrown for them from time to time. Lissa continued. "There is a pooper-scooper for weekly cleanups. The yard people try to do it, but at least one of them is scared to death of Mopp. Food is inside. I'll show you where."

The dogs were delighted to see the two women, and when they opened the gate to their enclosure both jumped and barked joyfully. Tay and Lissa picked up toys and played with the dogs until they were panting with exertion.

Finally they went back inside, picked up the boxes they'd set down in the hall and carried them up to the largest guest room. "I thought you'd prefer your own space, but please feel free to use any of my stuff," Lissa said, then sized Tay up. "Looks like we still wear the same size, so go for it, and don't worry about anything. You know how I enjoy buying more stuff, so if anything gets messed up, don't sweat it."

They made two more trips to the car and dumped the boxes in the large closet in the guest room. When the two women walked into Lissa's room, Tay's eyes widened. There were clothes everywhere, folded, dumped, draped and piled on every conceivable surface. "Lissa . . ."

"Okay, I know. But I can't decide what to pack."

Amazed but not surprised, Tay said, "You're going to be dressed in grubbies for the duration, so what's the big issue?" Then she grinned. "Okay, okay. In case of emergencies, right?" Despite the piles of clothing, Tay glanced into Lissa's closet, which was still full.

"Oh, Tay, you know me so well. Just in case I need something for a dinner somewhere, I want to have something I can dress up in."

Tay gave her what they both called the "hairy eyeball."

"Okay, I get the point." Changing the subject, Lissa said, "Why don't you wait to unpack until later? I'm ready for the pool."

The day hadn't been particularly warm, but they'd been wrestling with boxes and dogs for over an hour, so Tay was ready for a swim. "Love to."

Together, arm in arm like the dearest friends they were, they headed for the back of the house and opened the sliding door that led to the picturesque backyard. In the rear, a copse of willow trees was just beginning to get its green spring haze, and on the sides of the yard privacy was insured by an eight-foot fence covered with canes of the dozens of rose bushes planted there. In another month or two the yard would be filled with the scent of wild roses. Two dogwood trees stood in the center of the back lawn, flanking the heated pool, which had tendrils of steam wafting above it. "I'm really bad. I keep the heater on all the time and I swim almost every day when I'm here. God," she said with a long sigh, "I'll miss that. In the wilds of China I don't know whether I'll even get a shower."

To the left, out of sight behind the side of the house, was the dog run, and to the right, at the rear of the property, was the guesthouse, a one-story replica of the main building. Tay had stayed there on one visit and knew that it contained a small bedroom, living room, bath and a tiny kitchen area. It was small but comfortable and Dave often had friends stay over there for weekends.

Since it was late in the afternoon, the air had chilled, so the two women changed their clothes in one of the cabanas and, now dressed in two of the bathing suits that were kept there for guests, dashed across the putting green–like lawn and jumped into the warm water. "Laps?" Lissa said as she surfaced. They each did fifty laps, starting slowly and building to a blistering pace, each trying to outrace the other, and ended, laughing, barely winded. They splashed each other and played like kids.

After half an hour of that, they climbed out, rushed over to the hot tub and climbed in. "That was awesome," Lissa said.

"It will be great to be able to swim every day, without having to go anywhere."

"Don't rub it in," Lissa said, splashing her friend with hot water. "I still can't believe it's all working out. Plane tickets are booked, first class, mind you. Daddy won't have it any other way."

"I'll miss you," Tay said, getting slightly teary. She was becoming overwhelmed with the tasks she figured she'd have to do to keep up the house. Take out the garbage, laundry, the dogs, cats, rabbit, ferrets. . . . She'd be able to stay in touch with Lissa and her father by e-mail if she had questions or problems, of course, but it was quite a responsibility and Tay had always taken her responsibilities very seriously. This one was a doozie.

"You'll be fine, Tay," Lissa said. "I know you well enough to know you're in a bit of a panic right now, trying to figure it all out in advance. Just relax and roll with it. I promise it will all work out."

"I know you're right." Tay sat back, her head resting on the edge of the spa. She would overlay her anxiety with pleasure for her friend. "How are you dealing with being away for all that time? Excited?"

"Delirious. I can't wait. Daddy helped me pick out the most souped-up laptop we could find and I've been putting editing software on it so I won't have to disturb him. If we can get an Internet connection we'll be logging in to the setup here. By the way, don't turn the downstairs computer off, just leave it on all the time. And please feel free to use it and the network for whatever. There are some fantastic games and I've got lots of puzzle and game sites bookmarked. And, of course, there'll be e-mail. Write to me lots and I'll write to you from wherever whenever I can."

"You can really log in to to your computer system from wherever you'll be?" Lissa was a computer sophisticate, but from some remote outpost in China?

"Daddy says we probably can."

Later Tay dried off and changed upstairs. She did love the whole Bonner house, but as she pulled on a T-shirt, she thought about the things she particularly looked forward to having to herself.

There was the pool, of course, and the master bath. Once she was by herself she'd use that one exclusively. She remembered when Dave had had it redone. He'd just returned from a photo shoot in some South American country or other and had fallen in love with the tile bathrooms there. He'd had the walls of his bathroom covered with Spanish-style light brown tiles with hand-painted lizards embedded here and there, making it look like a jungle watering hole. The shower had been redone with jungle plants everywhere, kept green with recessed grow-lights, and the shower sprayed from three different angles. The floor was some kind of warm cork, and the sink was lined with more hand-painted tiles—florals, done in orange, red and green. Heat lamps and fans could be turned on to dry you without ever having to use a towel.

The other thing she loved was the fireplace. The wall dividing the living room from the den was constructed with a two-sided gas-log fireplace with glass doors that could be opened from either side and floor-level hearths fronted with fluffy rugs. Although she would be there during the summer, she knew she could, if she wanted, turn up the air conditioner and have a fire. Lying on the rug with a book, or better still a guy, if she could find one, was definitely in her future.

Dave Bonner arrived home on Sunday afternoon and they spent a wonderful dinner listening to him tell fabulous tales about his travels. At almost fifty, Dave was charming and good looking with a deeply tanned face that sported white laugh wrinkles around his surprisingly deep blue eyes. As she climbed into bed that night, Tay thought about how different he was from Steve. *Maybe I need to get acquainted with some older men. Steve was such a baby.* Then she shook her head as she listened to herself thinking, and almost laughed out loud. *Tay, you sound like such an age-snob. Face it, girl. You miss having a man in your life.*

She had taken the day off from work on Monday so she could finish unpacking, but Tuesday morning she said goodbye to Dave and Lissa over a quick breakfast and drove to the train station in Chappaqua. She had already gotten a train schedule from the Internet, so she arrived with just enough time to park and purchase a ten-trip ticket in the station. Since she would be using the railroad only three times a week, she'd calculated that this would be cheaper than a monthly commuter pass.

As she gazed out the window of the train, Tay realized that in the middle of the afternoon father and daughter would be off from Newark Airport for the beginning of an adventure the likes of which she'd never even imagined.

The train to Chappaqua that evening was relatively painless and as she drove back to Maple Court she realized that the entire routine really wasn't bad. Since there was no subway hassle involved, the whole thing added less than an hour to her workday.

As she parked in the driveway and let herself into the empty house, she felt a twinge of loneliness, so she microwaved a can of beef ravioli, did twenty-five laps in the pool, watched a little television and went to bed. "Have a great trip, guys," she said out loud as she turned out the bedroom light.

Chapter 4

After a month on Maple Court, Tay was bored to death. The commute had turned out to be less of a problem than she'd expected and the telecommuting was working out well. However, she found herself going into the office most days. There was little to do in suburbia. When she worked in the city she'd often stay in town for drinks with a few folks from the office and frequently remain for dinner with an acquaintance.

Westchester County, at least the part of it she'd visited so far, was a drag. The scenery was gorgeous and there were plenty of cultural sights to visit, but she couldn't spent all her days at museums and she wasn't the concert type. She'd seen most of the movies around and stopped at a few friendly neighborhood watering holes, but she hadn't met anyone worth the effort of dating, and there didn't seem to be anything else to do on the weekends.

What had she done when she lived in Brooklyn Heights? she wondered. Of course, she'd had Steve. As difficult as he'd become, he was company. It wasn't as if they had a date every night, but they'd gone to clubs, had a few beers and listened to whatever music was being performed and, of course, joined in from time to time.

So here she was, in suburbia, and again it was Saturday and she had nothing to do all weekend. She'd played with the dogs, fed the cats, rabbit and ferrets, tidied their cages and done a load of laundry. She'd stopped at the cleaners to pick up a few things she'd dropped off earlier in the week, then gone to the local library and found several books she'd been wanting to read. So, with little else to do she ate a peanut-butter-and-potato-chip sandwich and curled up in a recliner in the den with the stack beside her. As she was about to select something, the doorbell rang, which set the dogs in the backyard into a flurry of mad barking. It gave Tay a good feeling. No one was ever going to sneak up on the house with Mopp and Fred around.

"Coming," she yelled, delighted to have something break the monotony, even if it was just the UPS man.

She opened the front door and stared at a tiny, brown-haired woman whose age could have been from thirty to forty-five. She came up only to Tay's chin, but there was a presence about her that projected class. Her makeup accentuated her hazel eyes and her hair was casually chic. She was smartly dressed in a pair of casual tan slacks and a long-sleeved taupe blouse accessorized with chocolate sandals. Her jewelry was confined to several strands of deep amber beads and matching chunky drop earrings. Tay glanced down and noticed that the woman's toes and fingernails were polished in the same shade of red-gold. Her smile was warm and friendly. "Hi, is Dave around? I know I haven't seen him, or Lissa either for that matter, in a while, but I was hoping . . ."

"I'm sorry. Dave and Lissa are away on a photo shoot and they aren't expected back for several months." Looking at this classically lovely woman, Tay felt dowdy in a pair of old, comfortable jeans and a baggy "Save the Whales" T-shirt. She'd thrown all the windows open to catch the late spring breeze and turned off the "canned air," as she called the central air-conditioning system. She looked down at her bare feet, her toes polished embarrassingly flaming red, and almost apologized for her appearance.

"Oh damn. I'm sorry, too," the woman said. Then, as if just thinking about it, she extended her hand, graceful with slender fingers, wearing only a beautiful floral designed gold ring on her right index finger. No wedding ring, Tay noticed. "Pardon my rudeness. I'm Pam DePalma and in case you haven't seen me around I live two houses down."

"Tay Barwick. It's nice to meet you."

Tay hadn't noticed the woman but she had noticed the house when Lissa had pointed it out. It was set almost as far back from the road as possible, and from what she'd seen it was large yet comfortably doable, not palatially imposing the way that the Bonner house was. "That's certainly a lovely house," Tay said, taking the woman's hand. "I've been admiring it and all the others on the block. I'm house-sitting while Dave and Lissa are away."

"Taking care of all the animals must be quite a job. I'm sorry to have bothered you," Pam said.

"Oh, it's no bother," Tay said quickly, glad to have someone to talk to. "Can you come in for a moment? I'm a bit of a coffeeholic and I always have a pot on. Would you like a cup?"

She saw Pam hesitate for a moment, then walk into the large foyer, her heels making a clicking sound on the parquet floor. "I'd like that. Thanks."

As they walked toward the kitchen, Pam said, "I really like this house. He's done wonders with it. The old owners were here for about three years and lamented that they'd never be able to sell it. This whole area's now a wetland and no one's sure whether any changes or additions will ever be permitted."

"I didn't know that. I remember when Dave bought it," Tay said, entering the large kitchen. The counters were black granite and almost everything else in the kitchen was either white or black, from the place mats on the large white oak table to the canisters on the counters. It was a bit too organized for Tay's taste but it certainly looked put together. "He was so delighted."

"I can imagine. This is a great kitchen."

"Sadly I can't make much use of it. Not only can't I cook but I think I'd even burn any water I tried to boil. I can microwave and use a coffeemaker, but that's the extent of my culinary skills."

"I'm not much of a cook, either," Pam admitted. "But I've always admired this kitchen."

"Dave said that he didn't do much with the decorating when he bought the place. Instead, he just let a professional handle everything." Tay huffed out a breath and decided to be honest. "Actually the whole place is a bit too masculine and sterile for my taste. I'd love to add some color, maybe a few green plants in here, and a throw pillow or two in the living room."

Pam chuckled. "I've always thought the same thing, but I didn't want to insult the house in case you were a fan."

"Very tactful of you," Tay said, grinning, liking this woman immediately. "Have you ever been upstairs? The best bit of decorating is the master bath. It has to be seen to be appreciated. He had it redone just about a year ago."

A small smile crossed Pam's face. "Yeah, I remember the hoard of hunky guys in coveralls crawling all over the place during the construction. And I did see it once." She looked as if she could say more, but she remained silent.

While Pam settled at the kitchen table, Tay poured two cups of coffee into black and white patterned mugs and pulled a black and white striped cream pitcher from the kitchen closet. "Don't bother with a pitcher on my account," Pam said, "I'll just pour from the container."

"My kind of person," Tay said as she settled across from Pam at the kitchen table. "Although I've had the desire to go out and buy a pitcher shaped like a cow in bright green or something."

Pam's laugh was warm and inviting. Then the cats arrived. It wasn't time for their daily canned food and they disdained their dry crumbles, so whenever there was someone in the kitchen, they wandered around, purring loudly, hoping for a handout. As Precious started to climb into Pam's lap, Tay said, "Precious, stay down. This nice lady doesn't want your fur all over her slacks, nor your claws in her thigh."

"Not a problem," Pam said, but Precious, tail straight in the air, changed her mind and, thinking there might be something edible in the offing, paced impatiently beside her food dish. As Ginger climbed into Tay's lap, Tay was pretty sure that Honey was somewhere within earshot just in case food materialized.

The two women chatted for a while, about the weather and the town. They quickly discovered that they both frequently ate food from the same local Italian restaurant. "Their penne a la vodka is to die for," Pam said.

"I know. I eat out often in the city but I've never had it better anywhere. More often than my waistline would like, I stop on my way here from the train station and order something to go."

Chuckling, Pam said, "I do worse. I've discovered they will deliver for a generous tip."

"I'm really sorry you told me that," Tay said with a rueful grin. "Have you been able to find out where they get their green olives from? They're fabulous."

"I know. I always ask for extras and they indulge me since I'm a pretty good customer. I once asked the owner where he got them, thinking I could buy my own. However, he told me that he had them imported specially from Spain. He hates to admit that there's something that the Spanish make better than the Italians."

Tay nodded. "I can imagine."

"So, if you'll pardon me for being nosey, what do you do?" Pam asked as she sipped her coffee. "Do you commute to the city?"

"Most days. I work for a multinational you've probably never heard of. It's got its fingers in architecture, foreign manufacture, pharmaceuticals, but it's always the name behind the name."

"Interesting. What do you do for them? Or am I being too snoopy?"

Tay's laugh was warm. "Not a problem. I began in their Web-design department but several years ago, after one of those multiple firings they euphemistically called a downsizing, I was asked to work on a section of the in-house site that excerpts articles from scientific publications, in addition, of course, to doing all the things I used to do. Now I do all that and help with grant applications, edit papers for publication, do research, stuff like that."

"I'll bet you can even spell," Pam said.

"Actually you'd be wrong," Tay said, shaking her head slowly. "I can't spell worth a lick. I depend on spell-checker and the Web." Tay found that she liked this charming woman more and more. Maybe they could get together from time to time. She'd love to ask, but she didn't want to seem pushy.

"You must know everything," Pam said, obviously impressed.

"Not at all, but I've learned bits of everything and I can research the rest. I used to be a voracious reader, too."

"Used to be?"

"I read so much for work now that it's difficult for me to

get into reading for pleasure. I just found the local library and took out a few things I've been meaning to get around to."

"Did you study writing in school?"

"Graphic arts, actually. That's where I met Lissa. I read somewhere that seventy-five percent of college graduates aren't working in anything related to what they studied. I seem to be the exception."

"I can believe that," Pam said. "I meet and greet lots of high-powered executives and very few of them are in any field they studied in school. Actually most of them are scared witless that someone will find out that their job requires very little actual"—Pam made quote marks in the air—"'learning.'"

"True enough."

"What do you do on the weekends, for fun?"

Tay sighed. "I swim fifty laps a day, as long as the weather cooperates, and take care of Lissa's animals. I'm taking several online courses, one called American History Before the Civil War, one on astronomy. There are a lot of podcasts I subscribe to as well. Keeps me busy, sort of." She knew she was babbling a bit, but it was so nice to have someone outside the office to talk to.

"Sort of?"

"I get bored sometimes." No, she wouldn't whine.

"I can imagine. No boyfriends?"

"Not anymore. Steve moved out around Christmas."

"Bad breakup?"

"Sudden and a bit wrenching, but if I'd been more observant I would have seen it coming. I think I was too bookish for him. He's a musician and I think he wanted me for ego boosting and financial support."

"Ahhh. The old financial support. I think he gave up a lot when he split."

Surprised, Tay said a sincere "Thanks."

A considering look flashed over Pam's face, then vanished. "Good sex at least?"

From anyone else that question would have sounded out of place, but Pam was so warm and friendly that Tay just answered. "Frequent, at least, but I've had better. Not recently, however." Pam's laugh was infectious. What was it about this lovely woman that encouraged sharing of girlish secrets? Tay realized that it was the first time she'd been able to really laugh about Steve's defection. "And what do you do, if *I'm* not being too nosey?"

Pam hesitated slightly, then huffed out a short breath and said, "Not nosey at all. I host corporate and upscale parties. Business affairs, weddings, showers, charity gatherings and such."

"Ah, right," Tay said, wondering whether one could actually make a living doing that. "I think Lissa mentioned that. So that's why all the cars on most weekends."

"I hope there haven't been any problems for you."

"Not in the least. That must be an interesting business. How did you get into it?"

"Long story." She glanced at her watch. "And I don't have enough time to get into the tale of my life right now. I've got a charity tea today." She paused, then chuckled. "What a euphemism. A tea. No one actually drinks tea, but it does define the hour." She paused again. "I came over here to invite Dave and Lissa over. Would you consider stopping over for just a short while?"

"I don't think so," Tay said, tempted to do almost anything to relieve the boredom.

"I know it's an imposition, but the Steinbergs, who are hosting this event, are new in the area and don't have enough friends to fill the backyard. It should have been too cool at this time of year to have it outside, but today is so fabulous that the party will spill into the backyard. There won't be nearly enough people to make it look busy so I'm gathering everyone I can think of. I thought I'd drag Dave and Lissa over to fill out the crowd.

"The Steinbergs didn't want to invite their close friends for fear that they'd feel they had to contribute, but they are even calling a few of them. You don't have to give a cent, of course. Just stand with a drink in your hand, make conversation when you find someone who's convivial, and at other times just inhale occasionally and look like you're having a good time. It would be a great favor to me."

"That's a nice offer, but I won't know anyone and the Steinbergs will know I'm an interloper."

"Not at all. Everyone is asked to bring friends and they know I'll invite people, too. The Bonners wouldn't have known anyone, either. Please." Pam leaned forward and patted Tay's hand. "I hope I won't embarrass you, but I have to tell you that you make a fabulous first impression. You're such a charming person and it would really help me out."

Tempted, Tay asked, "What's the dress code?" She had a few things that might do, and she had Lissa's closet to work from.

"Summer casual." Pam stood and pirouetted. "This is what I'm wearing. How about an enticement? I'll give you the cook's tour of the house and maybe we can have a swim and a sauna afterward. And you'll get to meet Linc."

"Linc?"

"He's the main guy in my life."

"You're not married, I gather," Tay said.

"I was widowed several years ago. Long story. I've moved on with my life, in ways I can't even begin to explain to you. No children either, more's the pity. Maybe we can get together for lunch one day next week and exchange life histories. Right now, however, I have to get back home. Please come over this afternoon, even if it's only for a few minutes."

"Can I think about it? I'm not very good with people I don't know."

"Nonsense. You and I hit it off quickly so I'm sure you'll hold your own without any trouble. The guests will all be bright, interesting people and with your varied interests you'll fit right in."

"What time?"

"Come over any time after three. It probably won't last much past five or so but you can always run for the hills if you're bored out of your mind."

She considered, then made a snap decision. "Okay. I'll find something to wear and be over between three and three-thirty."

"Perfect." Pam put her cup in the sink. "I can't thank you enough."

The two women walked to the front door and as Pam stepped out onto the walk she impulsively leaned up and kissed Tay on the cheek. "I hope we can get together soon. I'll be pit deep this afternoon, but since I'm sure we have a lot in common, I'd love to get to know you a little better. I originally made the offer as a toss off, but I mean it. I would really like to have lunch with you one day soon."

Delighted, Tay said, "I'd like that a lot. I work at home a few days a week, usually Tuesdays and Thursdays, so maybe then."

"Great. Well, I'll see you later and then we'll figure something out."

As Pam walked back to her house she thought about the fascinating woman she'd just met and wondered whether she'd made a new friend and/or a new business associate.

She certainly looked good, not gorgeous by any means, but she had a classic attractiveness and a way of looking you right in the eye when she spoke to you. And when she smiled her entire face lit up. Her features were good and with a little makeup and a decent haircut—why in the world did she wear that long, awkward braid?—she'd be fit for any setting.

Pam thought about business. In addition to the obvious reason for the party, Jeff Steinberg had asked her to help him "entertain" several out-of-town business associates, so several of the women at the party would be wearing ankle bracelets with small heart charms, indicating that they were available for activities afterward.

What Pam hadn't told Tay and what even the Bonners didn't know was that many of Pam's parties were meeting places for men who wanted to hire women to have sex with. Her ladies, well-paid courtesans, would meet just about any needs the men might have.

If Tay was the kind of woman Pam suspected she was, she'd have to call her business partner, Marcy McGee, and see whether she might come up for a visit. They had recently discussed the problem of finding some new blood for their business. Several of their employees had either moved on or left the area and now they were having to turn down business or schedule weeks or even months ahead.

Since Marcy was busy with her children, Pam hadn't seen her face-to-face for several weeks. Yes. If Tay worked out as Pam thought she might, she'd ask for Marcy's opinion of Tay as a potential associate for Club Fantasy and the Madam of Maple Court. Marcy's instincts about the business were first-rate.

Tay was a bright, interesting woman who obviously enjoyed sex but was without male companionship at the moment. What could be better than getting paid for something she'd willingly do for nothing? Pam vowed that, if she could, she'd get to know Tay better and then mention the business. She'd tread gently, never wanting to take any serious risks, but this might just work well for all of them. First of all she'd see what Linc thought of her new friend.

Chapter 5

The weather was indeed beautiful for May. The sun was warm but the air was cool enough not to cause anyone to sweat. Tay had looked through her clothing to find something appropriate to wear, then, finding nothing that made her happy, decided to invade Lissa's closet.

She found a light blue floral chiffon dress with a full skirt and demure bodice, and as she'd anticipated, despite the difference in the two women's "endowments," it fit quite well. She kept her jewelry simple, several strands of small white and gold beads with matching small-drop earrings. White, low-heeled sandals completed the outfit. She gazed at herself in the mirror and smiled. These would be affluent people, and, dressed simply and classically as she was, she knew that she wouldn't look totally out of place. She brushed her blond hair until it shone, then French-braided it, leaving a few strands softly loose over her ears. She kept her makeup light and summery, with just a touch of blue shadow to bring out the color of her eyes.

As she walked down the stairs she wondered why she was even going to this silly gathering. She wouldn't know anyone, couldn't care less about meeting a bunch of stuffy upper-crust couples and didn't particularly want to be bothered. And, she realized with a start, she didn't even know what charity this shindig was being thrown for. However, she had nothing better to do. Actually she had nothing at all to do, better or worse, except a stack of books she ought to want to read and several courses she was taking on the Internet. Furthermore, she really liked Pam, and in addition to helping her out, Tay was eager to find a way to meet the woman again.

At three she closed the Bonners' door behind her, walked along the cul-de-sac and up the DePalma driveway. She wondered why there were no cars parked anywhere, but she quickly understood. Several nice-looking young men wearing red T-shirts and denim shorts stood around in front of the wide three-double-bay garage, chatting amiably among themselves. As guests arrived they helped the occupants out of their cars, gave them valet tags and whisked the expensive autos away to some off-site parking area Pam must have arranged for. They looked at her oddly, probably wondering where her car was. Two of the valets gave her the once-over and smiled appreciatively. *Nice,* she thought. She liked being looked over and it told her she'd selected her outfit well. However, they were all very young. God, she had to find a way to meet guys.

Even before she rounded the house she could hear the mellow strains of a woodwind quartet. *God, it must be nice to be rich. Woodwinds.* Holding a charity event that obviously cost more than would be raised seemed a bit ridiculous, but what did she know about this sort of thing? Maybe this gathering would raise more than she'd thought. The attendees were probably capable of writing checks with a significant number of zeros.

Her first view of the assembly was impressive and she almost walked back down the driveway, but she considered how that would look to the parking guys and kept going. *People do things for the strangest reasons,* she thought.

There were approximately seventy-five people standing around in the backyard, men and women of all ages, sizes, shapes and ethnicities. She even recognized a few faces, one or two low-level celebrities, a few county politicians and several business types she recognized from the financial TV stations. Movers and shakers all. The women were arrayed in spring and summer colors, slender slacks with bright-patterned blouses and blazers, dresses with bared shoulders and short skirts, long flowing caftan-like robes in a dazzling array of jewel tones. As she looked around she noticed that most of the women wore expensive-looking jewelry, coordinated with the fabric of their clothing. Sapphires with blue, rubies with red, emeralds with green and diamonds or large pearls with everything else. She thought about her simple white plastic and smiled inwardly. *Never mind,* she told herself, *you're as good as any of them. Not as rich, perhaps, but just as good. And don't you forget it!*

As she glanced around she became amused when she realized that, as varied as the clothing was on the women, the men seemed to wear uniforms. About half wore polo shirts, many either red or navy, and khakis, with most of the rest dressed in navy or dark gray blazers and tan or gray slacks. The shirts varied from yellow to light blue to tan, most open at the neck. There were very few ties.

Serving people of both genders wandered through the crowd, all dressed as the valets had been, red polos and denim shorts, skirts or long pants. Some held platters of fancy-looking hors d'oeuvres—no pigs in blankets for this crowd. Others had trays with glasses of wine or champagne and some offered soft drinks or bottles of water. Bottled water mystified Tay. The water in New York was some of the best in the world. Why would anyone purchase water, then take up space in landfills with the plastic bottles? Yet everyone seemed to do it.

The yard itself was fabulous. About two dozen small tables were situated around the lawn, covered with bright blue cloths, each with a floral centerpiece of tulips in different shades. Crystal and china gleamed. Several tables were occupied by couples or foursomes, nibbling, sipping and laughing. It was immediately obvious that everyone here was having a great time.

Farther back in the yard was a formal rose garden bordered by a massed planting of azaleas in every shade from deep burgundy to white, most of the plants in full bloom. Tay hadn't seen such an array of blossoms since her last visit to the botanical gardens. She wanted to go over and examine the bushes more carefully but she was afraid it would look like she was avoiding the guests.

As she watched the flow of people she was pretty sure she could pick out the Steinbergs, if only from their careful movement from conversational group to conversational group and from checks being handed over. Soliciting never stopped, she figured. The yard was certainly crowded so she assumed that Pam had been able to supplement the original number she'd invited. Why was she here? Why had Pam invited her? She was sure she wouldn't fit in, and wasn't interested in writing a check.

In a slight panic, unable to think of a graceful way to leave, Tay walked onto the enclosed patio, the floor covered with large gray flagstones. Several guests sat on soft, upholstered chairs, sofas and lounges, all covered in smokey gray linen with burgundy and moss flowers. Several glass-topped tables held drinks. The patio opened into the air-conditioned living room, where several more people sat around in a warm, comfortable room done in the same shades as the patio, a pale gray sofa with a burgundy satin stripe, several burgundy chairs and a love seat in navy and the palest gray. The feeling here was exactly the opposite of the Bonner house. Each piece of furniture was overstuffed, inviting-looking and almost begged a guest to make him- or herself at home. Cushions in matching tones longed to be shoved behind backs.

The decorations were understated, several surfaces showcasing a single leafy green plant, a few varieties of which Tay had never seen before. The walls were uncluttered, with only a few well-placed oils and watercolors, all landscapes. *Probably great art,* she thought. A piano stood off to one side and a man was playing show tunes while a few guests stood around and sang along. *Wonderful house,* she thought. *Opulent without being standoffish. The kind of rooms that make a person want to sit and chat. This is what the Bonner house could look like with a little softening. Oh well, it's not my house.*

She was still feeling very stiff, so she thought a little alcohol might make all this a bit more bearable. She made her way back outside and walked over to a freestanding bar set up on a small platform in front of the foundation planting and asked another hunky-looking guy, who stood behind it, for a glass of white wine. He was older than the guys in the driveway, probably closer to Pam's age, but he was dressed in the uniform of the day, red polo shirt and denim shorts. She couldn't help but notice that he had great legs and a tight, well-exercised body. Great, tight buns, too. God, she must be really horny. She was looking at every guy like the main course at a buffet. While she had been living with Steve she'd had frequent, if not too imaginative sex. She quickly counted backward and realized that she had been without sex for more than four months. She took a deep breath and let it out slowly. Damn. She'd have to do something about that.

She returned her attention to the guy behind the bar and she couldn't stop her mind from picturing him on the rug in front of the Bonners' fireplace. He was naked, build like a Greek statue, fully erect. Poised above her, he was supporting his weight on his sweat-sheened, muscular arms, his expression hot and hungry, obviously eager to enter her. When she found her pussy twitching, she yanked herself back to reality.

"Chablis, Chardonnay or Pinot Grigio?" the guy asked.

"Quite a selection. What would you recommend?" Was she flirting? Maybe just a little. It had been quite a while since she'd felt like starting something with a man. Since Steve, actually. This guy was really magnificent.

"The Pinot is really nice."

She nodded and, as he poured her a glass, she suddenly felt a woman's hand on her arm.

"I'm so glad you could come," Pam said. "I was hoping you wouldn't change your mind." Pam was still dressed in beige, tan and coffee and Tay saw that she looked efficient, yet feminine.

Not sure what to say, Tay said, "I love your yard. It's perfect for what you've arranged this afternoon. And your azaleas are amazing."

Pam's smile was warm. "Thanks, but I can't take much credit. I have lots of help. My landscaper is a gem. You should see the roses. They'll begin to bloom in a week or so, and then they'll continue all summer."

"Don't believe it's all her gardeners," the bartender said. "She works very hard on those flowers." There was a slightly proprietary tone in his voice that made Tay curious, but she couldn't ask about it. Instead, she sipped the wine the bartender had handed her, then said, "You seem so relaxed, Pam. Doesn't this all stress you out?"

"Pam's done this dozens, maybe hundreds of times," the bartender said. "She's really good at entertaining." A special look passed between them but vanished quickly.

"Linc's right, Tay," Pam said. "This is what I do for a living." She took Linc's hand. "Tay, this is Linc. He's my, well, the language hasn't quite caught up with the lifestyle yet. I guess the closest I can come is that he's a permanent part of my life."

"I'm her boyfriend," Linc said with a twinkle, "significant other, better half."

"Better half my ass," Pam hissed, then turned to Tay. "Don't mind him. He knows how I hate all those terms." Then she leaned a bit closer to the hunky bartender and winked at him.

Bartender? Wouldn't you think Pam's guy would be part of the party rather than part of the staff? Since he was Pam's she'd have to keep her fantasies to a minimum. Well, a deep secret anyway. He was too sexy to eliminate entirely.

"I've been trying to convince her to make our relationship more formal," he said, "but she keeps turning me down."

Pam cuffed Linc on the shoulder. "Enough." She squeezed his powerful upper arm. "Linc, this is Tay. She's housesitting for the Bonners for several months. Be nice to her. We're going to have lunch one day next week and I'm looking forward to getting to know her better." Something was going on here, Tay thought, realizing that there was an undercurrent of unspoken understanding between the two.

"I'd really like that, Pam," she said, now curious as to what was up. Maybe she'd never find out, but lunch sounded good for many reasons.

"Well," Pam said with a sigh, "I can't stand around any longer." She linked her arm through Tay's and gently guided her away from the bar. "Come with me and let me introduce you to a few people I think you'll like."

Although Tay would have felt more comfortable talking to Linc, she let the hostess lead her to a group of high-powered–

looking men. "Okay you three, enough business talk. You're here to enjoy yourselves."

"We are enjoying ourselves. Talking business is always enjoyable." The man who spoke was short and, well, *substantial* was the only word Tay could think of. He was dressed in khaki slacks and a navy polo shirt. "But we can certainly be interrupted for someone as lovely as your friend."

Oh, come now, Tay thought. But somehow he had made it sound sincere.

"This is Tay Barwick," Pam said. "She's a neighbor and doesn't know anyone here. I'm going to leave her with you three and I hope you'll get to know each other."

The man who'd spoken extended a well-manicured hand. "Tay, it's nice to meet you. I'm Carter Hamilton." He gave her a quick once-over, glancing at her legs and ankles. *Must be a leg man,* Tay thought.

"It's Carter Hamilton the Third," a second man said. He was solidly built, with deep brown hair, a neatly, carefully trimmed beard and eyes that seemed to smile even when his face was in repose. "Doesn't that sound imposing? You'd think he was the president of the corporation."

"Get over it, Mike." Carter's laugh took all the sting out of his words. Tay realized that this must be a running joke between them.

The taller man extended his hand. "Mike Cioffi. And just so you understand, he *is* the president of the corporation."

"Ah, now I get it. Nice to meet you," Tay said, shaking hands with both men.

The third man chimed in. "Peter Reid. And it's nice to meet you, too." A third handshake. She was beginning to feel like a politician as she plastered a charming smile on her face. Peter was the tallest of the three, lanky, with sandy hair and a small gold ring in one ear.

"What do you do, Tay?"

Tay was sure she'd be made to feel like a working stiff by these three executives but they listened attentively as she gave them a brief description of her job. Surprisingly she found herself slowly relaxing. "Sounds like you get to learn about the cutting edge of things, writing articles and grant proposals. Do you enjoy it?"

The question made her think for a moment, but she realized that she could answer firmly in the affirmative. "I love it, and we get lots of money and have lots of articles published. I guess that's pretty good. A job I enjoy and am good at."

"That's amazing in the world of corporate America."

"Not so unusual. I really love my job," Peter said.

"Right. Except when you have to interrupt your golf game to work on the weekends or attend things like this." His gesture included everyone in the yard.

Peter smiled ruefully. "Yeah, there is that."

During the next fifteen minutes they all seemed to make an effort to be charming and she totally enjoyed the conversation. It turned out that, like her, Peter was a history buff and eventually, when the two of them argued pleasantly about how much of the Renaissance resulted from the Black Plague, the other two men wandered off. They found that they'd also both watched and enjoyed a recent History Channel special on the French Revolution and as they talked Tay barely noticed time passing.

Later they were joined by two couples and Tay was unexpectedly fascinated by everyone. While the men separated themselves from the group and launched into a separate conversation about their latest round of golf, the women dissected the most recent disagreement between the President and Congress. When they couldn't agree on which side was right they agreed to disagree and moved on to discussing a recent finding on the growing obesity problem in the U.S. "Look around," a woman named Charlene said. "Half the men here look several months' pregnant, with their belts now drooping below their bellies. No wonder so many guys drop dead at fifty-five." She indicated her husband standing nearby, a man who'd introduced himself as Norman. "He considers riding around a golf course in a cart exercise." She looked exasperated. "For a while I tried to get him to watch his calories but he eats business lunches all the time and eventually I just gave up. It scares the shit out of me sometimes."

It almost shocked Tay to hear one of these polished socialites use the word *shit. Preconceived notions are so ridiculous,* she told herself.

"Many of the women," a woman named Carolyn said, "are overweight as well."

"Yeah, but on women like Pam it looks really good. Very feminine and Rubenesque."

"Most the women I know diet constantly. At least I do."

"You are so lucky," Charlene said, looking at the canapé in Tay's hand. "I'm sure you never have to diet. You're so beautifully slim."

Beautifully slim? She'd always thought of herself as skinny. She almost blushed. Slim. She liked that word a lot.

She wandered to the bar and with a wink Linc poured her another glass of wine. *Linc and Pam must really have something going,* she thought. *He's totally attentive to all the guests and pours very professionally, but any time he has a moment his eyes wander the party to find Pam.* The look he had on his face said *serious* to Tay.

Around four-thirty there were several speeches, requests for pledges for a fund to aid sufferers of a disease Tay had never heard of, pleas so passionate that she felt fortunate not to have brought her checkbook.

Later, as the crowd thinned, Pam walked up beside her. "The Steinbergs are delighted. They raised more than they had expected. I hope you had a good time."

"I'm really surprised, but I did. I've had more interesting conversations this afternoon than I've had in months."

Pam looked suddenly serious. "That's a very sad commentary on your life, Tay."

She sighed. "Yeah. I guess it is."

"Listen," Pam said, brightening, "which days are you home this week? I'd love to set up that lunch we've been talking about."

This was a slice of life Tay hadn't tasted in a long time, if at all, and now an invitation for a friendly lunch with a charming woman. "I'd love that. I'm planning to be in the city on Monday, but I'll be working at home Tuesday."

"Wonderful. Have you ever been to the Tea Pot?"

Totally puzzled, she frowned. "The Tea Pot?"

"It's a kitschy little restaurant in Chappaqua. It has to be seen to be appreciated and it's got an interesting menu with salads filled with things I'd never think to use cold. I'm particularly fond of their curry chicken salad with Craisins and pine nuts, but they also make a dynamite cold duck breast with macadamia nuts and bits of Maraschino cherry. And everyone needs to see the decor at least once in their life. You either love it or hate it. It's sort of the Vegas of Westchester County."

Okay. She was intrigued. "That sounds wonderful."

"Great. I'll pick you up a little after one, if that works for you. It's mobbed between noon and one, so if we get there a little later we won't feel rushed."

"Sounds like a plan to me."

As Tay walked home, she thought about the afternoon, then about Steve. Adults. That's what these people were. Not all were fascinating, but they were all grown-ups, able to carry on conversations that didn't center on music and celebrities. And themselves. Pam too was a grown-up, a charming woman who obviously did extremely well organizing parties. What a fabulous job to have.

"I think she'd be perfect for me, Linc," Pam said as they sat on the patio with their feet up on a glass-topped table and watched the cleaning crew remove the remains of the party. "I just knew she would be. She seemed comfortable with the people she talked to and they all seemed to be enjoying her company. Mike Cioffi asked me, very sub rosa, whether she was one of my ladies. He was hoping that the lack of ankle bracelet was an oversight."

"He's a very selective guy, Pam," Linc said, lazily crossing his long legs at the ankles, "so she must have charmed the pants off of him, if you'll pardon the pun."

"I won't pardon the pun," she said as she slapped him slightly on his bare thigh. "I know how critical Mike is about his ladies. I'll feel her out over the next few weeks, pardon the play on words, and then, when we've had lunch a few times, if she seems sympatico, I'll talk to Marcy. Then, with any luck . . ."

"Watch it, lady. Feel her out?" Linc said, slapping her back on her fabric-covered thigh. "I agree, though. I think she'll be quite something for you, if she's agreeable. When she first walked up to me she looked me over like a piece of rare steak."

Pam slipped her hand under his shirt and slid her fingertips over his flat abs. "You are a piece of rare steak, at least to a woman of taste."

He turned and lightly brushed his lips against hers. "Well," he said, "you can feast all you want. With or without A1 sauce."

"Hmm," Pam said, "I never thought of A1 sauce. Whipped cream, maybe."

"Umm." He straightened. "By the way, I didn't see Rob Sherwood here today."

Pam and Rob had had a thing going for almost a year, but she knew that Linc wasn't jealous. Although he'd asked her to marry him a few times, neither of them had a need to commit, to be anyone's one and only, so each of them granted the other total freedom. And yet, when things got difficult, she turned to Linc. Sometimes she wondered . . . "I've barely seen you since I found out, but Rob's leaving," she said with a sigh, "moving to London. I saw him last evening and we had a farewell dinner."

"You didn't tell me. I'm so sorry, Pam," he said, squeezing her hand and looking at her with genuine sympathy.

"Don't be. I think it was just as well. We enjoyed each other's company and he was damn good in bed, but I think we'd sort of worn thin. It's always better to end things before they wear out their welcome."

"Fair enough," Linc said, solicitously. "Are you really okay with it?"

Pam smiled softly. "Yeah, I think I am." She gestured with her hand to encompass the party remains. "He was responsible for this whole thing and I will always be grateful for it."

"Yeah. He started something very special."

"And lucrative," she said with a grin.

"That too," he said with a chuckle. "Just be careful with Tay. You don't know much about her yet."

"Within a few weeks I'll know what I need to know, and if she's the person I think she is, she'll know a lot more about me and my business than she ever imagined."

Linc kissed her again, more deeply this time. "Do you need to supervise the cleanup folks?"

"No. What did you have in mind?"

"If you think you can keep from screaming and scaring those folks," he said, indicating the workers folding tables and chairs, "I've got a few ideas."

Dashing ahead of him, Pam called back, "Last one to the bedroom is a horny bastard."

Chapter 6

Tay watched Pam's Lexus pull up the Bonner driveway, punched the "away" code into the security system and closed the front door behind her. Climbing into the passenger seat and glancing at the driver she was glad she'd taken a little care with her appearance. Pam always seemed to look—what was the best way to put it?—put together.

Today Tay had dressed in one of the outfits she wore to work when she had a meeting, navy linen slacks paired with a white silk shirt with thin navy and red stripes. She had a matching navy blazer draped over her arm and wore white flat-heeled sandals to try to minimize the height difference between the two women.

"We look like we do some kind of an act," Pam said, gazing down. Tay chuckled as it registered that Pam was wearing identical colors, hers a slender navy skirt with a navy blouse with a tiny red and white figure.

"I'm afraid I don't sing or dance," Tay said, enjoying the warmth of Pam's acceptance.

"Me neither, except the kind of dancing you do with a guy."

"I haven't done any of that kind of dancing in about forever."

Pam shifted into reverse, backed down the driveway, and headed out of the cul-de-sac. "That's too bad. Dancing is such fun."

"Yeah. Steve wasn't into that kind of thing."

"Steve's the ex-boyfriend?"

"Yeah."

"Miss him?"

"Like I'd miss a toothache. I cared for him at first, and the sex was frequent and satisfying. I think we did it on every horizontal surface in the apartment." Tay had surprised and embarrassed herself with the fact that she'd just outlined her sex life to a woman who was almost a stranger. Somehow it seemed natural.

Pam's laugh was open and infectious and Tay joined her. "Sadly, that was the best part of the relationship," Tay continued, "and he used it to the max."

Pam eased the car onto a main road. "Used it?"

"He used sex to get what he wanted from me. Namely money."

"You paid him for sex?"

Tay huffed out a surprised breath. "No. Well, not the way you mean. It was just that when he wanted money for something, like a new keyboard or a piece of sound-mixing equipment, he told me how I'd be helping him start this great new enterprise. Then he'd make love to me until I said yes and loaned him another chunk from my bank account."

"Smart guy."

"I beg your pardon?" Tay's shock at Pam's reaction must have been evident.

"He used what he had that you wanted to get what *he* wanted. That may be a lot of things, unethical, immoral, but it's not stupid."

Tay hadn't ever thought of things that way. "That's an interesting way to look at it. I guess that makes me pretty dumb."

"Not at all. You gave him money and he fucked your brains out. Not an unusual trade-off."

"Hmm. I guess you have a point," Tay said, trying to rearrange her thinking. She'd been busy remembering Steve and everything he did for so long that this new concept couldn't quite gel yet, but what Pam said made sense. She'd have to give it some thought.

"Listen, Tay, don't get me wrong. He was obviously a louse, not for what he did, but because he was dishonest about it. If he'd been open about the quid pro quo you'd have had the chance to decide whether he was worth what you were paying him."

Tay snorted, then found a bubble of laughter surfacing. "You know, you're absolutely right." Laughter filled her. "You're a wise woman."

The talk turned to other things, but in the back of her mind Tay was feeling freer than she had in weeks. She slowly began to understand Steve, and Pam's view of their relationship made more and more sense as it rattled around in her head. She had participated in an agreement, whether she was totally aware of it at the time or not, and Steve had known exactly what the bargain was. Sadly, she hadn't, but whose fault was that?

Tay spotted the sign for the Tea Pot as they turned off of the town's main street. The front window was edged in painted purple swirls, with tiny yellow and pink flowers interspersed with butterflies, and the name spelled out in letters constructed from tiny cups and saucers. The hours were listed in one corner. 11:00–4:00. The kitschy little spot must do well pretty well, at least well enough to be open only for lunch, Tay thought.

Pam parked in front of the restaurant and the two women walked in. The place was unlike anything Tay had ever seen before. The center of the floor contained about a dozen tables, most full of women chatting over salads and wraps. The rest of the room was filled with teapots, cup-and-saucer combinations and related knickknacks. There were floral and patterned china pots with matching tea services, several old-fashioned samovars, a Turkish pot on a stoneware tray surrounded by four tiny cups, a few old English-looking silver sets and a few items she had no idea what they did or where they came from. The walls were covered with pot holders, everything from Kiss the Cook to roosters. For long moments Tay just stood and gaped.

As the hostess approached, Pam whispered, "I told you this place had to be seen to be believed."

"You were certainly right," Tay said, eyes wide.

The hostess led them to a small table on one side of the room and handed each woman a menu in an ersatz leather folder with the teapot motif carried throughout, and a photocopied sheet of the day's specials. Then she stood a wine list in the center of the pristine pink tablecloth. Pam picked it up and handed it to Tay. "You've got to see this, too," she said.

What she had thought was a wine list was actually a multipage tome listing the teas the restaurant had to offer, with the country of origin, the caffeine content and whether it was available hot, iced or both. "You've got to be kidding," Tay said, her mind boggling.

"Not at all, and if you've never had some of those teas you're in for a surprise. Of course, if you'd prefer soda or ice water they will let you get away with that, too. They don't have coffee, however."

"I'm not much of a tea drinker but in a place like this it seems like a crime of some sort to drink anything else."

"That's the way I felt the first time I came here. A new client suggested meeting here and she fit right in." Pam paused, then grinned. "Her party would have fit right in here. I hated every minute of it, but it was her daughter's bridal shower luncheon so I did what she wanted. Tiny sandwiches, miniature pastries and kitschy centerpieces built around little floral ceramic watering cans." She gazed into space, obviously remembering. "Each place had a little basket filled with chocolate truffles with a tiny pair of crepe-paper wedding bells hanging from the handle. Fifty women of all ages sat around giggling, openly reveling in several hours of opening elaborately wrapped packages containing high-priced erotic lingerie, dildos and sex manuals. I thought I'd gag."

"I guess you can't enjoy all the parties you arrange."

"Actually I like most of them, and most of the time, like last Saturday, people take my advice. However, the mother of the bride knew exactly what she wanted and wouldn't change a thing. She just needed me to make the arrangements and see to it that the house where the shower was held was organized on the day of the event."

"She didn't hold it in your backyard? It's such a perfect spot."

"No, not that one. It was at the home of the maid of honor. I think she giggled most of all. God, was I ever that young?"

Tay grinned. "I don't think I was."

"Me neither. Have a look at the menu," Pam suggested, "and decide which salad you want. Frankly I'm starving."

"Do you know what you're having already?" Tay asked, noticing that Pam hadn't picked up the menu.

"They have a curried chicken salad with apples, raisins and almonds that I love, so I have it when I'm here. It sounds so dietetic, but they have the most fabulous cheddar-cheese biscuits. I'm going to chuck what dieting I do and eat several."

"Do you come here often?"

"It's not a place I would come to often," Pam said, "but I thought you had to see it."

"I wouldn't have missed it for anything," Tay said as she folded her menu. "That salad you're having sounds wonderful to me. Do you have tea with it?"

"I'm particularly partial to one called Lapsang Souchong. It's got a sort of smokey, bacony smell. According to the menu the leaves are smoke-dried over a pinewood fire."

"That sounds too unusual to pass up. Hot or iced?"

"Either one. I think I'll have mine hot."

"I think I'll try iced."

The waitress arrived and took their order. "I read somewhere that the leaves for Lapsang souchong were originally carried under the saddles of camels to create the flavor."

Tay raised an eyebrow. "You're kidding, of course."

"No. Want to change your mind?"

"Now I'm even more curious."

"You must be a taster."

"A taster?" Tay asked, unfolding her pink napkin and putting it in her lap.

"I divide the world into two groups, tasters and non-tasters. There are people who are interested in tasting new things, and I don't mean just foods, because there might be something wonderful out there, and non-tasters, who spend their lives worried that they'll taste something they don't like. I guess it's risk takers and non-risk takers."

"I never thought of it that way, but I guess you're right. I'm pretty much of a taster."

"I suspected that the first time I met you."

Again the conversation wandered onto other topics. Tay was amazed that there was never a lull. One comment led to another, subjects as far afield as the latest conflict in the states of the old Soviet Union to a recent blockbuster trade in the NBA.

The salad was as good as Pam had promised and the tea delicious. The dessert menu was so tempting that the two women agreed to split an apple tart with homemade vanilla ice cream.

By three, the restaurant was almost empty and still the women chatted. Tay regretted that soon they would go their separate ways. Maybe Pam would suggest that they do this again sometime. Why did she think like that? she asked herself. She could make the suggestion. There wasn't such a big gap between her and Pam.

Okay, Tay, who are you fooling? They seemed to have a lot in common, but get real. Pam probably made more in a month than she did in a year. Money wasn't everything, of course, but it did emphasize the differences between them.

"How did you get into the party-planning business?" Tay asked in the next momentary lull in the conversation.

"It's a long story, but briefly, when my husband died I was broke. Actually I was less than broke, stuck with my huge house that was mortgaged to the hilt and no way to pay it off. Sadly, unlike you, I had no salable skills, nothing I could fall back on."

Sadly? Unlike me? Was Pam sounding a little envious of her?

"Anyway," she continued, "a friend asked me if she could use my yard for a wedding and, as they say, the rest is history."

"I think yours must be the ideal job. You spend your time with upper-crust types, mingling with famous and interesting people and getting paid for it."

"Frankly, it's a lot of work. Nothing ever goes off without a hitch, or two, or a dozen. I've got to deal with finicky caterers, crazy chefs, stressed-out brides, grooms and mothers and fathers of both. It's not all the glitz and glamour you see from the outside."

"I didn't think of it that way."

"You're right in one way, though, I do get to meet amazing people. Celebrities, politicos, the rich and famous. You probably noticed a couple of famous faces at the gathering last Saturday."

"I recognized a few and there was one guy I was dying to talk to, to yell at him for what he did in the state senate a few months ago."

"But you didn't."

"Not the right venue for vitriol."

"Thanks for not making anyone feel uncomfortable."

With a small smile, Tay said, "Of course, but my palm was itching to slap his little butt."

"If you're thinking about the same guy I am, I couldn't agree with you more."

The visit continued for another hour, by which time the women felt like they'd known each other forever. Pam told Tay a few amusing anecdotes about parties she'd arranged and Tay told her a lot about Steve, about both their relationship and their breakup.

They talked about everything and nothing, and when Tay glanced at her watch and realized that they'd been chatting for almost three hours, she was amazed. Few people were interesting enough to keep her amused for that long. Usually she grew tired of companions after an hour or so, or at least she had with Steve's friends and the people she met at work.

The restaurant was empty and the staff was looking eager to close when Pam reached for the check. She pulled her credit card from her wallet and Tay added her own. No argument about who paid. Two credit-card slips were delivered back to the table by a relieved waitress.

When Pam dropped her off at her driveway, Tay said, "I'd love to do this again," and to her delight they made a date for the following week. Quickly their lunches became a once, then twice a week thing as the two women became fast friends.

Chapter 7

On a rare cool and gray Saturday afternoon in early June, thirty-four-year-old Justin Karalis pulled his slightly battered eleven-year-old Subaru up the driveway on Maple Court until it was nosed against the garage door beside Lissa's little Toyota. She was home and that was great.

He had just arrived back from a month-long photographic tour of the wine country of Northern California and had several flash drives filled with photographs and film clips that he was itching to get onto Dave Bonner's computer system so he could do all the editing that was whirling in his mind. He had been in such a rush that he'd stopped for only a few hours at his father's house in Cold Spring Harbor. He would like to have left even sooner but his older brother and his wife, his younger sister, her husband and their three children had been there to welcome him home. His parents had planned a catered buffet lunch for his homecoming, so it had taken him longer than he'd wanted to extricate himself and head north.

He'd thought about warning Lissa that he was in town and asking her if he could stay in their guesthouse but he hadn't wanted to give her the opportunity to say no. The last time he'd stayed there he'd overstayed his welcome and he'd finally taken the hint to move on. And anyway, he wanted to try again to get into Lissa's pants.

So as soon as he could gracefully leave, he'd jumped into the car his folks kept for him and headed for Maple Court. Wearing faded jeans, a longsleeved deep green polo and tennis shoes, he climbed out of his car and, hearing splashing sounds from the backyard, rounded the garage and strode toward the pool.

The woman swimming laps certainly wasn't Lissa. The hair was wrong. Lissa's was short and deep brown while this woman's long braid was blond. The body was similar, a swimmer's physique with great muscle tone that was evident as she plowed through the water with long, powerful strokes then executed an excellent flip turn. He stood, wondering who she was and why she was doing laps alone in the Bonners' pool.

Finally, when she reached the shallow end, she stood up, her back to him, grabbed a towel from the side of the pool and, with effortless grace, climbed out. Still not seeing him, she began a dash toward the spa.

"Excuse me," he said.

She whirled and placed a startled hand against her breastbone. Not bad, he thought. The simple black suit was so tight and the fabric so worn that it left little to the imagination. She had a nice, if reed-thin body with nipples that had tightened in the cool air. Those certainly weren't Lissa's generous boobs, but they'd do in a pinch. "Holy shit," she said. "You scared the daylights out of me. Who the hell are you?"

"Who the hell are you?" he retorted, giving her body another once-over, partly because he enjoyed the view and partly to unsettle her. He liked to shake people up from time to time.

"Okay." She let out a long breath and, seeing his eyes roam over her, wrapped the towel around herself, tucking it in over her breasts. "One of us has to start. I'm Tay Barwick, a friend of Lissa's. Your turn."

He walked forward and extended his hand. "Justin Karalis. I'm also a friend of Lissa's. Actually I've heard her talk about you. College friend, right?"

He could see her shoulders relax. "Right. You're the photographer she met in one of her classes. You lived here for a short time about eighteen months ago."

"Right on both counts," he said, glad to have them on a civil if not friendly basis. "Is she or Dave around?"

"As of yesterday they were somewhere in the western part of Quinghai Province. That's in Western China, I looked it up. They're photographing an amazing assortment of unusual animals, some I've never even heard of, and getting great shots. She and Dave have sent back some fabulous pictures and videos."

"Don't tell me her father finally agreed to take her along on one of his safaris."

"Not without a lot of arm-twisting." Her laugh was warm. "And whining. I'm house- and critter-sitting while they're gone."

"Ah yes, her critters. How many now?"

"Two dogs, three cats, two ferrets, a rabbit, and a ball python."

"Lissa Bonner, girl wildlife photographer, who never met an animal she didn't like."

"Or adopt. Maybe that's what makes her pictures so wonderful. You can almost feel the affection."

"That could certainly be." Justin heaved a great sigh. With Lissa gone there wouldn't be any reason why he couldn't stay over for a few days and use the Bonners' advanced editing equipment and software. *Stay cool, Justin,* he told himself. *Don't be too obvious.* He looked the woman over. There might be a few fringe benefits here as well. "However, I guess her being out of the country puts a kink in my plans."

"Listen, I'm freezing here. Would you mind continuing this conversation while I soak in the hot tub?"

He looked at her skin and saw gooseflesh. "Of course." Together they walked across the lawn and Tay quickly immersed herself in the steamy water, dipping her head to warm the water in her hair.

"Okay, what were the plans that I've loused up?" she asked when her teeth stopped chattering.

"Not you," he said, dropping onto a bench beside the spa. "Just Lissa's not being here. I had intended to wheedle my way into crashing in the guesthouse for a couple of days so I could use Dave's computer setup. I probably won't be here most of the time. I've got meetings with several magazine editors next week and I'll probably crash for a few nights with friends in the city."

Tay looked skeptical. "Lissa didn't write anything about your arrival."

He did feel a little sheepish. In addition to overstaying his welcome, he'd asked Lissa out a few times the last time he was in the area but she'd said something about a boyfriend and made it plain she wasn't interested. This time he had been afraid that she'd feel awkward so he didn't want to give her any time to make up excuses not to see him. "I didn't tell her. I just thought I'd surprise her."

Tay's grin was genuine. "Surprise!"

"I'm sorry I bothered you." He stood. "I'm out of here."

"Don't rush off. I don't see any reason for you to leave. There's no one using the guesthouse and I'm sure Lissa and Dave wouldn't mind if you bunked there for a while and used the computer system. Let me drop her an e-mail and make sure it's okay with both of them."

Tay knew the name Justin Karalis, of course. Lissa told her all the juicy details of each of her encounters with men, and there had been plenty. Justin had showed up about eighteen months before and Lissa had been involved in a very hot relationship with another guy which was, at that moment, exclusive. She had mentioned to Tay that she'd had to brush Justin off but he'd stayed at the guesthouse for a while and been a bit more persistent than she'd liked, although she'd enjoyed the brief flirtation. "He's a real ladies' man, with fabulous eyes, and if I hadn't been involved I'd probably have jumped at the chance to fuck him senseless, and let him do likewise." She also warned that "He isn't a relationship kind of guy, though. He's got girlfriends everywhere. When he was staying here he only spent one out of three nights in the guesthouse. He said he was staying in the city with friends or on Long Island with his family, but personally I think he was having grown-up sleepovers."

She'd said he was really cute, Tay remembered, but she'd understated tremendously. He was gorgeous. Tall, with shaggy chestnut hair that hung over the collar of his polo shirt and skin that looked soft but was deeply tanned, as if he spent considerable time out-of-doors. He filled out the shirt nicely, as he did his jeans. Nice body altogether. But it was his eyes that attracted her. They were a shade somewhere between blue and green, and were fringed with long, almost black lashes. She knew women who would kill for bedroom eyes like that, and Tay really liked the sexy way he looked at her. His look made her nipples swell and her pussy twitch. God, she hadn't felt this sexy since Steve left. Down, girl!

"Did you just get back from somewhere? I mean needing a place to crash and all. No apartment of your own?"

"I'm gone more than I'm here," he said, "so I let my apartment go. If you're not comfortable with my staying here I can always go back to the Island and stay with my folks. However, I don't really like the intrusive atmosphere there and I would love to get my film into Dave's computer. Would you really let someone you don't know bunk in the guesthouse?"

"Lissa mentioned you occasionally a while back, so I'm pretty sure you're legit." She climbed out of the tub, grabbed another towel from the cabinet beside the tiled path and wrapped herself tightly. "Let me dry off and change and I'll drop her and Dave a note. You can put whatever things you've got in there," she said, pointing to the guesthouse, "until I hear back, but I can't imagine there'll be any problem."

His smile was—well, all Tay could think was "dangerous." "I can't thank you enough," he said, almost purring.

Okay. Keep it light. "No problem. What do you photograph?"

"Buildings and people mostly. And grapes."

"Grapes?"

"I just got back from the wine country of Northern California. I do travel stuff to pay the bills. That allows me to go wherever I want, and as long as I get articles published from time to time, I get to write all my travel off on my income tax."

"It must be wonderful to do something you enjoy and get paid for it. Where before California?" she asked as she dried herself off.

"London, and before that Mali. In London I did an article about the restoration of an old baronial country house and in Mali I photographed the changing life in a native village as they evolved into the twenty-first century."

"Timbuktu's in Mali, right?"

"Right you are. That's amazing. Most people haven't even heard of it."

"Sounds fascinating. I read a lot but I haven't traveled much, so I envy people who have."

"How about you?" Justin asked. "What do you do?"

"Nothing glamorous. I design Web sites, do grant applications and edit articles for publication for a multinational."

"Sounds complicated and high pressure."

"Sometimes." She shivered, the warm towel no longer

keeping her body heat up in the cool air. "Listen, I need to change. Why don't you get settled and I'll write to Lissa and Dave?" She was repeating herself but she found herself out of things to say.

"That works for me." He looked at his watch. "It's about five now. How about I treat you to dinner at that great Mexican place in town to say thanks for indulging me? Assuming it's still there, that is."

"Casa Manaña? It's still there. I've seen it as I drove by but never been there." This was not a date, she assured herself, although Lissa had commented on how quickly he operated the last time he was around. But he was nice to look at and as usual she was bored. Why the hell not? "Sure. I'll knock on your door in about an hour. That should give you time to get settled."

"Great. See ya then."

Casa Manaña was a typical Tex-Mex restaurant decorated with hanging lamps with intricate metalwork shades, dark wood tables, banquettes and chairs upholstered in red plastic and dark wooden tables covered with snowy white tablecloths. They had a standard menu of tacos, fajitas and combo plates, with an interesting assortment of main dishes. The place was quieter than many she'd been to in the city, with no roaming guitarists playing "Guantanamera" and looking for tips. The tables were spread out a bit more than at other restaurants so that conversation was encouraged. She'd have to suggest this place to Pam for lunch one day, Tay thought. "You've obviously been here before," she said. "What do you recommend?"

"What do you like?" Justin asked with a subtle dropping of his voice.

"I like most things," she said with a slight smile, willing to go along with the sexual innuendo.

"I like a woman who likes everything," he said, glancing

at the front of her butter-yellow blouse, then gazing into her eyes. No doubt about it, he was a fast worker.

"I didn't say everything, just most things." She knew that neither of them was talking about food and the banter was fun, but right then her stomach was empty. She held up her hand, palm out. "Okay—enough for now. You promised me food. Remember? Dinner?" Was she objecting to the flirtation? Not in the least.

He sighed, and his sexy smile left no doubts that he was thinking about ending the evening in bed. "Okay. Dinner first." He glanced at the menu. "They make a great Shrimp Ajillo but it's very heavy in garlic and we'd both have to eat it or neither of us should."

"Garlic's fine with me," Tay said. Bad breath be damned. From a quick look at the menu there would be no way to avoid it.

"Then here's my suggestion. How about we start with Alitas de Pollo, that's chicken wings. They're sensational here and the portion is monumental. Then we could split the shrimp and a dessert. I don't want to stuff myself so early in the evening." He raised an eyebrow.

At another time Justin's obvious intentions might have turned Tay off, but it had been so long since a man had come on to her that she was enjoying the byplay. "Neither do I. That sounds like a great idea. We can decide on dessert later."

"Fine with me. Wine? Beer?"

"Do they have sangria?"

"They make a wonderful white sangria."

"I didn't know it came in white."

"Willing to experiment?" he asked, with another obvious double meaning.

"Sure."

"Good girl. I'll join you."

After Justin ordered for both of them they talked about

their lives, with most sentences carrying an innuendo of one sort or another. Finally Tay had had enough. "Justin, I have to admit that I'm getting worn out with the constant sexual banter."

"I'm sorry, but I'm glad you said something. I find you very attractive and I think you're interested as well. Shall we agree and declare a truce until later, when we can decide what our last course should be?"

"Truce," Tay said, offering her hand across the table. Justin shook it, but instead of shaking it, he kissed the inside of her wrist. She pulled her tingling fingers back with a light, nonverbal admonishment, and the rest of the meal proceeded more calmly. Although she relaxed, she was always conscious of the decision they'd make later, and she was pretty sure she knew what she'd like for dessert. She certainly wasn't averse to a one-night stand, and that's what Justin was probably interested in as well. After all, she was on the pill and carried condoms in her purse at all times, just in case. She was a modern woman who missed sex greatly.

They finished the meal with a very good flan and cups of strong espresso. Justin waved away her efforts to split the check and tucked an American Express Gold Card into the leather folder. "No need. This is my party to say thank you for letting me use the guesthouse, and other things." When she looked slightly dubious he smiled and said, "I'm not an itinerant photographer, if that's what you're thinking. I do good work and I'm paid a decent wage for it."

"I wasn't saying anything."

"Sorry. I know you weren't. I get a little defensive sometimes. My folks always treat me as if I were a kid playing with my cameras until I get a real job."

"You won't get that from me. I know Dave and Lissa too well, and anyway, I'm all for doing things that give you joy."

He squeezed her hand. "I know what would give me joy." He twisted his face into an overly obvious leer.

"I get the message."

The waiter returned at that moment and Justin signed the credit-card receipt. In the parking lot Justin opened the passenger-side car door for her, then climbed behind the wheel. He reached over and gently cupped his hand on the back of her neck, pulling her toward him. His lips were warm and firm and his kiss was long and lingering, savoring her like a special treat. When they separated, he said, "You still taste like flan."

He was a fabulous kisser, and she found it difficult to catch her breath. Her heart was pounding and she knew she was wet with desire. She didn't respond to his comment, couldn't answer, and not another word passed between them as they made their way back to Maple Court. He drove expertly with one hand while the fingers of the other stroked the nape of her neck. Getting hotter and hotter as they entered the cul-de-sac Tay turned and kissed his palm. She licked the sensitive pulse at his wrist and nipped at the base of his thumb. God, she was hungry. She needed what he could provide, so what the heck? Why not?

Justin pulled the car to the top of the driveway and the two almost ran to the front door. Once inside, clothing began to litter the stairs. Toward the bottom Tay pulled off her sneakers, dragged the belt from Justin's jeans and tossed it into the entryway. Several steps higher, he kicked off his shoes and pulled off her slacks, and she dragged his shirt over his head. Her blouse landed on the next-to-the-top step along with his jeans and their socks. At the top of the stairs he took her in his arms and kissed her deeply, his fingers playing with the elastic on her bikini panties, her fabric-covered breasts rubbing his skin.

Tay pushed her palms against his shoulders until, panting, they separated so she could look at him. He was gorgeous, with a well-developed, almost hairless chest, narrow hips and long legs.

She watched Justin as he gazed at her appreciatingly. Steve had always said that he liked her slightly angular body with its small but firm breasts and she was now glad she'd selected a lacy peach bra. Matching panties just barely covered her well-trimmed mound. From the leer on Justin's face she knew he wasn't disappointed.

He cupped her head and kissed her again, then they hurried into her bedroom, turning on the small dressing-table lamp. He looked mildly amused while Tay summarily grabbed Honey and Ginger off the bed, tucking one under each arm. Without a wasted motion she tossed them out the door and closed it behind them.

With a deft flick Justin flipped the spread off the bed and sat down on the edge of the mattress. He pulled her close between his spread thighs and nuzzled her belly. Catching the top of her panties with his thumbs he slowly pulled them down, nibbling a path from her belly button to the top of her pubic hair.

"I love the scent of a turned-on woman," he said, surprising Tay. Steve had always been a silent lover.

As he held her hips against his lips she closed her eyes and let her head fall backward, concentrating on the feel of his mouth. Then he pulled her onto the bed beside him and found her already-erect nipple through the soft fabric of her bra. He bit down hard enough for her to feel it through the material, wetting the cloth with his saliva. Then he blew on the moist fabric, making her nipples harden still more. He repeated this until she thought she would expire from the sheer pleasure of it all.

When she could wait no longer, she rolled on top of him and straddled his thighs, noting the large bulge in the front of his briefs. She took him in her hand, feeling the thickness of his erection, then squeezed his testicles lightly through the stretchy cotton. White cotton briefs had never looked so sexy. While she played, Justin unhooked her bra so he could play with her naked breasts.

"Enough of this, woman," he growled, flipping her onto her back and yanking her panties all the way off. He stood, pulled down his briefs, then stood frozen and cursed. He started toward the door. "My wallet's in my pants pocket."

"Here," Tay said, reaching into the drawer of the bed table and pulling out a foil packet. "Is this what you're looking for?"

"I love a woman who's prepared for anything," he said, quickly unrolling the condom over his cock. As he did so, Tay gazed at the size of him and wondered whether it would hurt. She knew that a woman's body could accommodate most men, but he was really built.

She needn't have worried. She was so wet that he slid inside easily and slowly stroked her with his cock. He moved in and out with agonizing deliberateness, teasing and tempting her. His fingers found her clit, and as he fucked her he rubbed, pushing her higher and higher.

Finally her impatience got the better of her. She wrapped her legs around his waist and, with sudden pressure of calves and heels, thrust upward, pushing him deeply into her. "And I love a woman who takes what she wants," he said, his voice gravely.

"Oh God, fuck me good," she cried as he pounded into her. "More, more."

"Yes, yes, yes," he screamed as he came and Tay came with him. Hard. Fast. Waves of incredibly violent spasms sucked on his erection. Eventually his motions slowed.

Replete and exhausted, their breathing heavy and rapid, they collapsed onto the bed, side by side. "Shit, Tay. That was amazing," he said when he was finally able to catch his breath.

"Yes," she said, barely able to get the word out. "Amazing."

A while later Justin climbed off the bed and, with some confusion, found his clothing and dressed. He pulled the spread over her. "I'm going back to the guesthouse."

Leaving? He was probably wise. "You're right," she said. "It's much too soon for sleepovers."

He grinned, flipped off the light, and moments later she heard the front door close.

Chapter 8

"You look like the cat that swallowed the canary," Pam said the following Tuesday as the two women settled into chairs at a new Indian restaurant a bit north of Maple Court. "Who's the guy?"

It was difficult for Tay not to smirk. She and Justin had spent Sunday in bed, making love in a few adventurous ways. In the middle of the afternoon, she'd thrown on clothes to exercise the dogs. Although she knew they didn't really need the workout she found she needed a little breathing room to keep things in proportion. Lust was a powerful motivator, but it had been with Steve, too. She wasn't going to get caught again.

From time to time she and Justin wandered to the well-stocked kitchen and Tay put together a meal wearing only an apron. "That is the sexiest thing I've ever seen," he had said while she scrambled eggs for a late breakfast. His left hand slipped beneath the bib front to fondle her breast, then he cupped a bare buttock. She'd reluctantly gone to work on Monday while Justin spent the day hunched over the computer. Today he had gone into the city to meet with several new magazine contacts. He'd already said he'd probably stay with friends and most likely wouldn't be back to the guesthouse until later in the week. "I'll call and let you know." Tay took advantage of the respite to have lunch with Pam.

"What guy?" she said, being a little coy.

"Come on, Tay. That guy I saw in the front yard yesterday?"

"Oh, that guy," Tay said, grinning from ear to ear.

Pam nodded knowingly. "It must be very good sex."

Tay let out a long breath and decided to be honest. "It's been so long for me that I think any sex would be good sex, but Justin's very adventurous."

"So," Pam said, her smile still bright, "you've been—adventuring?"

"Steve thought he was God's gift to lovemaking but he wasn't particularly imaginative. Justin's pretty terrific."

"I'm happy for you. Is this something with a future?"

"Probably not. I gather from Lissa that he's got a girl in every port, so to speak, and I'm just the local interest. I thought quite a bit about what you said about Steve and the rules of the relationship. So I decided that I'm not averse to great sex as long as we both know what's what."

As they usually did after lunch, the two women wandered into Tay's kitchen for coffee. She'd learned to use Lissa's espresso machine to make mocha lattes that were as good as any the local Starbucks could concoct. While Tay got mugs from the cupboard Pam sat at the table and watched as the machine chugged away. When there was a momentary lull in the conversation, Pam asked, "What did you think of that business last year with Eliot Spitzer?"

The out-of-left-field question caught Tay by surprise, but sudden twists in their conversation weren't unusual. "You mean the call-girl thing? I thought he was an arrogant idiot, thinking he could do something like that and not get caught."

"You're right there. But what about the whole prostitute thing?"

"That was his business, and his wife's, I guess."

"You don't blame the girl?"

"Blame her? Why should I? She was being paid for a service. What goes on between them is their business."

"I'm glad you feel that way. I was sure you would."

"Glad? That's a funny thing to say."

"I think the coffee's done. Can I help steam the milk?"

"I can handle it." She always did. Something was going on.

As Tay dealt with the milk, Pam hesitated, then said, "I have a few things I would like to tell you, and I don't want you to be shocked. At any time, if I say anything that upsets you, just let me know and I'll head back to my house. I don't want anything to get in the way of our friendship. I really treasure that."

Pam watched as Tay foamed milk and added chocolate powder. She'd felt an immediate connection to Tay, although she had no idea exactly why, a connection that had only deepened over the past few weeks. Tay was an amazing woman, head and shoulders above the idiot she had been dating. Why did women seem to go for the grungy, rocker types who were capable of great sex, and used it for their own purposes?

Now there was Justin, a one-night stand looking for a place to happen. No strings, just the way good sex could, and maybe should, be under the right circumstances.

She watched Tay's crisp, capable movements in silence. Pam liked her more and more. Maybe it was the way she looked people straight in the eye; or maybe it was her easy smile and direct answers to direct questions. Maybe it was her ability to be, or at least seem to be, interested in everything. Maybe it was the unconscious sensuality in certain of her movements. It was probably all that and more.

Pam had thought from the beginning that Tay would be a great addition to Club Fantasy, and now was as good a time as any to finally bring the subject up. If Tay proved to be as open-minded as Pam was almost positive she was, she would really enjoy the people that Marcy and Pam surrounded themselves with. Despite Justin, the woman was also sexually frustrated, ready for a real adventure. The question was, did Tay know that and would she be ready for the Club's kind of games?

"You know," Pam said as Tay put a mug of foamy latte in front of her, "I've known Lissa casually, and Dave better, for several years," she began. "They're great people and very open-minded."

"Okay," Tay said when the silence lengthened. She looked a little puzzled at the new shift of the conversation. "I've known Lissa since college, but then you know that."

"Did they tell you anything about me? To watch out for me, or about what I do to earn a living?"

"No," Tay said. "Listen, Pam, I'm not used to you beating around the bush. I think you're trying to tell me something and you sound very serious. I'd like to think we're friends. Is there a problem I can help with?"

Pam huffed out a breath. Help with? In a strange way she'd be helping Tay. "Not in the way you think. I want to tell you about myself."

Tay looked concerned. "We've talked so much that I didn't realize there was something I didn't know. Are you ill?"

Pam reached out, squeezed Tay's hand and smiled reassuringly. "No. Not at all."

She watched Tay's shoulders relax. "Good. I'm glad. You had me worried for a moment. So now that it's not medical, you've got me really curious. What's up?"

Pam took a deep breath. In for a penny . . . "Where to start? When I was left with my house and no way to earn a living, I put together a party for an acquaintance. A friend suggested that I expand my horizons and cater to big-business types, the ones with the money."

"I know that, and I can see that it worked. You certainly do cater to the upper crust."

"Yes, but not just in the way you mean. I entertain men and at my parties sometimes men and women hook up. Financially."

She watched the puzzled expression on Tay's face change to amazement as she caught on. "Oh shit. That question about Eliot Spitzer. You were feeling me out." Tay suddenly blushed at her unintended double entendre.

"If we're going to have this conversation we've got to get past the problems with words and double meanings. Just say the things that come into your mouth and we'll be okay. I cater to men, and occasionally to women, who want companionship of a sexual nature."

Tay's eyes widened. "You're telling me that you're a prostitute."

"I prefer courtesan, but yes." There was a long silence while Pam let Tay digest what she'd just heard.

"You throw parties, so you're also a madam of sorts?"

"That too." Pam paused to let Tay absorb what she'd just said. "I hope that doesn't make you hate me."

"No, not at all. Quite the opposite, actually. I'm fascinated. Tell me about it."

"It's pretty simple. In addition to connecting hungry men with willing women, I entertain men myself. Many are from out of town, looking for an intelligent woman to have dinner with, talk with and have sex with, not necessarily in that order. Although I will occasionally go directly to someone's hotel room, the guy and I frequently have dinner first, go to a show or a business function, then make love afterward."

"As you can imagine, I have a thousand questions."

Pam couldn't have gotten a better response. Tay didn't seem shocked, just curious, exactly as Pam had hoped. "I'll answer most of your questions as best I can, but no names of clients."

"Of course not. I assume these men pay for privacy."

"That's a big part of it. They pay big bucks for anonymity, for no strings, for, oh, let's just say flexibility."

"I'm blown away. You seem so . . ."

"Normal?"

"I'm sorry. There's no way this will come out right," Tay said ruefully. "You don't look like what I'd expect a courtesan or a madam to look like."

Pam chuckled. "I know. I felt the same way when I started. I thought all call girls—and that's a big part of what I am—were in their late teens or early twenties, big-breasted, long legged and gorgeous. I learned very quickly that some men want real, bright, well-read, easy-to-talk-to women, not eye candy."

"That surprises me, but it makes sense, I guess. Are most of your johns, I mean customers, I mean men, regulars? God," she sighed, "no offense."

"Relax. No offense taken. This is difficult to talk about without using incendiary words. Feel free to say whatever you like, use whatever words you want, and I'll assume you mean no offense. Deal?"

She could see Tay's chest rise and fall with another big sigh. "Deal."

"Okay. To answer your question, yes, most of my clients are regulars, men who've been with me before, enjoyed our time together, and have enough money to indulge their pleasures. They call and set up a new date or, in the case of two at the moment, have monthly appointments."

"Are most of them married? Why don't they just do things at home? I mean, I can understand if a guy's out of town, but I assume not all are."

"Most of them are married and some of them do live locally." She caught Tay's hesitation. "That gave me pause when I first started entertaining, too. In the beginning I asked a few guys why me and not their wives. One said that his wife wouldn't be interested in the things we do together. Another said he just wanted something different, someone different. Many of my clients are just bored or lazy, with money enough to spend on evenings out."

"Okay, more nosey questions. They said that the woman who entertained the governor made over one thousand dollars per. Is that possible?"

"Amazingly enough, yes. The money's really big, and I earn it doing something I love. I love good sex, along with good conversation and going out to expensive restaurants. I've seen most of the shows on Broadway, the good and the god-awful. One of my regulars is a hockey fan, although I've no idea why, and I've been to several Ranger games. It really varies."

"You talk about shows and dinners. Don't most just want sex?"

"Many do, and if that's what they want, I oblige."

Her voice lowered. "Kinky sex?"

"Sure. For the prices we charge, men want—oh, let's just say different stuff."

"And you connect men with other women, too? And take a cut of the profits?"

She decided not to mention Marcy just yet. "Right again."

Tay paused. The entire conversation was just too weird. Pam was quite attractive and seemed so normal. However, she didn't doubt for a moment that her friend was telling her the truth. She intimated that Dave Bonner knew. Was he one of her customers? He was single and certainly able to do whatever he wanted, but would he pay for it? She wondered. It was all totally mind-boggling.

Tay thought about the hunky guy who'd been behind the bar at the party. Pam's boyfriend? What was his name again? "You introduced me to the bartender at the party."

"Linc, and I'll answer your questions before you have to

figure out how to ask them. Yes, he knows, and yes, he's also in the business, although only part-time now. He's a male model and recently he's been getting lots of magazine work."

"I thought he looked a little familiar. I must have seen his photo somewhere." She took a deep breath. "So women hire—what would you call him?"

"He's a male prostitute and, yes, more women than you'd imagine are interested in uninhibited sex. Sure, many women want someone who looks like Linc to wear to parties and such, like new, expensive jewelry, but most also want the fringe benefits."

"Aren't you jealous?"

"Actually no, and he isn't, either. I love him very much and I know he loves me, too. It might sound unbelievable, but our other activities don't interfere with that." She took a deep breath. "What we do with our clients involves lots of caring. If we didn't care about our counterparts we wouldn't be any good at what we do. But caring isn't loving." She thought for a moment. "Maybe that's not right. What we feel toward each other is something special, different from any other feelings. That's the best I can do to describe it. If he's enjoying himself, that's great. Neither his activities nor mine get in the way of what we have together."

"That's an astonishing attitude and I'm not sure I'd feel the same way. However, putting that aside, now I have to ask the sixty-four-dollar question. Why are you telling me all this?"

"I had hoped not to get to that so quickly, but here goes. I'm looking for someone to have the occasional date with some of my newest clients."

It was all Tay could do not to let her jaw hang open.

Pam continued. "You seem to have an open attitude toward sex. I watched you at the party and you made great conversation with lots of different people. You're obviously bright, attractive and charming and now I know you're not averse to good, hot sex. I hoped you'd be interested in my business."

"Phew. My mind is reeling. Are you serious?"

"I wouldn't have told you all this if I weren't." She twinkled. "Like the T-shirt says, 'So many men and so little time.'"

"I don't know what to say."

"Of course you don't. Not right away. You need time to absorb all of this and I certainly understand that." Pam finished her coffee and stood. "Think about what I've told you and digest it all. I only ask that you keep it to yourself."

"Not a problem. Who would I tell? Who'd even believe me?"

"Good. Let's have lunch again, maybe on Saturday, and we can talk more. I'm sure you'll have lots more questions and I'll answer what I can without breaking confidences. Will you think about it all?"

"I can't imagine I'll think about much else."

Pam's smile was genuine. "Good." She turned and headed for the door. "I'll call you and we'll make plans for Saturday."

"Great."

Chapter 9

Pam had asked her to come in through the house to the back patio. The day was warm but gray, with a hint of drizzle in the air. Despite the gloom the patio looked festive and inviting. Tay didn't think Pam could do things any other way.

A table had been set with a picnic-style tablecloth and napkins, colorful paper plates, plastic glasses and bright metal utensils with matching-colored enamel handles. A platter in the center of the table held flame-grilled chicken breasts, several kinds of grilled vegetables and salad greens. Several bottles of different dressings were also in evidence. "I hope you don't mind, but I thought that, despite the dreary weather, we'd eat out here today."

Pam immediately noticed that the table was set for three. At that moment a matronly looking woman walked out through the sliding doors from the living room. She was wearing an untucked man-tailored shirt that hung over well-washed black denim pants. "Sorry, but I find that I need to use the ladies' room rather frequently these days."

"Tay Barwick," Pam said, "this is my friend Marcy McGee and she's expecting child number four in a few months." Pam patted Marcy's almost nonexistent belly.

"A few months?" Marcy said with a groan. "More than five months, actually."

"Nice to meet you," Tay said. The woman was nice looking with carefully cut mahogany-brown hair and stylishly applied makeup. She put out her hand and found Marcy's grip strong without being overpowering. "This is your fourth?"

"I have twin boys, Patrick and William, who are now almost seven, and Eliza will be five soon. Spoiled rotten, every one, but I love them dearly."

"Where are they today?" Tay asked.

"My husband, Zack, is with them. He's taking them to the Bronx Zoo, if the real rain holds off." She pulled out an envelope and waved it under Pam's nose. "I've got new pictures."

"Great," Pam said. "I haven't seen the kids in forever."

Marcy handed over an obviously professionally taken photo of a delightful-looking family. The twins each had big grins, revealing missing teeth, and the little girl, perched on her father's knee, was holding a stuffed elephant. There were matching stills of each of the children and of Marcy and her husband.

"God, I'm jealous," Pam said with a slight catch in her voice.

"Of the family?" Marcy asked. "I didn't realize that you still regretted not having kids."

"I get a twinge occasionally," she said, handing the photos to Tay for a closer look. "Back when I was married I thought about it a lot but I think Vin was just as happy to find out I couldn't have any." She turned to Tay. "We had all the tests and nada."

Marcy patted her friend's shoulder and Pam ended the brief awkward moment. "Changing the subject, I saw Zack last week and he looks great. How's his job going?"

"He's thriving, and now works from home from time to time so he gets to spend more time with the kids."

"I assume he's happy about the baby."

"After Eliza he said he didn't think he wanted any more but he's discovered how wonderful kids are—most of the time. Anyway, he's ecstatic and, like always, treats me like I have some life-threatening condition." Marcy turned to Tay. "Sorry for the family talk. Pam and I haven't seen each other in a while."

Tay handed the photos back. "Do you live around here?" she asked.

"Nope, although part of me would love to. I grew up in a small town upstate and I've always wanted to move back into a house, but we've got an apartment that makes Zack and me happy. I wouldn't give up the comforts of being in the big city now anyway. I understand you're a city girl, too."

"I grew up in nearby New Jersey and we came into the city often. Since college I've lived in SoHo and in Brooklyn Heights."

"God, I love both those areas. Brooklyn Heights has some of the benefits of the country but is within a quick subway ride of midtown. Zack and I looked there last year when we realized we'd need more space but we settled on a four bedroom on Riverside Drive."

Tay's eyes widened. That was the really high-rent district. Zack must be doing very well for them to be able to afford something that pricey. "What does your husband do?"

"He's in human resources with a company that manufactures plastics for a zillion industrial uses." When she mentioned the name, Tay had heard of it. "I gather you're part of corporate America, too. Pam tells me that you commute to the city a few days a week."

"I've finagled it so I go in Mondays, Wednesdays and Fridays and spend the rest of the days telecommuting."

"Great invention, computers," Marcy said, putting a napkin on her lap. "How about we eat? I find I'm hungry all the time now. My doctor tells me I'm eating for two, but he keeps reminding me how little that second one is."

"Second one?" Pam said. "Only one?"

"I had another sonogram last week," Marcy said with a long sigh of relief, "and it's definitely, definitely not twins." She turned to Tay. "We had a little scare last month but it's definitely a single. My twin sister, Jenna, just had her second set of twins, boys again. So now she's got four boys, all under six, and a big sister—no one uses her name any more—who's seven."

"That's quite a collection," Tay said. "Does she live in the city, too?"

"No, she's upstate where we came from. Her husband, Gary, is a lawyer, and like Zack he dotes on the kids."

With enthusiasm the three women scooped up chicken, vegetables and salad. Marcy eschewed the dressing. "Calories," she said. Tay couldn't imagine why this lovely looking woman was worried. Pam poured glasses of Chablis for herself and Tay and iced tea for Marcy. "No alcohol for me until after Junior is born, more's the pity."

"Boy or girl?" Tay asked.

"Zack and I decided not to find out this time."

For the next half hour they chatted and got to know each other a little better. They talked about movies they'd seen, TV shows they liked and didn't, and Tay regaled them with a few interesting anecdotes she'd gleaned from a course on Western civilization that she was taking over the Internet.

As they settled back after lunch, Tay asked, "So, Marcy, where do you know Pam from?" She wondered whether Marcy knew what Pam did for a living. Would a woman with little children want to be associated with a prostitute?

The two women smiled at each other. Then Pam said, "I work for Marcy."

Tay almost choked. Pam must mean in some other capacity. Marcy quickly said, "Pam works *with* me. I own and run a very high-class brothel."

"Okay, joke's over," Tay said, chuckling. "What do you really do?"

Ignoring Tay's incredulous look, Marcy continued. "It's called Club Fantasy. Its run out of a brownstone on the East Side of Manhattan and caters to very high-class people. Although we didn't have Eliot Spizter as a client, it's that kind of business."

Tay didn't know what to say so she remained silent, ideas and images whirling in her head. Nice pregnant lady with three kids and a husband in human resources who runs a brothel. Holy shit. Pam filled the conversational gap. "I didn't mean to ambush you like that but I really wanted you two to meet."

"You don't look like a call girl," Tay said, then realized what she'd said. "I mean—"

"Relax. Actually I'm not a call girl. I run the operation but I'm not one of the ladies. Never have been. It's not my thing."

"But I am," Pam said. "In addition to the party planning, I work for, or with, Marcy to 'entertain'"—she made quote marks in the air—"and many of my parties employ Marcy's women to 'hook up' with some of my 'guests'"—more quote marks—"after the festivities."

"Okay," Tay said. "I knew about you, Pam, but Marcy? You seem so motherly. A housewife or a career woman. I would have never suspected that you'd be part of this kind of professional operation. I mean a brownstone. What did you call it? Club Fantasy."

Pam said, "You know what I do and it didn't shock you. I hoped you wouldn't be too negative about Marcy and the club."

"I'm not negative or shocked really, just surprised," Tay said. "Actually flabbergasted. Okay, I'd like to ask about a million questions, if that's okay." She selected one from the many swirling in her brain. "Club Fantasy. Why is it called that?" It was one of the least-threatening questions she could think of.

Marcy sat back and folded her hands at her waist. "Club Fantasy was started by my sister Jenna and our friend Chloe. We fulfill fantasies. If a man, or a woman for that matter, wants to make love to a bride, play doctor, be the Sheik of Araby, be part of a threesome or even join an orgy, we make it happen—for a hefty fee, of course."

Tay thought about it for a moment. "Sounds like something men would be interested in, but women?"

"Yup, women too. I'll shock you again. Zack still has a few clients."

"Your husband Zack? He's a male prostitute? You don't mind?"

Marcy's smile was easy. "We came to an agreement long ago. He entertains maybe once a month and gets paid well for it. And he enjoys it. He loves women, and making them happy makes him happy."

Pam said, "Like what I told you about me and Linc."

"Mind-blowing." Tay focused her mind on Pam's boyfriend and wondered about Marcy's husband, Zack. Linc was a hunk, and Zack was probably also a babe magnet. Tay shook her head slowly. This was a little more information than she could process all at once. A four-months'-pregnant matronly looking woman with three kids and an apartment on Riverside Drive and a wealthy suburban woman with a house to kill for worked together as, as hookers. Well, damn! The money must be quite something. "I read that Spitzer was paying all that money to the woman to join him in Washington."

Marcy and Pam both nodded. "He probably did pay that to the agency that booked her and much of it went to the lady in question. We now change about thirty-five hundred dollars for an evening at the club. The woman gets seventy-five percent and Pam and/or I keep or split the rest depending on the circumstances."

Tay's breath caught in her throat. That certainly was quite high-priced. It sounded like Marcy and Pam took in about one thousand dollars per night per client and the woman got to keep the rest. Holy shit. "Okay, how did the club start?"

"To make a very, very long story very, very short," Marcy said, "a few years ago my sister and her friend, with the help of a wonderful woman who is now happily married and lives on the Island, converted a brownstone into Club Fantasy. After a rocky time, I joined them. Then Jenna retired, Chloe moved to southern France with a man she met through the club and I took over running the building and the business."

"You said you live on Riverside Drive. Does anyone live in the building?"

"Our only live-in is our caretaker, bouncer and general good guy, Rock."

Marcy looked at Pam, who picked up the story. "As for my connection to the club, I investigated some of my husband's credit-card charges and it turned out that the debts were to the club. I met Marcy through a detective, and, as they say, the rest is history. I still see the detective and his wonderful daughters from time to time, now as good friends rather than lovers, as we once were."

"And in a nutshell," Marcy said, "that's the story."

"Phew. I thought I'd digested what Pam told me last Tuesday, but I'm blown away again."

"You have obviously thought about what I suggested at our last lunch. We've become friends," Pam said, "and although it's only been about a month I think I know you pretty well. As I told you, we are always looking for bright, charming, good-looking and sexually active women to help us out at the club and with my party business, and you seem to be a good candidate. It's difficult to find anyone really right for this." She giggled. "After all, we can't very well take out a help-wanted ad in the *Times*."

Marcy chimed in, writing an imaginary advertisement in the air. "Wanted: attractive, intelligent, sexually creative women to entertain men and get well paid for it."

"Oh, we'd get applicants, all right," Pam said, laughing, "but, well, you can see the problems."

"There must be loads of problems in all this," Tay said. "What about the law? Aren't they all over you, especially since all the publicity about our ex-governor?"

Pam answered. "I think they'd like to be, but we're pretty careful."

Marcy added, "And we have a client list that won't quit. If you remember during a couple of recent, high-profile cases several congressmen lost their jobs. No one wants to see that happen again."

"But there are prosecutions. People go to jail. Aren't either of you worried?"

"Sometimes," Pam said honestly. "But you have to realize that the ones who get caught are only the tip of a very large iceberg. There are hundreds of businesses like ours all over the country and very, very few prosecutions. It's a minor risk, one that I think we're all willing to take."

"I guess. Are you really inviting me to become one of your . . ." Tay floundered for a good word.

"We like to call them courtesans," Marcy said.

"One of your courtesans, then. Why me? I'm not particularly pretty or"—she looked down—"well-endowed."

"I've discovered over the years I've been doing this that well-endowed, as you put it, isn't everything," Marcy said. "If I guy just wants eye candy he can have that for a hell of a lot less money than we charge. Sure, some guys want a 36DD and we have a few women who qualify. However, many more want someone personable and let's say sexually flexible. It doesn't have to be kinky sex, but someone who's experienced and willing, or even eager, to play the kind of games he wants to play, to act out the fantasies he wants to act out. Someone who'll be Maid Marian to his Robin Hood, the serving wench to his traveling power broker, an eighteenth century English maid to his lord of the manor, the sweet young thing who's just been saved by the sheriff from the stagecoach holdup. You get the idea."

Pam continued the story. "In addition they demand someone who's totally discrete. Famous people have liaison opportunities all the time but most of those are with groupies who will immediately put the gory details up on their page on Facebook and brag to their friends."

"Okay, I get that part. But isn't this all allowing men to cheat on their wives? I saw the press conference and Mrs. Spitzer looked awful." That issue nagged at Tay.

"I'll admit that wives do get hurt," Marcy said, "and we have an elaborate interview process before we set up any fantasy or party. When I meet the guys I suggest strongly that they talk to their wives about their needs, desires and fantasies. They usually flatly refuse. Then, I guess I've rationalized that if it isn't our service it will be someone else. Well, it might as well be us.

"Women blame the 'other woman,' but who's the cheater, really? The other woman has no agreement to love, honor and cherish anyone—the hubby does. Why is it always her fault?"

"Very practical. But maybe these guys will go home and stay home."

"Maybe, but I doubt it. They'll probably find someone else," Pam said. "Maybe they will go to a bar and pick up a woman or invite their secretary out for drinks. For the cost of dinner and a movie they can get some of what they want."

She thought about Justin. She'd certainly had that experience.

"And," Pam continued, "with a person they pay, there's no danger of entanglements, no next morning. No hurt feelings or disappointments when he or she doesn't call. No strings. It's strictly a cash deal."

"My reasoning has always been this," Marcy said, leaning forward and resting her elbows on the table. "Why shouldn't a woman be able to take something she owns, like her body, and rent it out for a period of time? You rent out your talents with computers and research and no one gets bent out of shape. Why not your erogenous zones?"

Tay realized her head was shaking. "This is all too much to process. You're really offering me a job."

"Yup," Pam said. "I think you'd be perfect, either at the club or at one of my parties, or both."

Marcy stood and started toward the door to the house. "Sorry to interrupt, ladies, but I've got to go back to the ladies' room. I think I know the location of every toilet on the West Side of Manhattan. Don't let my absence stop you, just keep discussing. I'll be right back."

Tay thought for a few moments while Pam poured coffee out of a pot that had been sitting off to one side on a warmer. Finally, as she stirred milk into her cup, Tay asked, "About your parties. How do they work?"

"Sometimes corporate executives want to throw parties for one reason or another. And sometimes they have clients or other executives in from out of town, or out of the country. They can request courtesans to entertain people after the gathering, or even during it in one of my upstairs bedrooms. If that's what they want, I invite several of Marcy's ladies and they get hooked up." She giggled. "I call myself the Madam of Maple Court. Only among my closest friends, of course."

Tay made a little snorting sound. "Like that first party I went to?"

"Jeff Steinberg had a few guys with big checkbooks who

wanted companionship. I provided, and they wrote checks, to the club and to Jeff's charity."

"I didn't see anything."

"That's because nothing happened here. We'd hired a very discrete limo service and several guys went back to the city with a few of the ladies."

Tay shook her head. "I didn't see anyone that day who looked like a hooker."

"That's just the point. They don't look any different from anyone else."

"So how do the guys know who's who?"

"Ankle bracelets. Each of the available ladies wore a gold ankle bracelet with an identifiable charm. I change the charms frequently and keep them unique so there are no accidental slips. Did you by any chance notice anyone glancing at your legs or feet?"

Tay thought back and realized that several of the men had looked down.

"I'll take that for a yes." Pam sipped her coffee. "It's just that simple."

"They thought I was for sale? That's both flattering and a bit insulting."

Marcy rejoined them, having heard Tay's last remark. "Be flattered, not insulted. If a man wondered whether you were available, it was because he was interested in you and wanted you for a partner."

"You both are truly serious about all this."

"We certainly are," Pam said. "There are very few people we would even consider talking to about this. It's that simple."

"You say it's that simple, Pam," Tay said, "but it's not simple for me. It takes quite a bit of getting used to."

"You're right, of course. It's not that simple," Marcy said. "Pam and I have been doing this for a while and we've both worked out our own ways of dealing with it all. I'm sure you'll have to do some thinking about all you've learned today."

"I will, but I will freely admit that I'm intrigued."

"I hoped you would be. How about visiting the club one afternoon after you're done at work?" Marcy asked. "I'd love to show you around. Maybe Pam can come down, too."

Tay thought only a moment. "I'd like that."

"Great," Marcy said. "How about Monday? Will you be in the city then?"

"I will, and I'd love to meet you and see the place. It's a bit difficult for me to picture it all."

"Wonderful. How about five-thirty? The club is closed Mondays and Tuesdays, so we will have the place all to ourselves. Except for Rock, that is. Pam, can you make it?"

"I don't know. I think Linc and I have plans, but I'll see. Do you ladies need me to referee?"

Tay gazed at both women. "Not at all. I think Marcy and I will get along just fine."

"Please try to get to the city, Pam," Marcy said. "We don't need you, but we'd all love to have you. You haven't been down in quite a while, and I know Rock would be delighted to see you, too.

"For now, I'm ready to get home. By the time I get there Zack will be pit deep in overstimulated kids. What's the train situation, Pam?"

Pam looked at her watch. "If we hustle you can just make the three-twenty-three train."

"Great." The three women rose and Marcy extended her hand again. "Tay, it's been great meeting you. I'll look forward to Monday. I hope you'll decide to play with us, but should you decide that this is not your cup of tea, that's fine, too. There's no pressure."

Tay released Marcy's hand. "I appreciate that, Marcy, and it's been an eye-opening afternoon."

"I'll bet," Marcy said.

* * *

Justin arrived back on Maple Court on Sunday afternoon with no discussion about where he'd been staying or with whom. Tay enjoyed sharing dinner with him at a local Chinese restaurant, with hot sex afterward. However, except when she was carried away by arousal, her mind kept flipping to Club Fantasy. What would it be like to have this kind of good sex and get paid for it? And what about more kinky stuff?

As he dressed at about one AM Justin told her that he'd be away for several weeks doing a film project in Montana. As he left, Tay thought that under other circumstances she'd be upset about the impending lack of sex, but now maybe she'd have other options. *Let's hear it for options,* she told herself as she fell asleep.

Chapter 10

Monday dawned with bright sun and moderate temperatures for New York City in late June. Tay dressed a bit more carefully than usual, selecting a slender, knee-length, tan skirt and pairing it with a soft coral blouse. She kept her jewelry simple, a thick gold chain necklace that rested at her throat and matching gold earrings. She slipped her stockinged feet into tan pumps.

Her day at the office was busy, but seemed to pass slowly. Her mind kept drifting to a brownstone in the east fifties. She was disappointed to receive a phone call from Pam saying that she wasn't going to be able to make it to the city, but they agreed to have lunch the following day. They'd certainly have a lot to talk about.

At just after five, Tay left work and, eschewing the subway, treated herself to a taxi to the building that housed what she believed was one of the best courtesan agencies in the city. Club Fantasy. When the taxi pulled up in front of the unassuming building, she paid the fare, gave the cabbie a generous tip, climbed the stairs and rang the bell.

Tay's eyes widened when a giant of a man opened the door. "You must be Tay. It's nice to meet you. I hate my real name so please just call me Rock." His voice was soft with just the hint of a slight Southern accent. She shook his large hand and was ushered inside a plush-looking entryway that led to a comfortable living room. The place looked like a typical home and she almost expected to hear the voices of children recently home from school. Brothel? It certainly didn't look like one. If he hadn't called her by name she'd be sure she was in the wrong house.

"Come in and sit down. Marcy called and apologized that she wouldn't be here to greet you. She's doing an interview and is running a little late so she sicced me on you."

As she settled into an overstuffed, oatmeal-tweed chair she looked at Rock. He was—well, the best word Tay could think of was *substantial.* He was a big man, but there wasn't an ounce of softness on him anywhere. An obvious bodybuilder, he had heavily muscled arms, shoulders and chest, bulging beneath a soft black silk shirt. Below his shirt cuff Tay could make out a tattoo of a thick linked chain. His black slacks were tight over his muscular thighs and his head was completely shaved, a large diamond stud winking in each ear. According to Marcy, Rock was the club's bouncer. He wasn't particularly good looking, but he exuded masculinity and sex through every pore. He also made it plain, without any effort, that he brooked no interference from anyone about anything. Built the way he was, she thought his mere presence would be enough to deter anyone from getting out of line.

"Marcy says you're a friend of Pam's," he said. "She's a wonderful woman who triumphed over truly ugly circumstances. I like her a lot." Rock's voice was a complete contrast to his looks, soft and melodious. Sexy even. "Can I get you something to drink? I make a mean mojito."

"Okay, you've got me. What's a mojito?"

"Basically it's rum, soda, sugar and mint. Want to give it a try?"

"Sounds good. I'd love one. Can I help with something?"

"You can follow me into the kitchen and keep me company if you like."

Tay followed Rock to the back of the brownstone. "I gather you live here."

"I recently bought a condo near my parents in California, but I spend most of my time here. After I make you that drink I'll show you around."

The kitchen was modern and efficient, with immaculate beige cabinets and countertops covered with shiny appliances. There was evidence of dinner preparations, with cutting boards and utensils neatly arranged on the counters. "I'm a pretty good cook and Marcy and I were hoping we could entice you into staying for dinner. Gazpacho, salad niçoise with homemade bread and a great white wine." He raised a questioning eyebrow. "We'd really like to have you."

Tay considered only a moment. "I'd love to."

Rock's smile lit up his face. "Fantastic. I get to show off yet again." He quickly made drinks, using fresh mint from the refrigerator, and handed one to Tay. "Pam called earlier and she told me that she's not able to come down here this evening. I'm sorry. I haven't seen her in ages."

She sipped and said, "This is wonderful. Thanks."

He motioned to the door to the back of the brownstone, his huge hand holding his drink. "Let's sit outside for a little while. Marcy said she'd call as she was leaving, and the place is just around the corner."

The backyard was totally unexpected, a special treat in the middle of Manhattan. Flowers bloomed in pots and a small area was filled with well-developed seedlings. "What's growing?" Tay asked.

"I planted vegetables last year, but I discovered that they really are only marginally better than the store-bought stuff. By the time I considered what I spent for fertilizer and the cost of my time, they're far cheaper at the little grocery on First Avenue. This year I've planted zinnias, snapdragons and petunias."

Tay tilted her head to one side and gazed at Rock. "Somehow you don't look like the zinnia and petunia type."

Rock's laugh was spontaneous and ingratiating and Tay quickly joined him. "You're certainly right about that."

Ice now broken, Tay set her drink down on a small glass-topped table and sat beside Rock on a soft upholstered patio chair. She was filled with questions but she wasn't sure what she should ask. Rock broke the silence and continued. "I don't know what Marcy and Pam have told you and I'm sure you're really curious about what goes on here. Shall I give you the spiel?"

"Thanks. It's difficult to know what to ask, where to start."

"At the risk of repeating what Marcy's already told you, Marcy's twin sister, Jenna, and her friend Chloe started this business several years ago. They learned a lot from a dear friend named Erika who was already in the business. Her firm was called Courtesans, Inc. We were friends, Erika and I, and when she realized that the women needed a little protection, she introduced us and I moved in. I get room and board and the use of the place, particularly on Mondays and Tuesdays when it's closed to customers. Tonight I'm not entertaining until quite late."

"You do that kind of work, too?" Tay asked, unable to keep up with the new concepts. His raised eyebrow and considered silence answered her question. "Oh."

"Yeah. Right. And I have for many years. I occasionally use the upstairs, but mostly I entertain downstairs. I'll show you around later and you'll understand more. Suffice it to say that I like to play heavier games than most of what goes on here, lots of BDSM stuff. We have a fully-equipped dungeon downstairs with all the accoutrements."

Tay swallowed hard, finding some of the pictures that flew through her mind both scary and intriguing. She was certainly no stranger to ordinary sex, and although she'd never actually tried anything, she had often found herself curious about the kinkier aspects. "Oh," was again all she could say. Then she took a gulp of her drink.

"I'm sorry if I shocked you," Rock said, looking genuinely chagrined.

"*Shocked* isn't the word, at least in the negative sense. It's just that all this is a lot to take in at once. The contrasts are overwhelming."

"Contrasts?"

"You planting flowers and playing bondage games. Marcy being the mother of three-plus and running this place. Pam being the high-society matron and connecting men with prostitutes. It's all a bit much."

Again Rock laughed. "I can imagine. I remember when I first met Pam and told her about myself. I thought her brain would explode."

"Mine might, too."

When Rock's cell phone played "Für Elise" he opened it, listened and nodded. "Marcy will be here in about five minutes," he said, snapping the instrument shut. "Want another drink?"

"Not right now. I think I need my head clear."

"Right. I wish you could meet Zack and the kids. They're as much my family as if they were my own. You can add bouncer and delighted babysitter to my list of contrasts."

Tay moved her fingers as if taking notes. "Right. Added to my list."

"You're very quick on the uptake. No wonder Marcy and Pam like you. You're a lot like them."

"I consider that a compliment."

"It was meant that way. I'm a pretty good judge of character. I have to be in this business because trust plays a large part in everything we do here. Yup," he said, nodding, "you're okay."

She beamed. "Thanks."

"I'll let Marcy show you around. This is quite an operation."

"How many men at a time can be here?"

"For obvious reasons we have to be careful that no one sees anyone else, but we juggle pretty well. We have six rooms upstairs plus we do play outside of this building."

Tay made a few quick calculations. At a thousand dollars per for Marcy and Pam, it figured roughly to five thousand a night. Even with the upkeep on the brownstone, that added up to a great deal of money. A very great deal. "You said that Marcy was doing an interview—a new employee?"

"A new client. Since neither Jenna nor Chloe are around to do them anymore, Marcy does all the talking to prospective clients."

"I don't quite understand. What's to interview? Does she worry that someone's a cop?"

"No, not really. The people who come to us have been fully vetted. To even get to the interview one of our current clients has to recommend you, and a very discrete investigator, who's also an old friend of Pam's, does a thorough background check. No, this interview is to find out what the—in this case, guy—wants. What are his innermost desires and can we fulfill them?"

"Ah, you mean what should the woman look like, like that?"

"That's a very small part of it. The crux of it all is the scenario he wants to act out. Who does he want to be and who does he want his vis-à-vis to be? It might be as simple as wanting to make love in a garden in the country—that's Pam's department—or do it in a hot tub—also Pam's. Maybe he wants to play the burglar and rape the woman he finds in her bedroom. Some men want to be overpowered and forced to dress in women's clothes. I told you there's a dungeon downstairs and it gets a lot of use, by both men and women. Lots of people want a member of the opposite sex at his or her mercy and there are just as many who want to be subjugated. Clients come with all the desires under the sun."

"I guess if they just wanted a partner they wouldn't have to pay what Club Fantasy charges."

"True enough."

With that, Marcy walked into the backyard from the kitchen, dropped into a chair and put her feet on the chair opposite. "I'm beat," she said with a long sigh. "This poor guy was so nervous it took me almost an hour to calm him down enough for me to learn his story. He finally told me that he wanted to make love to his virginal new bride on their wedding night and when I told him that his desire wasn't unusual it was as if the weight of the world fell from his shoulders. So many men think that what they want is beyond the pale that they get almost as much satisfaction out of knowing they aren't crazy as out of the act itself."

Rock went into the kitchen and returned immediately with a large glass of iced tea, which Marcy drained. "Thanks, Rock. You're a prince among men. And welcome, Tay. I hope Rock has been keeping you entertained. I'm so sorry I'm late."

"Don't even think about it," Tay said. "Rock has been filling me in on your interview process."

"It's both rewarding and wearing. To do this I have to be a combination sex therapist, marriage counselor, animal handler and intuitive guru. Right now I'm a bit worn out."

"Listen," Tay said. "We don't have to have dinner. Let me grab my purse and I'll make the next train to Westchester."

"Don't be silly. I'll be fine. I think my body's still adjusting to this pregnancy thing and I merely need a few minutes with my feet up. And anyway, Rock's doing all the cooking. Please. I really do want to visit with you and Rock. Zack has the kids and I'm blessedly by myself. If you leave I'll have no excuse not to go home and play mommy." She looked at Rock. "Okay, I love to play mommy most of the time, but there are times . . ."

"You're really happy about the baby?" Tay asked.

"We're all delighted, even the kids. I feel a little twinge about Pam, however."

"Why?"

"Although she seldom mentions it, I think she's still really upset at her lack of children. She and Vin were tested and she can't conceive. Part of me is a little embarrassed to get pregnant so easily, so I really hate to talk about it when she's around."

"I didn't realize she wanted kids that badly."

"Please don't say anything. She's only in her late-thirties, so theoretically there's still time if the doctor was wrong. There's so much they can do now, but I don't know whether she'd want to go through it all."

"I met Linc at the party Pam had a month ago," Tay said, "and since then the three of us have had dinner a few times. He's really quite a guy. Are they going to get serious?"

"They are serious, and I think permanent. I know he'd love to make a home and family with her."

"What about their . . . uh . . . extracurricular activities? Doesn't that complicate matters a little?"

"I don't know. It hasn't with Zack and me. And Pam and Linc seem to be fine with each other's lifestyle." She shrugged. "Anyway, who knows what people think? Actually, that's my job. To find out what men think and want." She reached down, kicked off her shoes and rubbed her arches. "But enough of Pam's life. Please stay for dinner. I'd really like you to."

"Yes, please, Tay," Rock added. "I don't get to cook for folks nearly often enough."

Marcy and Rock's desire seemed genuine, so Tay relaxed. She did want to stay for a little while and see the upstairs. She could decide later when to leave and let Marcy rest.

"Good," Rock said, "because I have a great dinner planned." To Marcy he continued, "I'm trying new recipes. A slightly different take on gazpacho, a recipe I got from watching Emeril last week, an upmarket tuna salad with olives, walnuts and diced apricots with home-baked French bread."

Marcy let out a long sigh. "You're my hero. If I weren't already married to Zack . . ."

"Sweetheart, if I were ready to settle down and you weren't married to Zack . . ."

More contrasts. "Okay, you two," Tay said, laughing, "enough hearts and flowers."

"If you don't mind," Marcy said to Tay, "I'll let Rock start the tour." She pulled her cell phone from its holder on her waist band, and said, "I've got a few calls I have to make."

"I'll be delighted," Rock said. "Dinner is already made so I'll take Tay upstairs, then we can eat. Say in half an hour?"

"Sounds wonderful," Marcy said.

Chapter 11

Rock and Tay walked slowly through the kitchen toward the main part of the house. Rock motioned to a doorway in the hall. "That leads to my rooms. Marcy had this section of the house remodeled about a year and a half ago and created a bedroom and studio for me. She's such a great person and really thoughtful, protective of my privacy."

"Everyone must feel very safe with you here. I can't imagine anyone messing around with you in residence."

"That's the idea, and I'm truly happy here."

Tay thought for a moment. "What about Pam? What does she do about security when she hosts one of her parties?"

"Linc's usually around, and although he's not as formidable looking as I am," Rock said, posing, displaying well developed biceps, "he'll do for mild intimidation. And we're all very, very careful."

"I can imagine." As they approached the foot of the stairs Marcy rejoined them. "I'm feeling much better so I thought I'd add my two cents' worth during the grand tour."

"Great," Tay said.

The three climbed the stairs and Rock indicated an ordinary-looking room with a plain motel-type dresser, with matching bedside tables and a large double bed. "For example, this is our all-purpose room. Let's say our guy wants to be a burglar. He can hide in the closet while his chosen 'victim' gets ready for bed. He can jump out of the closet and have his way with her."

"Or someone wants to do it with a prostitute, or a virgin," Marcy added. "Maybe she wants a gigolo to seduce her or another woman to force her to have sex."

Women's fantasies? She could imagine it for others, but not for herself. "I really do get it, and what a fabulous place to set it all up."

"It really is," Rock said. "People who get recommended to us here want something special, something they can't get from the Acme Brothel Company. We do whatever it takes to provide it."

"You bet," Marcy said. "Much of this has been here since the first year Chloe and my sister set it up, but we've upgraded since as well."

"Okay, show me more."

Rock crossed the hall. "This is the sheriff's office. Many men who want what I call the 'gratitude fantasy' agree on playing the lawman who's just saved the sweet young thing from the desperados." The room looked very much like a stage set for an old-fashioned Western, with a wooden desk, Wanted posters on the walls, a rack with gun belts and barred windows.

"I almost expect Marshal Dillon to appear," Tay said.

"Exactly what we intend," Marcy said as she opened the door to a third room. "The doctor's office."

It looked just like a medical examination room, with white walls covered with shiny white cabinets. A desk stood to one side covered with lots of jars and containers for various tubes and pills. A real doctor's office scale stood against one wall. The center of the room was dominated by a padded, paper-covered exam table and a little roll-around chair. "This seems like such an elaborate setup. Is it used often?"

"You can't imagine," Marcy said. "So many people want this kind of thing, either becoming the patient or the doctor. There's a large adjoining bathroom for shower games as well."

Rock draped his arm around Tay's shoulders. "Upstairs we have a room with a desert motif, sand on the floor and a mock-up of the side of a bedouin tent, and another made to resemble the cabin on a pirate ship. Want to see those?"

"I think I get the message." Tay wandered into the sheriff's office and perched on the edge of the desk. "I'm overwhelmed, but I can certainly see that this operation would thrive. I would guess that there were dozens of men who would enjoy this sort of thing."

"Hundreds, and more. I think if it weren't illegal," Rock said, "we could franchise this and make a fortune, not that we aren't making a fortune now."

But it is illegal, she told herself. Then she consciously put that out of her mind.

"What about Pam's business? How does that work?"

"As you know, she arranges parties for the upper crust. Quite a few business types also employ her to find ladies to entertain out-of-town visitors and the like. The ladies get their salary and Pam and the club get a piece of the action."

"You used the word *salary.* You mean a real salary?"

"We're an escort service, and as such we pay on the books. Escort services and phone-sex companies aren't illegal as long as no actual intercourse takes place. Many of the ladies are 'consultants' and some are actually salaried, with medical benefits, taxes, all the right stuff. We can claim that what our ladies do afterward, on their own time, isn't our concern."

"Loophole?"

"Of sorts. I don't spend too much time on the legalities of it all. It is what it is and that's that."

"Good attitude."

"It's stood me and the club in good stead for quite a while."

"Would you like to see the downstairs?" Rock asked.

"Sure." Tay remembered talk of a dungeon. "I gather it's quite a setup."

Marcy's cell phone rang, and as she looked at the caller ID her face softened and a small smile curved her lips. She waved her hands at Rock and Tay to say that they should go on without her. "Hi, honey," she said into the phone, "how was work today?" She walked into the all-purpose room and stretched out on the bed.

Rock's smile was a bit wolfish as he led Tay back down to the ground level, through a small hallway and down another flight. When he flipped on the light she couldn't suppress a small gasp. The room was the size of a large living room, but that's where any resemblance ended. Three of the walls and the ceiling were mirrored, and the fourth wall was covered with dark wood-fronted cabinets. In the center of the room stood a flat table not unlike that in the doctor's office upstairs and other large items were draped in velvet coverings to conceal what was beneath.

Rock crossed the room and moved one of the mirrored panels to reveal several hooks, chains and straps, obviously for bondage sessions. Without any thought, Tay's tissues swelled, her nipples hardened and her hands shook. She could picture some of the games that went on in here, extrapolating from stories she'd read. She'd always had to masturbate afterward.

Silently Rock moved behind her. "Maybe someday," he whispered in her ear. She felt his heated breath but said nothing. Together they walked back upstairs.

"Okay," Marcy said when they walked into the backyard. "I'm done. Zack is taking the kids and the nanny for pizza, so I have the evening off."

"You should have invited them for dinner. I always have enough."

"Zack had work to do after dinner, so he needs to stay close to home."

"Too bad, but in that case, let me set up for supper." Tay moved to help but Rock took her hand and squeezed. "No need to help. I've got everything ready."

She forced any kinky thoughts about Rock down and said, "Your husband's good with the kids?"

"He's the best," she said. "I've got only one lingering problem now." She huffed out a breath. "The guy this afternoon. His name is Henry. He's a huge man, not fat but big all over, probably goes six foot four and weighs at least two-fifty. He's blond, with a neat, slightly curly blond beard and thick, bushy eyebrows. He has seven older brothers and sisters, and when he was a kid he was teased about being Henry the Eighth. It stuck with him and he developed a fantasy about it. He actually grew the beard and combed it the way the real Henry did. Then, several months back, he saw the film *The Other Boleyn Girl* and he became still more obsessed. Now he wants to order some innocent courtiers like Mary or Anne into his bed. Regally, of course. That's the fantasy he wants us to create for him."

"That must present no end of problems," Tay said. "You'd need costumes, stage sets and all."

"That's not the problem. We have a company that we deal with and it can provide the costumes and trappings and he's agreed to defray all the costs. The problem is the woman."

"That's your problem? You must have dozens of likely candidates."

"Oh, I do, and playing the innocent is something most of my employees do well. That part of his fantasy is common enough. However, he's spelled out his physical desires quite explicitly. He's not fond of small women since he's so big. The lady of his dreams is tall and slender with blond hair and blue eyes."

"Tall? That surprises me." She'd always hated being taller than most of the women she knew. "I always thought that men who want something like what he's describing would want someone of small to medium height and, you know, built. Like Pam, for instance."

"You'd be amazed at the varied tastes in the male population. I can usually accommodate just about anything, but I'm short on tall women." Marcy obviously listened to what she'd just said and snickered. "Sorry, poor choice of words." She sipped her iced tea. "Several of my women are tall, but none of them are available just now. The summer's vacation season, and many of them are away. I hate to put this guy off so I merely told him I'd get back to him."

Tay was catching Marcy's drift. She would fit the bill to a tee, if she were interested in becoming one of Marcy and Pam's employees. Was this some kind of setup between Pam and Marcy? "Surely if he's waited this long . . ."

"True, but I always hate to turn someone down. You never know whether he'll find some other way to scratch his itch."

"You've got me in mind, haven't you?"

Marcy looked at her pink polished toes. "Busted. Yes, I do. I didn't know about this guy specifically, but Pam and I agree that you'd be great working with us."

"Mary Boleyn was only fifteen. I haven't seen fifteen in almost fifteen years."

"Not a problem. Age is only a matter of frame of mind.

You'll look the way we want you to look and he'll see what he wants to see.

"Listen, I don't want you to think there's any pressure here. Pam and I both want you with us, but we'll both love you either way. You're a wonderful person and you'd be a great friend in any event. However, you're also everything we want in a business sense, too. You're bright and charming, well-rounded with a good sense of humor and a sensual presence that can't be faked. You carry yourself well, straight and tall, as though you're proud of who you are. Men will really enjoy everything about you."

Tay was flattered and couldn't quite control her smile. "What do you mean by a sensual presence?"

"There's a barely hidden erotic side to your nature. It's nothing overt and not everyone will recognize it. But to someone who's dealt with that side of the world for as long as I have, it's difficult to hide. And even if men don't see it directly, they'll sense it. You are looking for erotic adventures, even if you don't know it yourself."

Tay could feel herself blush. "Is that what you see in me?"

"I can't deny it. You can, if you like, but you'd be missing a lot, things that Club Fantasy can offer you. Many of the women who work for me got into this for the money, and I won't deny that the pay is stupendous. You, on the other hand, could do this for the thrill, the newness, the ventures into sexual realms you've never dreamt about, or, if you have, you never thought you'd actually be there."

Tay's flesh was tingling. Marcy was right. She'd thought she had scratched that itch with Steve but after he was gone she'd missed frequent sex. It was obvious, to her at least, that the minute Justin came along, she'd jumped at the chance to make love to him. Why be coy? "I have to admit that I'm intrigued."

"I thought you would be. I want you to think about joining us. Give yourself a chance to really consider everything," she said, waving her hand at the building, "so don't say anything right now. There's a sexual charge to the atmosphere around this place and I don't want that to sway your decision. Let's have a nice dinner and talk about inanities. Take the train home and get yourself into less intense surroundings. Go to work, live your life for a little while, talk it over with Pam and get her take on everything, then let's talk again, maybe in a week or so."

Tay wanted to say yes right now, but she realized that Marcy was right. She did need to get back into a normal routine and see how the idea of becoming a prostitute felt. Prostitute. Hooker. Whore. She had to bounce those words off her brain and see what came out the other side. "That sounds like a good plan. I assume all that talk about not putting this guy off was just that, talk?"

Marcy grinned. "Okay, I'll admit that some of it was. I can accommodate him with one of my existing women, but I do think you'd be right for this. You could play the innocent without trouble and for a first experience it would be perfect for you. I told him that his fantasy was delightful and that I'd thought I'd be able to set it up but that it might take a few weeks. He said he was willing to wait if it will be as great as I promised."

She panicked. If she decided to do this, maybe she'd be a failure at it. "What if it isn't?"

"You mean if he's dissatisfied? We give him his money back, of course. Anything we set up must work out well, not perfectly but well enough to please him, or we credit our fee back to his card, no questions asked."

"You take credit cards?"

"Sure. CF + Co. is what they see on the receipt. An

anonymous company that, if a person needs to, can represent anything he wants to tell anyone."

"Of course."

"So will you think about it?"

"You can bet I will."

Chapter 12

Dinner was delightful and Tay quickly realized that Rock was a superb cook. The soup was cool, with just enough spice to make it interesting but not painful. The salad was a mix of greens, raisins and pine nuts with a raspberry vinaigrette: salty and sweet, crisp and smooth. The bread was perfect, served warm with a light center and a crispy crust. A plate of pale green olive oil combined with herbs and spices sat in the middle of the table for dipping.

When she raved to Rock about the crust on the bread, he preened. "It's really difficult to get a good crust in the summer with all this humidity. I'll make a copy of the recipe for you, if you want."

"I'd love to think that I could do it, but my cooking talent consists of peanut-butter-and-potato-chip sandwiches, cans of ravioli, frozen dinners and takeout. Without a microwave I'd be lost."

No further reference was made either to Tay's joining Club Fantasy or to the scene in the lower part of the house. Both Marcy and Rock were charming dinner companions, making clever conversation on topics as far ranging as the latest Yankees pitching prospect to a new reality TV show they had all watched and hated immediately. Tay put down her fork. "Why do the people who create those shows think folks out here will enjoy watching a bunch of idiots making fools of themselves for money?"

Rock answered. "Because a significant portion of the TV-watching public does enjoy that sort of thing. I guess it makes them feel superior. And the programs are cheap to produce with no big stars to pay. Sponsors eat it up."

"I suppose. I guess I just resent all those Hollywood guys treating me like I'm a blessed idiot," Tay said.

"I'm not sure I completely agree with you, Tay," Marcy said. "I can't stand *Survivor* and that sort of stuff, but I will cheerfully admit that I watched and fully enjoyed *Dancing with the Stars* and Zack and I love *American Idol.* We like the performances and the contest format. I like to judge for myself who I enjoyed watching and then compare my opinions with the hosts and the American public. We seldom agree, of course, but it's fun anyway.

"Frankly I like those shows much better than the overdone sexuality and R-rated stuff they have on the cable channels. With many of them I think they put in sex scenes and four-letter words just to keep the guys in middle America watching."

"I'm surprised," Tay said. "I would think that you'd like the racier type of fare."

"Why? Because I run this place?" Marcy said, raising her eyebrows and waving her hand around the room. "I'm no different from normal folks."

"Marcy, I'm really sorry," Tay said quickly, sure she'd screwed everything up. *Why can't you shut up from time to time?* she asked herself. "I didn't mean to insult you."

"Hey," Marcy said, putting her hand over Tay's, "don't ever be ashamed to express your opinion, with me or Pam or Rock, or with clients. You are who you are and there's no need to hide that. If any of us wanted an insipid, slightly vapid female with none of her own opinions, we could find them by the dozens at any watering hole in the city."

Rock had made coffee and now filled three mugs, offering milk and sugar. "I hope you don't mind, Tay," he said. "It's decaf in deference to the baby."

"No problem." They took their cups to the backyard and made themselves comfortable.

"You really want your women to express their opinions? I would think that ladies who do what your courtesans do would have to be—God, words do present a problem—let's say biddable, as they say in those romance novels."

"Not at all. I wouldn't flat-out insult a client, but having your own opinions and being able to express them is what makes our ladies different from the run-of-the-mill call girls."

"It's true," Rock added. "I spend time with many of the men who visit here while they wait for their appointments and they often comment on how the ladies who work here are real people, not bimbos. That's their word, not mine."

"Okay," Tay said, "I'll have to take your word for that. Just so I know what I'm thinking of getting myself into, any rules and regulations?"

"Of course," Marcy said. "First and foremost, condoms. All the time, no exceptions. Every man who visits knows that rule and you mustn't let anyone violate it, even for an extra fee. Period. I have only had to ask a woman to leave once and it was for playing with a customer without protection. You probably take birth-control pills."

"Sure."

"Great, but that's no substitute for the use of condoms. You don't want to end up with a souvenir you didn't intend."

"Absolutely fine. No problem there."

"No extracurricular activities with a client without letting him know that he's going to pay for it. Anything you two do is fine, just let us know that you've done something outside of what was contracted for so we can charge his credit card accordingly. Most of the men are quite willing to pay extra for whatever goes on."

"Like different kinds of sex?"

"No, that's not what I mean. When a person contracts with us it's for a time period, like a few hours or a weekend, not an activity. The partners are encouraged to do anything that they both will enjoy. What I meant was more time, or another meeting."

"What if I like a guy so much that I want to meet him socially, you know, off the books?"

"We can talk about that if the situation arises," Marcy said. "A few of my employees have dated customers and one married an ex-customer, but it's pretty unusual for anyone even to ask."

Tay continued, "Anything else?"

"No drugs of any kind. Period. No pot, no anything."

"Sounds reasonable. Do many men try to do drugs or to get the girl to?"

"Happily no, and it's made very clear in the agreement that they sign."

"They sign an agreement?"

"Remember that this is a business," Rock said. "A guy can use a pseudonym if he likes but he has to give a credit-card number, so he's connected to us that way. Sometimes a guy gets a special credit card just for us to use so his family, or company, knows nothing. Maybe under a different name. Then he'll pay the credit-card bill from a separate checking account and no one's the wiser."

"The agreement we negotiate spells out what he's agreed to and what he gets in return," Marcy continued. "That almost always eliminates conflicts later. It happens, of course, but it's unusual. The agreement won't hold up in court, of course, but it clarifies things, and if it's broken, the client will not be allowed to return.

"Getting back to rules, I have a few guidelines of my own. No pantyhose unless specifically requested. Most men hate them but we do have at least one guy who enjoys cutting them off his lady with a large pair of scissors."

"Hate them, hate them, hate them," Rock said under his breath. "Whoever invented those torture devices should be severely punished. And I'm just the guy who can do that."

Tay felt all her blood rush to her nipples and pussy as she saw Rock's gaze on her.

Marcy seemed not to notice. "No garlic or onions before or during, unless you both indulge. And watch gassy foods, too."

"Makes sense. What about safety?" Tay asked. "Anything I should know there?"

"If you decide to play, I'm sure Marcy will start you here," Rock said. "Everyone's been thoroughly checked out, but, just in case, there are panic buttons in each room and I'm always here. It's never been necessary but it's comforting for the employees to know that help's immediately available if needed."

"Actually the button has been used a few times. Remember the guy with chest pains?" Marcy said to Rock. "We called an ambulance. Fortunately he was still fully dressed and Rock carried him down to the living room. It was merely indigestion, but it gave us all a scare. I've no idea what he told people about why he was here but we gave him every chance to brush it off."

"Right," Rock said, snickering. "I'd forgotten."

"They've never been used for someone who got hostile?"

"Never for anything we couldn't handle," Rock said.

"You don't smoke, do you?" Marcy asked.

"Not a chance."

"Good," she said. "The smell of smoke on someone's skin and clothing is a real turnoff for most people. None of my ladies smoke, and I can usually tell who the smokers are during a client interview. I won't pair that person off without warning the lady or gentleman in advance. I will also warn the courtesan of any off-center activities that the guy, or woman, is interested in and make sure it's okay with him or her."

"Or them," Rock said, winking so only Tay could see. "Off-center, like bondage, or anal sex."

He's teasing me, Tay realized. *He knows what's going on inside of me and he's playing a game and, I guess, asking me a question. One of these days I might even answer him. For now, I need to concentrate on what I'm going to do.* "Anything else, guys?"

"Not that I can think of offhand," Marcy said. "Rock, can you think of anything?"

"Nope. I think you covered it all." As Marcy sipped her coffee, Rock winked at Tay again. She looked down, picked up her mug and swallowed so quickly that had the coffee still been hot she would have burned her mouth. As it was, she almost choked and Rock laughed, enjoying her obvious combination of excitement and discomfort. *Damn, the man's an inveterate flirt*, Tay thought. *And it works.*

"Remember that Marcy pairs ladies and clients so each has a good time," he said. "It's tough to keep up a pretense, so if the lady doesn't enjoy what's going on it's not going to be a totally wonderful experience for the guy who's paying the money."

"That's what we all want," Marcy said, finishing the remainder of her coffee. "I'm going to get going. I will admit that I'm pooping out and Zack's got the kids waiting up for me." When she stood and picked up her now-empty mug, Tay stood, too.

"You don't have to leave yet," Marcy said. "I'm sure Rock can answer any more questions and entertain you for a while."

Right, Tay thought. *Not just yet.* "I think I'll head for Grand

Central myself and catch a train home." The sun was setting and the sky was turning a magnificent deep azure blue in the east.

"Sure you wouldn't like to stick around?" Rock asked.

"Not tonight, thanks," Tay said. Did that sound like an agreement to stick around another time? *Tay, stop it!* She followed Marcy through the building, grabbing her purse. "It was a fabulous dinner, Rock, and thanks for the food and the conversation." *Don't pause,* she thought. "Marcy, thanks for everything and for the very flattering offer you made me. I will certainly think about it. Pam and I have a lunch date on Friday, so if you don't mind, I'll discuss it with her and get back to you over the weekend."

"That's great," Marcy said, opening the front door. She kissed Rock's cheek and walked toward the curb.

"Good night, Rock," Tay said, keeping the slight quaver out of her voice with effort. "It was nice meeting you."

"Nice meeting you, too," he said. Then, as she passed through the door, he brushed his knuckles over the nape of her neck. "Anticipation," he whispered, "is a great aphrodisiac." He closed the door behind her.

She turned down Marcy's offer to share a taxi and flagged down her own. "This was wonderful," she said as the yellow car came to a stop behind the one Marcy had hailed. "I'll call you over the weekend."

"I hope you'll agree to everything," Marcy said, climbing into her taxi as Tay climbed into the one behind.

The following Friday Tay sat across from Pam on her patio. "Of course I've been thinking about it. I've been able to concentrate on little else. I've been waffling about the idea of getting paid for sex. It seems so wrong, but once I get past the initial knee-jerk reaction, which frequently kicks me in the gut, I can't think of any reason why not to do it."

"That's wonderful," Pam said, refilling her glass with iced

tea. Their lobster salads sat in front of them, untouched. "I'm glad you're going to join us."

"I hate the idea of doing something I can't tell my family about, but I wouldn't endanger anyone by blabbing."

"How do you think they would react?"

"Actually, I think my mom would have been tickled. She was a very open-minded woman and wanted me to do things that will make me happy. She'd have worried about the legalities, too, and would probably have had a mental picture of bringing me a cake with a file inside while I was in the slammer. She'd probably have pictured me on the evening news with a newspaper held in front of my face to hide my identity." Was she projecting and deliberately exaggerating her own fears?

Pam propped her chin on her palm. "Yeah, I know what you mean. Your dad's still around. What would he think if he knew?"

"He's always been a bit more conservative. He still hasn't figured out why I'm not married, raising babies." She sipped her tea and sighed. "He met Steve a few times and thought I had finally settled down. I thought so too for a short time."

"And now?"

"He wasn't the one. To be honest, I don't think I'm interested in settling down right now, my dad to the contrary notwithstanding. I like my job and my life, most of it, that is. But I'm bored, too. I want something more, and maybe the club is that something. I really like and respect you, Linc, Rock and Marcy."

"I envy Marcy," Pam said, leaning back in her chair. "She's got it all."

"Which *all* is that?" She agreed with Pam, but was curious as to which aspects of Marcy's life particularly appealed to her friend.

There was a small smile on Pam's face as she answered.

"She's got a guy who loves her totally, a job she really enjoys and kids. What more is there?"

"You've got Linc and he seems to love you the way Zack must love Marcy."

"Oh, he does. He keeps asking me to marry him, or at least let him move in and become more of a real couple. That counts for a lot."

"Why don't you let him do that?"

"I don't know. It's a little scary sometimes. He knows what I do, and I know what he does, and we're both okay with it. I worry, though, that if we make our relationship more traditional, things will change, and I like everything the way it is."

Realizing that they were getting into sensitive areas, Tay changed the subject. "Marcy really does seem to enjoy what she does for a living."

"She feels in some ways that she's serving an important function in society. She's counseled several men who've decided to actually talk to their wives and scratch the erotic itch at home rather than at the club. She's made zillions of men happy, and maybe once that itch is scratched they will return to their life as it was before, home and happy."

"That's great."

"You sound like you've decided to do it."

"I think so, yeah. What could be better than getting paid for doing something I really enjoy doing anyway?"

"That's my take on it. Any problems with the possibly kinkier aspects of it all?"

Trying not to think about Rock, something she was doing more and more of late, she said, "I don't know. Steve was a frequent, if not so creative lover. We loved oral sex and I had my collection of toys."

"Had?"

"Okay, I still have." She tried not to blush. She'd have to

get more used to plain speaking and doing things she hadn't tried yet. "I haven't ventured into the really offbeat stuff. I've never tried anal sex although I'm not opposed to it." She lowered her voice. "Have you tried it?"

"Yes, and it's really hot. You have to get past the knee jerk, as you said before, but once you do, if you and he do it right, it's terrific, and very arousing. As for other kinky stuff, it's all a matter of individual taste. Take your time, keep an open mind and make your decisions one step at a time. Marcy is a great interviewer and will be able to match you to men who want the same things sexually that you do. You don't have to worry that your partner will get into something you don't want to do."

"What if he does?"

"Then just say no. Tell him that if that's what it takes to make him enjoy his fantasy, then he can either have his money back or the club will set him up with a different woman."

"Won't you and Marcy be angry? After all, it's your money."

"It's your enjoyment too and no, we won't, I promise."

"I'll take your word for that. The more I understand about the club and how careful and considerate you all are, the more eager I am to participate."

"Great. Shall we call Marcy and tell her?"

"Let's."

Later that evening Pam and Linc lay stretched out beside each other on the bed. They'd just finished watching through their toes a documentary on the builders of the pyramids. "She's really going to do it," Pam said as the credits rolled up the screen. Linc had gotten to know Tay during their dinners together, and was as much a fan of hers as Pam was.

"I'm glad. I think she'll be really happy with it. She's outgoing, vital and so bright. And really, really hungry for good sex."

"I know. I guess it takes me back to when I began this thing. I wish, when I started, I'd been as comfortable with creative sex as she seems to be or wants to become."

"You can't mean she isn't nervous about becoming a courtesan."

"Like anyone else she's got her reservations, but she's doing it for all the right reasons. She wants to experience it all, and get paid for it. I was driven into it by my need for money."

Linc turned so he was facing her. "Money's not a bad reason, and anyway you were good with it once you got over your initial reluctance. Right?"

"I certainly was, and you were my island of sanity. It did take me a while to get into the whole idea, but I've got no regrets." She kissed his cheek. "Not a one. Remember that without Club Fantasy I never would have met you."

"That's the best reason of all." He kissed her more soundly.

Chapter 13

So this was what it felt like, Tay thought as she rang the bell at Club Fantasy's brownstone the following Monday evening after an almost useless day at work. Before she left for work that morning she supplied extra food for the caged animals, cleaned litter pans and added more kibble to the cats' bowls. Now her heart was pounding and it was difficult to catch her breath. She was about to become a prostitute.

The club was usually closed on Monday, but Marcy had decided that this scenario and Tay's first experience needed the rest of the club to be empty, so she made an exception in her usually hard-and-fast rule. That way, if Tay made a complete ass of herself and either she or Henry the Eighth ran screaming, no other clients would be involved.

Rock answered the door and guided her inside. "Remind me before you leave later to give you a key and show you through the security system."

"Right," she said, unable to gather her thoughts for more than a one-word answer.

Rock closed the front door behind her and gathered her into his arms, surrounding her with his warmth. There was nothing sexual about his embrace, and she realized it immediately. No, he was offering her security. That was exactly what she needed, and she was glad he realized it, too. She rested her head against his hard, muscular shoulder and inhaled the spicy scent of the man. He was taller than she was, so she felt cosseted as he leaned over and kissed the top of her head. "You'll be great."

She took a deep breath and stepped back. "I know."

"Good."

With Rock's arm around her shoulders, Tay walked up the stairs to an all-purpose room on the third floor. When she walked inside she was amazed at the change in the look and feel of it. Marcy stood up, having put the final touches on the throne room. They'd had props delivered and now the area was dominated by a massive, jeweled throne resting atop a small platform. Three walls were hung with heavy velvet drapes and the fourth with a gigantic tapestry. Marcy pulled one of the velvet drapes aside and reminded Tay where the panic button was. "Just in case."

"Thanks, and this is truly fabulous," Tay said, amazed. "It's difficult for me to remember I'm in midtown Manhattan." She gestured toward the large brocade and velvet pillows scattered along one edge of the room. "The pillows are for lovemaking, I assume," she said. "I was wondering how you'd provide for comfort."

"The room did turn out well," Marcy said, looking around. "Sometimes I surprise even myself with what we can do, and this is one of the most elaborate setups we've ever created." She motioned to the room across the hall. "Your costume is in there and if you want, I'll help you dress."

The previous Saturday Tay and Marcy had paid a visit to the costume company in Long Island City that the club used for their "theatricals," as the owner called them. They'd found the perfect outfit. Fortunately, except for her height,

Tay was a pretty standard size ten and the owner had been able to let down the hem of the gown they selected while they waited.

The costume guy had assured them that the dress they had selected was appropriate for a woman who might have been one of a sixteenth century English queen's ladies in waiting. Made of heavy champagne brocade, the gown had a deep square neck trimmed with narrow lace and studded with small pearls. The long full sleeves were turned back so the cerulean blue facing showed. The waist was tiny and required a tight corset that flattened Tay's already small breasts and pinched her waist. As she pulled the dress off in the dressing room, she said, "Those women sure went to great lengths to conform to fashion. I don't think I can breathe and this dress weighs a ton."

"Verisimilitude is a bitch," Marcy said, chuckling.

"Do I really need this corset thing?" Tay said in a mock whine.

"It's part of the outfit and Henry will expect it."

"Whatever you say. Anything for a client."

Together, she and Marcy selected large gold and faux sapphire earrings with a matching heavy necklace. She would wear white knee-high stockings and soft slippers that matched the blue of the sleeve facing.

"What about Henry's clothing?" she asked.

"He gave me all his measurements when we first met and I got his stuff while you were being fitted. I didn't want you to see his costume before Monday, so everything will be delivered to the club then."

Now, when it was finally real, Tay took a deep breath to try to relax. "Nervous?" Marcy asked as she guided her into her dressing room.

"Very."

Rock again hugged her shoulders. "Try not to be," he said, his voice soft and comforting, "but your nervousness will work nicely in the scenario. You're supposed to be a maid called to the king's chamber, to be with the most powerful man in England. You're in awe and very jittery."

"Rock probably told you that we've got no other customers tonight, so you won't be disturbed. I'm going to head home once you and Henry are settled but Rock will be here if there are any problems. That okay with you?"

"Of course. I certainly don't need both of you here, and I don't expect to need even him."

"Good," Rock said. "Okay. I'm going back downstairs. Marcy will help you get dressed." He winked at her. "Knock 'em dead." As he headed for the door he continued, "I'll be here to help you out of your costume afterward if you need me and maybe we can have a drink together. Just press the button in any room and I'll be up." She heard his muffled footsteps as he descended the carpeted stairs.

Trying to relax, Tay looked at her watch. "It's seven-thirty now. What time is Henry due?"

"He'll be here around eight," Marcy said, grinning. "I spoke to him this afternoon and he's as excited as any man I've ever dealt with. This has been his fantasy for a long time, and I'm sure he never thought he'd get to act it out."

"Any limits on what happens?" Tay asked.

"Only ones you want to set, which I hope will be few. From my talks with him, I don't think he's going to ask for anything too off-center. Maybe oral sex, but that's pretty on-center for us. It's the situation that will turn him on. The only thing I can advise is to try to go slowly. If he climaxes in half an hour it might not be as rewarding for him."

"Got it. Okay," Tay said, "let's get me dressed."

Slowly Tay transformed to a sixteenth-century woman. Marcy handed her a pair of lightweight cotton pantaloons. Tay noticed that part of the stitching that closed the seam between her thighs was missing. "I don't know whether women back then wore split-crotch undies. but in case he wants to do things while you're still dressed, I think that these should do nicely. I don't think Henry will argue about the authenticity."

"God, these clothes are really as uncomfortable as I remembered," Tay said a few moments later as Marcy put the stomacher around her waist. "It's a minor miracle anyone survived. I won't be able to take more than shallow breaths," she gasped as Marcy pulled on the laces, "and I think back then these were probably laced even more tightly."

"I think this will do," Marcy said, tying the strings and laughing, patting her slightly expanded waist. "I'd certainly never fit."

"God, this is so damned heavy," Tay added as the rich brocade dress was lowered over several petticoats. She kept talking so as not to have to think about what she was doing. "It's a wonder anyone back then ever got pregnant. But they must have."

"I think they probably removed the dresses long before that step," Marcy said, her voice deliberately calming. "Put on a little makeup but keep it very light. There's a hood-type thing here, too. I looked it up and all the paintings I found show women wearing them and the costumer agreed."

Tay took the hood, black velvet studded with pearls and what looked like diamond chips with a long velvet drape in the back that covered her hair, as Marcy said, "I didn't think a wig was necessary. I'd love to see you modernize your hair, but for tonight it will work well just as it is."

Tay brushed out her French braid, parted her soft, blond hair in the middle as she'd seen in a few of the pictures she'd looked at on the Internet and used a little styling foam to slick the front away from her forehead. Loose and kinked from the braid, her hair hung partway down her back. "Do you really think I should cut my hair?" she said, gazing into the mirror.

"Not cut it so much as have it shaped. I'd love to see you

get a real makeover, you know, hair, manicure, pedicure, makeup tips, like that. When we get more into this you'll probably find that there will be a lot of opportunity for really upscale wining and dining. You might as well look the part."

Tay continued to gaze at herself. She had to admit that she could use some help. She'd never had reason to care before, and now appearances would be important.

"There's something else about tonight," Marcy said. "One of the things I like about you is the way you carry yourself. Your back is straight and you look people in the eye when you talk to them. With Henry, that won't work. You've got to be subservient. Walk with your eyes downcast. Let your hands shake a little as they are right now."

"You noticed," Tay said. She'd been shaking inwardly for hours and it did show in her hands from time to time.

"Yeah," Marcy said, "and it was expected. Work with it. Become a frightened little maid who's been summoned by the most powerful man in England. The more you can get into the part, the better. Don't fight him when he wants to take you, but be reluctant. That's what he's looking for in this fantasy."

"I'm far from a virgin."

"Of course, and he knows that." She snorted. "We can't do everything, although we've been asked a few times. However, you can squeeze your PC muscles to make your channel tight. Make it a little difficult for him, and he'll love you all the more for it."

Tay clenched her vaginal muscles reflexively. She thought that she would be able to give a good account of herself in that respect when the time came. "Okay. Advice taken." Tay took a deep breath and heard soft footsteps in the hall.

"Henry will take a while getting into his costume, so you've got another few minutes. Rock will help him, then tap on this door when he's ready." Marcy looked into the bag that had come from the costumer. "Oops, we almost forgot your earrings." She reached into the bag and handed them to Tay, who hooked them into her ears.

Another deep breath. "Right. Well, I think I'm as ready as I can be."

"Would you mind if I took a few pictures of you in this outfit? I'd like to offer them to Henry for souvenirs. Rock will take some of him in costume, too."

"If you want to take photos, that's fine with me."

Marcy took out a digital camera and snapped from several angles. "Great."

"I'm surprised Henry would let you take his photo. Isn't there some risk of blackmail in situations like this?"

"That's one of our strengths. We're completely trusted and trustworthy. If we take stills or movies we guarantee that the client gets every copy. Nothing that goes on here has ever leaked."

"That must be a great relief to your customers."

The two women talked quietly for another fifteen minutes, then Tay heard a soft knock. Rock stuck his head in and Tay saw his familiar wink. "It's showtime, love. Oh, and he's already ecstatic about the clothing. I gave him information on how he can purchase some of the articles for himself."

As Rock headed downstairs, Tay took a deep breath, dropped her shoulders slightly into a more subservient posture, pinched her cheeks for a little added color and, with a pat on the ass from Marcy, crossed the hall and opened the door to Henry's throne room.

The man who greeted her looked so authentic that she almost felt she'd stepped into a time warp. Massive, with reddish blond hair and a curling beard, the man actually looked like the portraits she'd seen of King Henry the Eighth. He was seated on his throne and Tay quickly dropped her gaze and curtsied. Despite her quaking knees, she executed the move flawlessly, glad she'd practiced over the weekend.

She gazed up through her eyelashes. Henry was dressed in a costume closely resembling the one the real Henry wore in the famous Hans Holbein painting. Tight hose with soft leather slippers covered his legs and feet, and his torso was encased in a brocade, skirted, heavily embroidered jacket in deep purple, with long sleeves, all covered with a knee-length golden cloth coat. Rather than a crown, he wore a matching headpiece. Around his waist hung a bejeweled scabbard containing a small dagger. His three necklaces were weightier and finer than hers. She wondered whether he'd be able to move in all that finery. Well, they'd both find out.

"Cardinal Woolsey summoned me at your request, sire," she said, her voice barely above a whisper. She'd always been interested in the Reformation, both in England and on the Continent, and had listened to several Internet and podcast courses on it. She thought the reference might add some verisimilitude.

"You know of the cardinal?"

"Oh yes, sire. Everyone in the kingdom knows of him. He's a very powerful man. Almost as powerful as you are."

"So you know of the power I wield."

"Yes, sire."

His smile was brilliant, white teeth shown above his russet beard. In some silly part of her brain Tay wondered whether the real King Henry ever brushed his teeth. "Come here."

"Yes, sire." Head still lowered and hands shaking, she slowly crept toward the throne, stopping about three feet from Henry's feet. *Slowly* was the watchword, Marcy had told her. Draw out the tension, and thus the pleasure, for as long as it seemed feasible.

"You may look at me," he said.

She raised her head but said nothing.

"Come closer."

She moved until her skirt was almost touching one slightly extended royal foot.

"I am your lord. You understand that, don't you?"

"Oh yes, sire." She decided to play this as her great honor. "I know I've been favored by being invited into your presence."

His grin told her that he liked the way she was portraying herself. "Good. It is your job to please your lord."

Her slightly shy smile was her only answer to him.

"I want to touch you. Come closer still." When she leaned over his knees he reached down the front of her gown and cupped one breast. She didn't change her expression and he nodded. "Good. You understand why you're here."

"I only want to please you, sire," she said, her voice still soft and whispery.

He lifted the front of his jacket and parted a cleverly concealed slit in the front of his hose. "Does the look of this please you, impress you?" he asked.

"Indeed, sire. You are a man of unique proportions." His cock was fully erect.

"Then you may take it into your mouth."

Her smile was his answer and she knelt between his spread knees. She made sure she had lots of saliva in her mouth, then licked the precome from the tip of his cock. She wrapped her lips around the head, then created a small vacuum in her mouth and drew him inside. She took as much of him into her mouth as she could, but she knew she couldn't deep throat him. It didn't seem to matter. He sighed and slid his hips forward so she could continue her sucking. When she sensed he was getting close to orgasm she pulled back. There was no hurry. "May I touch you as well, sire?" she asked.

"I think that would be all right," he said.

She slid her hand through the slit and beneath his hose to cup his bare testicles. He groaned loudly, then pulled away and started to laugh. Horrified that she'd done something wrong, she gaped at him.

"Let's not rush, my little maid. This is all wonderful and my fantasy is wonderful, but I can't have any fun with both of us in all these clothes."

Her smile was warm. "I was wondering about that myself, sire."

"I'll help you undress, if you'll help me."

When she started to remove her hair covering first, he said, "Leave that on and the jewelry, too. It keeps everything more real for me."

"Of course, sire. But our clothing should be removed. I can't imagine even the queen wears all these clothes in your private chambers."

"So true," he said. With intermittent giggles they disrobed until both were naked. "That's better." Then he arranged several pillows into a soft, flat surface, then lay down with her beside him. "You're really lovely, and so tall. I won't crush you, will I?"

Keeping to the fantasy as best she could, she said, "No, sire. I love a man of substance."

His loud laugh was her best reward. "Now, my little lady in waiting, let's wait no longer." He leaned over and took one nipple in his mouth, while his hand covered her belly. Her hand found his cock and she held it while his fingers threaded through her pubic hair and touched her clit. She hadn't been particularly aroused, but now, with his fingers playing with her and his mouth on her breast, she felt familiar twitches in her pussy.

When his fingers slipped into her channel, she was well lubricated. "Ah, you are a forward one," he said, "all ready for the king's dick."

"Oh yes, sire," she said, stroking him and scratching his balls and the sensitive area between his sac and anus. "I am more than ready for you." And she was. "But, sire, we must be protected. No royal bastards for me."

Again he laughed and found a condom he'd obviously put beneath a pillow for later use. "Of course, my lady."

He covered his cock with the latex, then climbed over her and slowly pressed his large erection into her. "Many of the maids at court find my member too large for them. I'm glad you can take it all," he said as he sheathed himself to the hilt.

She lifted her legs and wrapped them around his waist, linking her ankles. Then they thrust together and she heard his harsh breathing. "Oh, Henry. You fill me so well."

With little preamble, he came with a bellow. Although she hadn't climaxed Tay was delighted with the amount of pleasure Henry had taken from their encounter. It took several minutes for them to catch their breath. "It happened too fast," Henry said. Tay's face must have reflected her immediate distress, so he quickly added, "That was my fault, not yours, my little maid. Otherwise, it was exactly what I dreamed of," he said, rolling over onto his back. His wide grin told Tay as much as his words. So did his completely limp penis.

"I'm glad, sire."

"Yes, let's keep the fantasy until the very end."

"Did you enjoy your evening with your lady in waiting, my lord?" she asked.

"More than I could have possibly imagined. Can we play this again?"

She wasn't sure why he'd want to do it again. Hadn't he lived his fantasy? Did many men act out the same fantasy over and over? She'd have to ask Marcy or Pam. "If you like, sire."

"Oh, I do like. Let me say one thing to you personally.

The fact that you mentioned Cardinal Woolsey was a fabulous thing to do."

"I wish I could take credit for looking something up just for this evening but I've been a history buff for many years and I've been particularly interested in Renaissance and Reformation England. I've taken a few online and audio courses recently."

"Really? You're even more fascinating than I suspected. Maybe we could get together and talk about it some time."

She lowered her eyes. "I'd like that, sire."

His wide grin was her reward.

After a few minutes, Henry stood. "My clothing is in the next room, so I will bid you good night." His eyes roamed her body, dressed only in the hood and her earrings and necklace. "Yes, my little maid, we'll have to get together again soon. What's your real name?"

"Tay, sire."

"Ah, Tay, you're magnificent."

As he exited the room, she turned his final words over in her mind. *Magnificent. Wow!*

Chapter 14

The muted footsteps of Henry going down the stairs were Tay's cue to head for the shower. She washed quickly, put her own clothes back on, carefully folded her costume and stacked it on the bed in the room she'd changed in. Rock had taken care of Henry's outfit and it now lay beside hers. It was done. She was a prostitute.

Her still-wet hair again braided, she walked downstairs and found Rock in the living room. "I heard lots of laughter so I gather things went well," he said.

"Amazingly so," Tay said. "He was delightful and said he'd be back to act out this fantasy again. Is it common for people to want to repeat a fantasy?"

"I was surprised in the beginning when men wanted repeats, but now I've gotten used to it," Rock said, rising. "Okay, enough about him, how about you? How are you holding up?"

Almost giddy from happiness and relief that it was finally over, she said, "I'm doing much better than I'd expected. I was truly okay with all this in contemplation, but I wasn't sure how I'd react in actuality. I have to admit now that I had a great time."

"That's wonderful," he said, beaming, "and very important both to you and to Henry the Eighth. Did you climax?"

Tay blushed. She wasn't used to such direct questions, but these folks probably had little reluctance to discuss the more intimate aspects of what went on in the club. "No, but that's all right. He did and that's what counts."

"Right you are," Rock said, "but it's too bad you were left hanging."

She felt his unspoken offer, but didn't want to take him up on it. "I am really fine with things just the way they are."

"Sorry if I embarrassed you. I guess we're pretty 'out there' around here and I'm sure you're not used to it. Yet." He started toward the back of the brownstone. "With nerves and the newness of it all I would bet that you haven't eaten all day. Are you starved?"

She looked at her watch. "I am but I really had better make my way to Grand Central. I can grab something at the station."

"There are trains until after one AM so I'm sure you can spare a little time for yourself. And it's Monday, so you probably don't have to go into the city tomorrow. You know, next time you should arrange to stay over. We've certainly got enough rooms and Marcy has all kinds of toiletries stashed away. I'm sure you could ask Pam to take care of your animals if necessary."

Tay shook her head slowly. "You really know everything about me, don't you?"

His almost boyish chuckle was in such contrast to his kung fu physique. "I'm the truly nosey type and I'm an inveterate eavesdropper. Sorry yet again." He waved her toward the kitchen. "Come on back. I can make you something substantial but I seem to remember that you're a fan of peanut butter and potato chips. I've got both," he said.

"I really am ravenous and since you've got pb and chips I'll consider you for sainthood."

As Rock turned she saw his now-familiar wink. Those frequent winks were so charming that she wondered whether she could get more serious about this guy. He wasn't the type with whom to form a relationship. But for some temporary fun?

"I think I'm the last person who might qualify in that department," he said, "but I'm an expert about food. As you get more experienced at this sort of thing, you'll be able to eat beforehand, but even then I find that hot, sweaty sex really works up an appetite."

I'd guess you'd know, Tay said to herself, thinking again about the room downstairs. "By the way, I hope you don't mind but I gave him pictures of each of you in costume. He was delighted with them. I can picture the many evenings of pleasure he'll get from the memories of this encounter. No doubt he'll be back."

"I hope so. That will make me feel like I really made him happy."

"Judging from the shit-eating grin on his face when he left, you did."

While Rock found a jar of chunky peanut butter and a bag of Ruffles with ridges and put them in the center of the small breakfast bar, Tay sat on a stool and kicked her shoes off. "Toast or plain bread?" he asked.

"You must be a peanut butter eater to ask about toast. Non-peanut butter people assume white bread. Makes it gunky."

"As you might have noticed, since I am most certainly a peanut butter kind of guy, I've taken out bread for both of us and the toaster is ready. I've never tried chips, though. I'm a bacon bits person," he said with a grin that showed off his white teeth. "I've never gone for the sweet stuff, you know, jelly or marshmallow fluff."

"Me neither. Hmm. Bacon bits," she said, tilting her head to one side. "Sounds good. How about we go halvies? I'll take half of your sandwich with bits and you can have half of my chip one."

"Done," Rock said, adding a jar of bacon bits to the table, then popping slices of bread into a four-slice toaster. "This is certainly an evening of new experiences. Drink?" he asked. "We've got everything from water to vodka."

"Diet Pepsi?"

He reached into the large refrigerator, and while the door was open she saw that it was filled with cans of soda and beer of every description, as well as bottles of wine and champagne. "We offer drinks to most of our clients, if it fits with their fantasy, of course. We've also got a well-stocked bar in the living room plus I make a great assortment of blender drinks for those who desire." He looked at her questioningly. "Glass?"

"No thanks. And I should have realized you'd have just about everything. The club is truly a full-service facility."

"And then some." The toast popped and Rock put two slices on each of two light blue and black striped plates and settled across from her. In a companionable silence they each put crunchy goo on one slice of crispy toast, and while Tay piled on the Ruffles, Rock sprinkled a generous amount of bacon bits on his. He grabbed a knife and they each cut their sandwich and then exchanged halves.

Tay's bite of the new combination was delicious. "Not bad," she said, then took a bit of the chipped one. "Both excellent."

"I couldn't agree more," Rock said, taking bites of each. "You've got good taste, Tay."

"You're an interesting man," Tay said, crunching her sandwich. "How did you get into this business?"

"Several years ago a wonderful woman named Erika, for whom I then worked as a male prostitute, introduced me to Jenna, Marcy's sister, and Chloe, who between them started the club. Erika convinced them that they needed someone like me to live in and be on-site protection. I loved the idea, since I got to redecorate and then use the room downstairs for my particular clients, and my friends. Some of the friends play with me, others use the room to be with their friends and pay for the privilege. I get to keep those funds, in addition to my salary here, and room and board."

"And the rest is history."

"Right."

"But what about you personally? Family? Childhood? Like that."

"I was born Martin Rockford, like that old TV show the *Rockford Files*. I was small for my age, a skinny kid with big hands and feet, but with no idea how to use them to defend myself. If you can believe this, when I was fourteen I was the shortest kid in my class. So, since I was constantly picked on, my folks hired what you would now call a personal trainer. In addition to spending thousands of hours working with weights and machines, he instructed me in tae kwon do, which, along with other self-defense techniques, taught me to move gracefully despite my increasing size. By the time I was sixteen I'd grown almost a foot, put on about eighty pounds, most of it muscle, and was well on my way to what I now hold, a third-degree black belt. If you ever want to see me break wood with my feet, let me know."

Tay giggled. "Maybe not. I guess the kids didn't fool with you after that. Did you ever bust anyone's chops?"

Rock grinned. "I never actually had to mess anyone up. My feelings about myself changed about a hundred and eighty degrees and it became unnecessary. I became firm without being pushy and the other guys sensed my newfound strength, both outer and inner. I quickly learned that attitude is more important than actually beating anyone up."

"Brothers? Sisters?"

"Neither. My folks now live in California but I was raised in Louisiana. You probably guessed I'm originally from somewhere south of the Mason-Dixon Line. I can't seem to lose the slight accent even though I haven't lived there in twenty-five years."

Tay had finished her sandwich. "Another?" she asked.

"Not for me but help yourself."

Nice, she thought. *He's treating me like a member of the family and I guess I am.* She toasted two more slices of bread and made herself another sandwich, half chips and half bacon bits. "Do you enjoy working and living here? It must be a little confining."

"Not really. It's become my life and I like it. I'm free every day until late afternoon and all day Mondays and Tuesdays. Tonight being a delightful exception, of course."

As she ate her second sandwich, Tay told him about Steve and Lissa, moving to Maple Court and meeting Pam. "She's the greatest, isn't she?" Rock said. "I like her so much. I wish she and Linc would make a more permanent arrangement. I think they're great together. I introduced them."

"You did?"

"Pam needed someone to do for her, on Maple Court, what I do here and Linc was the perfect person. So Marcy and I got them together, and as you said before, the rest is history."

"They're both so great. I wonder though whether their work might get in the way. It must be difficult to deal with natural jealousies, both of them being what they are."

"I'm sure that there aren't many who could deal with it, but Marcy and Zack do. Erika, the woman who introduced me to Jenna, is married and lives on the Island. Her husband is the guy who got her into the business in the first place."

Tay looked at her watch. Henry had left just before nine, and now it was well after ten. "I'd love to continue our visit, but I've got to run," she said, putting her plate in the sink. "I can just make the ten-fifty train."

"I was hoping you'd stay over. You don't have work tomorrow and I thought you might want a more complete tour of the downstairs. I sense an interest."

Tay's pulse jumped and her pussy twitched. She hadn't climaxed with Henry and she was filled with unused sexual energy. However . . . "I have Lissa's animals to worry about, so I really have to get back." It was as good an excuse as any. She wasn't ready for Rock. Not yet.

Rock cupped the back of Tay's head and kissed her, his lips playing with hers. When he finally pulled back, he said, "Rain check? I think we can have lots of fun together."

Tay took a deep breath, and let it out slowly. "Rain check."

During the trip home, Tay relived the scene she'd just acted out and smiled. She'd done it and she'd had fun. She couldn't overlook the fact that she'd earned a chunk of cash as well. In addition she considered Rock's unspoken invitation. She realized that eventually she'd take him up on it. Not yet, though. She had a ways to go before she was ready for sex with a professional, and the dungeon was something she would leave for the future—the not-too-far-distant future, she thought. For now, things were great. The evening had made her realize that she was in need of a regular sexual outlet. She wondered whether Justin would be back on Maple Court soon. She'd e-mailed him a few times since he'd been gone, but he answered only sporadically. Damn.

She had itches, and was beginning to understand more of the reasons that men hired prostitutes.

She didn't overlook the fact that women hire men for sex as well. She couldn't see herself doing that, yet. Another "yet." Right now she was really frustrated and the more she thought about the evening, the more frustrated she became.

Chapter 15

Tay slept fitfully that night, the result of erotic dreams and strange images of handcuffs and powerlessness, all played with a sixteenth-century backdrop. She awoke just after six, took a quick shower and, to take her mind off everything that had happened the previous evening, grabbed a bowl of shredded wheat and attacked the mountain of work that awaited her on her laptop. Just before ten o'clock her cell phone rang.

"So how did it go?" Pam said without preamble.

"It was just great. I have so much to tell you, but I've got lots of work, too. Can we make lunch late?"

"Sure. We can stay really local so you'll be able to get back quickly, but I want to hear everything. How about I pick you up at one-thirty?"

"Works for me. See ya."

Ten minutes later Marcy called and Tay told her all about her evening with Henry, and her after-party with Rock. "Rock's a sweetie," Marcy said. "Did you know he used to be a corrections officer before Erika found him and, eventually, introduced him to Jenna?"

"No, but I can see it. He's one powerful guy."

"He certainly is, and his customers really enjoy that about him."

"I gather he entertains in the club on the evenings that you're closed."

"He's got more clients than he can handle, pardon the pun. Men and women both really go for his dominant personality." She chuckled. "A few even like playing the dominant to his submissive. He can play either role well."

"Somehow I can't picture him being submissive."

"I can't either, but it must be a thrill for someone to wield power over someone with his physique."

"I can imagine."

"You must have made quite an impression on Henry. He called me first thing this morning. He seems to think you know something about the England of King Henry's time. He wants to meet you for dinner so you can talk about British history or whatever. Do you really know something about that or was that a con?"

"Actually it's an interest of mine. One of many."

"Would you like to have dinner with him? On the books, of course."

"I'd love to. He's a really nice guy."

"Up for more encounters, too, Tay?" Marcy asked.

"I sure am. I can't decide which is more motivating, good sex or cash."

Marcy's laugh was warm and rich, even through the phone lines. "Right you are on both counts. Let me see what turns up and I'll call you when I know anything. If Pam's having a party and she can use you, so much the better."

Tay hung up soon after that interchange and got back to work. Around noon she read an e-mail from Lissa. The two women kept in frequent contact and Lissa's letters were filled with tales of her adventures in China. She'd told her friend about her bedroom encounters with Justin, and had been warned yet again that he wasn't the permanent type, something she knew all too well.

Tay had also written about her friendship with Pam. However, she hadn't told Lissa anything about the club, the Madam of Maple Court or about her adventures with it all. That would have to wait until she could discuss things with her friend face-to-face.

She considered what Lissa's reaction would be. She'd probably cheer and ask how she could get into the business but a little voice in the back of Tay's head told her to go slowly. People were funny. She wasn't sure how she'd have reacted before she'd learned to get past the PC responses if the situation were reversed.

By the time she heard Pam's car in the driveway she had put in almost six hours at the computer and had whittled her to-do list down to a manageable size. For long periods of time she had been able to shut down thoughts of the previous evening so she could concentrate totally. She'd edited three grant proposals, looked over and done a written evaluation of a set of plans for an expansion of the company's Web site, including several proposals for advertising, and answered a stack of e-mails from people in the company who couldn't take a step without asking her advice.

Finally she put her computer into sleep mode, slipped on her shoes and was at the door as Pam beeped the Lexus's horn. "You said you wanted to stay someplace local," Pam said as Tay climbed into the passenger seat. Just the walk down the front walk was enough to start her sweating in the heat of New York in July. "How about the diner?"

Not only was it hot but the humidity was astronomical and almost immediately Tay's T-shirt was stuck to her back. Her heavy jeans hung on her legs and, despite the Lexus's air-conditioning she was quickly drenched. It was difficult to keep track of the weather outside when the whole Bonner house was air-conditioned. "The diner's great." She wiped her forehead and leaned forward, sopping up the cool air pouring out of the air conditioner. "Good lord," she said. "It's like a sauna today." She looked at Pam's neat denim blue slacks and crisp red short-sleeved blouse. "How do you always manage to look so cool?"

"I haven't been out today. I remote-started the car so the air conditioner had a chance to cool it down, and stop teasing me, you beast. I don't give a damn about the heat. Tell me about last evening."

"Okay. But first let's get going. I really do have lots more work to do so I need to make it quick."

"The diner's always subarctic, so that should do us," Pam said, shifting into drive. The local diner was just a few minutes away. "Damn, you're right, it is stiflingly hot," Pam said, flipping the car's climate-control system up to its highest level. "Now, enough dawdling. Tell me everything."

By the time Pam parked in the lot of the local diner, Tay had given her the outline of her evening with Henry. "I found myself enjoying it all more than I thought I would. It took maybe five minutes to get over my jitters, but I never let him know I was anything but dazzled by his presence."

"That's one of the keys to all this. Staying in the part you're playing is everything."

"I slipped in a reference to a person of the era and now he wants to have dinner with me and talk about English history. I think he's a Henry the Eighth groupie but he's also a very nice guy."

They got out of the car and walked quickly into the cool interior of the diner. "Are you going to have dinner with him?"

"Sure. Why not?"

"Just be sure you get paid for it."

"Marcy mentioned that it would be on the books. I'd be willing to have dinner with him anyway."

"Don't mix business with pleasure," Pam said softly. "It's a bad habit to get into. Keep your professional life, the one you get paid for, separate from your dating life and especially from your friends. It's simpler all around. That way you don't get confused into thinking all these guys are serious about you as a person. Remember that the men you serve can afford to pay for your company and you know that you'll give them pleasure equal to what you receive and more."

"Aren't you being a little mercenary?"

"Several of the women who've worked with Marcy and who I cared about have gotten hurt by doing what I'm warning you against. I don't want to see you join them."

"Hurt?"

"They began to think 'relationship' while the guys were thinking 'lust.'"

"What about you and Linc, or Marcy and Zack?"

"That's different. They weren't customers."

"Hasn't it ever worked out?"

"Oh sure, a few times, but it's the exception."

They were shown to a booth and quickly ordered, Pam a grilled-chicken Caesar salad and Tay a bison burger with fries. "Gotta keep up my strength," she said.

"After last evening I can imagine. Sounds like you really scored with your first client."

"I did and not only did he go away happy, but he's going to see me again. What better compliment could there be?"

"That's great. My next few parties are of the ordinary kind. I have a shower scheduled for this weekend and a summer office party, without benefits, the following. However, I'm having a party in a few weeks that will require ladies for companionship. Interested?"

"Sure. Will you arrange it through Marcy?"

"I never handle any of that part of it by myself."

"Good. I'm definitely up for it." She sipped her coffee. "So, how's Linc?"

"He's great, but he's thinking of getting a real job in addition to his modeling and working for Marcy."

"Real job?"

"One of the companies he does catalog work for in White Plains is looking for someone to take over their entire online sales and advertising department. Ordering, scheduling, shipping and God knows what else. When he found out about the opening he told them of his background and they're considering each other."

"What kind of background?"

"His father is big in retailing in the Midwest and in college Linc was tracked to join his dad's business. After an MBA and a few years sitting at a desk he got restless and decided he didn't want to be tied down to a nine-to-five job so he took himself off to the Big Apple."

"How did his folks react to that?"

"Actually they were very supportive. I've met his parents several times when they've come to New York and they are great people. His mom's a history teacher, which is why his name. It's actually Washington Lincoln Truman Frawley."

"Ah, thus Linc."

"Right. Anyway, he decided to come to New York to make his way in the world of acting and modeling. That was almost seven years ago. Now he's thinking of dusting off that degree and showing everyone that he's not just a pretty face."

"How do you feel about that?"

"I'm in favor of Linc doing whatever will make him happy."

"Amen to that. Will you be happy when he's out of Marcy's business?"

"First of all I don't know whether he'll leave the business. I know it's difficult to understand but I've really got no problem with him doing what he does. He enjoys it and it makes him a great living."

Tay's eyes widened. "There's really no jealousy?"

"There was, at first. In the beginning I had vivid pictures of him with other women but at the time I was doing the same thing. After a few months, as our relationship developed, I relaxed and let it all go and I think he did the same. Now it's merely a job." She grinned. "With benefits, of course. And I don't do much actual fucking anymore. The party business suits me well and pays more than enough to keep me in hors d'oeuvres."

"What about getting married, or at least moving in together?"

"As you know, Linc wants to, but I don't know. I don't want him to feel tied to me. I want him to be with me because he wants to, not because he has nowhere else to live."

"That's pretty silly," Tay said. "It's obvious to everyone that he's really in love with you."

Pam's eyebrows lifted in surprise. "Why do you say that?"

"Oh please," Tay said. "You can see it in the way he looks at you, particularly when you're not paying attention to him. You should have seen him at your party."

"Really?"

"Oh, Pam, be serious." Tay felt like an older sister. "You can't mean that you don't know how he feels. Get real. Does the idea of something more permanent scare you?"

Pam thought a moment. "Yeah. It scares me to death. Toward the end my marriage to Vin had deteriorated to the point that we were two strangers living in the same house. He was using the services of the club and I knew nothing about it. After he was killed I realized how bad things had gotten, and we'd loved each other so much in the beginning. I'm terrified that if Linc and I make this more formal the same thing will happen, and he probably wants kids. I don't want to deny him that." She took a deep breath, wiping moisture from her eyes with the back of her hand. "Phew. I didn't see all that coming and I'm sorry to dump on you."

"Don't be ridiculous. We're friends and between friends there's no dumping. I'm glad you're being honest and I'll just put in my two cents' worth, then shut up. First, talk to him about the kids thing. You might be surprised. And about the idea of marriage itself, you and Vin married very young and still had a lot of maturing and growing to do. You grew in different directions with different values. The same isn't true with you and Linc. You're two mature people, capable of making mature decisions."

"But what if we can't make it in the long run?"

"The old saying 'nothing ventured, nothing gained' has a lot of truth to it. You can protect your heart only so far. Then you begin missing out on many of the good things about relationships. I've done a lot of thinking about Steve and me. Of course it wasn't marriage and was a lot shorter than you and Vin, but it was still really difficult for me when he left. But you know, there were really great times, and lots of sex. Had I protected myself from getting too involved I would have missed a lot. No real lows, but no highs, either."

"Interesting way to look at things."

The waitress arrived with their meals and for several minutes Pam was involved with salad dressing and Tay with ketchup. Pam picked up a few of Tay's fries and shoved them into her mouth. "So much for diets."

"Diets are for wimps," Tay answered. "So, now that I've been initiated, how about some war stories? I'm really curious about what goes on inside the club."

"And outside, too," Pam said. "My backyard and hot tub get a lot of use. Men love the idea of fucking in the great out of doors. Not only does it feel good, but there's a thrill about the possibility of being caught in the act."

"No one would walk in on you. Your grounds are too well protected."

"True, but the guys don't know that. Remember that much of what we do is illusion."

"What about other kinky stuff?" She again thought about Rock. "Ever gotten into more off-center stuff?" She didn't say what she was thinking. Things like the dungeon.

"Sure. Some I like, some I don't and Marcy makes sure to pair me with guys who have the same ideas of what's hot and what's not."

"If this question is too personal just tell me to mind my own business. What's beyond the pale for you?"

Pam heaved a deep sigh. "That's not too personal at all between us. Let's see. Marcy told me one guy wanted his dog to participate."

"You're kidding."

"No. And she found a woman who was willing to go along. Another thing I'm definitely not into is water sports."

"I guess I'm naive. Water sports?"

"Peeing and like that."

Tay felt her face wrinkle. "Ugh. I'm with you. Not my thing. But I guess there are folks who enjoy that sort of stuff, too."

"If you surf the Net, and I suggest that you do, you'll find sites devoted to really off-center stuff. People like all sorts of stuff: serious pain, whipping, feces"—her face wrinkled, too—"enemas, like that. I don't have to participate, however."

"Sane, to say the least."

"Just don't put anyone down for their beliefs, as long as the activity takes place between consenting adults. No drugs, no drunks, no one incapable of giving real consent. That's all I ask."

"I assume Marcy knows your preferences."

"And those of every woman who works for her, and she works very hard to match clients with employees. She'll question you once you've had a chance to adjust to all this."

"I'm amazingly adjusted even now, and I'll look around and see what's out there so I'll know in advance what I'm willing to do."

"Great. Just don't close any doors, either. You might not think something will be pleasurable at first, but in reality . . ."

"Like?"

"Like me and anal sex. I thought it would be painful and icky. Eventually I decided to try it with Linc and I found it to be"—a small smile lit her face—"not bad at all."

"I've never tried it, but with that recommendation . . ."

"Don't take anyone else's word for anything. Keep an open mind and relax. If you ever get into anything that doesn't work out, just tell the guy he'll get his money back if he wants."

"Right." Tay was finding all this talk about sex was making her really horny. Again the picture of Justin flashed through her mind.

The women finished their lunch and returned to Maple Court, agreeing to get Linc to barbecue over the weekend. Tay plunked herself in front of her laptop and put in another two hours of work. At around four-thirty she finally called it a day, put on her bathing suit and headed for the pool. If anything it was hotter than it had been earlier and she was looking forward to doing laps. She became aware of the dogs barking and wondered why all the noise.

"Hey, I'm really sorry," a male voice called as Tay crossed the lawn. She looked toward the sound and saw a young man, maybe in his late teens or early twenties, guiding a long-handled skimmer over the surface of the pool. He was of medium height, with light brown skin and deep brown hair and eyes that were almost black. He was dressed in only tan shorts and sandals. He was shirtless and his shoulders and hairless chest were deliciously developed. From across the pool she could make out a tattoo on his right calf.

It might have been a sword or dagger, stabbing through a dripping heart.

"I usually do this on Wednesdays," he continued, his voice tentative, "but I have something else I have to do tomorrow so I thought you wouldn't mind if I came today."

Came today, Tay thought. Why did such an innocent remark sound like such a double entendre? But she knew the answer.

She looked at him as he looked at her. Was she detecting a spark of interest? He wasn't particularly good looking, with badly cut hair in several shades of gold and brown, ears that stuck out from his head and large brown, puppy-dog eyes. But he was young and probably virile and she was so damned hungry. She mentally slapped herself. *Stop it, Tay*, she yelled at herself.

Why should I? she argued. *He's of age. If he's interested . . .*

Chapter 16

"I've no problem with you being here today," she said to the young man. "I'm Tay, by the way."

"Nice to meet you, ma'am. I'm José."

She slowly unbuckled the strap on her watch, put it on a small table beside the pool and kicked off her sandals. "Glad to meet you too, José. You know, it's very hot this afternoon," she said, trying to think of a graceful way to ask him if he wanted to fuck. "Uh, do you have many more stops to make?"

"No, ma'am. You're my last one."

"Well, then, why don't you join me for a swim to cool off?"

He hesitated. "I'm really not supposed to use the customers' pools."

"I'm sure that doesn't apply when you're invited." She made her way down the pool's stairs and walked through the water to where he stood, cupped a handful of water and splashed it all over him.

He barked a laugh. "That wasn't nice," he said, his face a mirror of his uncertainty as to exactly what she was suggesting. His shorts, however, indicated his body's reaction.

She splashed him again. "You're right. It wasn't nice. What are you going to do about it?"

"I don't have trunks," he said, water dripping from his face and down his chest. He shook himself like a puppy.

"Who cares?" *Don't rush things, Tay,* she told herself. "You can swim in your briefs."

He looked embarrassed. "Er, I'm not wearing any."

"I guess it's either in your shorts or in the buff for you. I'll bet you have a very nice body."

He blushed and Tay watched as he seemed to become more sure that he was reading her comments correctly. She saw the "things like this don't really happen" look in his eyes and the hope that he was interpreting the situation correctly. "I don't want to soak my pants. But if you're sure. . . ."

She splashed him again. "I'm sure." Was she sure? *Stop waffling,* she told herself. *You want to play, and if he does as well, what the heck!*

To ease his embarrassment she put her face in the water and swam a lap, ending up at the deep end of the pool, opposite from where he'd been standing. She heard the splash as he landed in the water, then, as she turned, he surfaced in front of her, hands on her shoulders, shoving her under. She opened her eyes beneath the water and, as she'd suggested, he was nude. The cool water diminished the size of his erection, but she could see that he was still aroused. And quite sizeable. She broke the surface and splashed him.

He looked at her through the water streaming through his eyes and said, "That wasn't nice."

"I think it's very nice."

"I'm at a disadvantage," he said, seeming to gain confidence. "You're still wearing a suit and I'm not."

"Ah," she said. "A definite imbalance." Bracing her hands on the edge of the pool, she vaulted out and stood on the surrounding tiles. "Let me remedy that." Slowly she wriggled out of her one-piece and watched his eyes as he saw her body revealed. *Yes,* she thought, *why the hell not!*

"Now we're even," she said, jumping back into the water. Since she'd made the initial move, she decided to let him set the pace, however tentative. She needn't have worried. He all but attacked her, hands everywhere. "Hold it," she said, gently pushing him away and backing up. "Let's slow down a little."

He looked chagrined. "I thought . . . Y-y-you're just so beautiful," he stammered.

"Thanks," she said, "and you're really good looking, too."

Reassured, he grinned and grabbed at her again. God, the mating dance was fun. "Not so fast," she continued. "Let's take this a little more slowly." She dove beneath the water and came up beside him, slithering her body against his as she surfaced. She snaked her arms around his neck and pressed her cool lips against his. When he reached for her breasts she again backed off. "Hey, look. Let's make a deal. I know what you want, and you'll get it, I promise. But let me lead." She guided him to the shallow end of the pool. "Keep your hands at your sides and let me do the work. Okay?"

He nodded, seeming a little reluctant. Then she kissed him, slowly rubbing her lips over his, then allowing her breasts to rub against his hairless chest. She cupped the back of his head and guided his mouth. "Umm," she purred. "I love to kiss. Don't you?"

"Umm." His purr joined hers, but she could still sense his impatience. *Too bad, but we're going to do this my way.*

She slid her hands down his neck to his well-developed shoulders, slick with pool water. He must get a good workout skimming and vacuuming. "Nice," she whispered. "Very nice." He now stood completely still, and as their bodies brushed against each other she could feel his cock stiffening despite the coolness of the water.

She allowed her hands to drift over his body and when he reached for her breasts, she again admonished him. "I'll tell you when you can use your hands."

He gazed at her, fingers curling and uncurling. "Please. I want to touch you."

"You'll get your chance in due time. Remember that patience is a virtue." Her hands found his buttocks and she cupped, then squeezed his cheeks. Then she stroked her way around to the front, not touching his package, caressing his belly and flanks. "You know," she said, "I really should allow you to reciprocate." She lifted his hands and placed them on her breasts, her nipples already hard and tight. She held his palms against her flesh, moving her body slightly so that her hungry tips rubbed against his hands exactly the way she liked. Finally he let her lead and he was now getting the first of his rewards.

Letting her head drop back she reveled in the sensations he was causing. She arched her back so that her pubis brushed his erection and heard his gasp. "Let's get onto dry land," she suggested and climbed the steps. She settled on a lounge chair with one leg on the cushion and one foot on the tile. She patted the cushion so he sat between her spread thighs. "Do you like to perform oral sex?" she asked.

As his answer, he leaned down and positioned his head between her thighs. "Slowly," she said. When his mouth found her clit, she gasped. "Oh yes. Just like that. Long and slow."

His licks traveled the length of her slit and she knew he could taste the juices that flowed freely. He slid his hands up her torso until he could cup her breasts and, in rhythm with his licks, squeezed her flesh and pinched her nipples. She came. Right then, without any penetration, she came. Hard. She tried not to scream and wake the world to her climax, but deep moans of pleasure escaped.

"Now?" he asked.

"Condom," she managed to say and he dashed to find his wallet. It took only moments until he was sheathed in latex, then his urgent cock found her opening and thrust inside.

Her legs wrapped around his waist, his buttocks bunching and pressing him forward, it took only a moment before he came, and she experienced her second orgasm in just a few minutes. "Feel it," she moaned. "Feel me come on your cock."

"Shit, shit, shit," he croaked. Their groans mingled, then the only sound was of their heavy breathing. "My God, I don't know what to say. I never thought anything like this would ever happen and I'm so glad it did. I want to see you again."

"Don't get carried away, José," she said. "This was something that just happened. Today. It was wonderful, but it wasn't real. Pretend I was a fantasy, something your mind created, and remember it that way."

His face fell. "But I want it to happen again."

"Fantasies are always best if you don't see them too clearly in the harsh light of reality." She knew that wasn't necessarily true, but it was the best way to lower his expectations. If he was here when she was horny she might invite him to make love to her again, but he mustn't count on it.

"I'm usually here around noon on Wednesdays. Will you be here next week?"

"I usually work in the city on Wednesdays."

"Oh. That's why I've never seen you before. I can be here on Tuesdays from now on. I'll rearrange my schedule."

She thought of Pam's words. Don't confuse sex for money—or in this case to scratch an itch—with a relationship. José needed to learn this, too. She quickly realized that she didn't want him here when she was hoping for more interludes like this one. She didn't want him to be continually disappointed. "No. I probably won't be here any more often on Tuesdays."

"Oh." He looked still more crestfallen. "Is there any day?"

"Just keep to your regular schedule and if, on occasion, I take a day off, I'll remember that you're here. That's the best I can do for you. Okay?"

Looking totally disappointed, he said, softly, "Okay."

She untangled her legs from his body and reached for a towel. Wrapping it around herself, she said, "You'll always have the memory of the wonderful time we had. Yes?"

"God, yes," he said.

"Good. I'll go inside and leave you to finish with the pool. Maybe we'll meet again."

"I hope so," he said to her back as she walked toward the house.

"Pam, tell me I'm not a slut," Tay said into the phone an hour later.

"You're not a slut," Pam dutifully replied. "Why are you wondering? Having second thoughts about your evening with Henry?"

"I just fucked the pool guy."

It took a minute for Pam to stop laughing. "You didn't."

Suddenly seeing the situation for what it was, ludicrous and fun, she was able to laugh with Pam. She felt considerably better. "I did. After you dropped me off I worked for a few hours, then started outside for a swim. He was here and convenient, young and randy as hell, and I was hungry. Tell me it was okay."

"Did he object?"

"No. He was all in favor. I had to tell him not to expect this kind of thing every time he comes over. That I'd be at work."

"So what's the harm?"

"I'm ruining the younger generation."

Pam laughed again. "Right. Younger generation. He's what,

ten years younger than you are? Maybe fifteen? He could have been your date rather than your target."

Tay huffed out a breath. "You're right, of course, but he seemed so young."

"That's because you've matured a lot in the past few weeks. Relax. If you both consented and had fun, what's the harm?"

"I don't know. It just seems so slutty."

"Don't be ridiculous, and stop taking yourself so seriously."

"Is that what I'm doing?"

"I think so. You're not the morality police. My theory is, if it feels good, and doesn't hurt anyone, go for it."

"Is Linc coming over tonight?" Tay asked.

"Not until late. I was just going to make myself a frozen dinner. I've really been off my diet so far today, so I'm going to try to be good for the rest of the day. Want to have dinner with me? You can bring something or scrounge out of my fridge. Or we can have something delivered."

"I thought you'd never ask. I'll make a sandwich and wander over. I need to pick your brain about a few more things regarding the business."

"Great. See you in a few. . . ."

Tay made a peanut-butter-and-potato-chip sandwich and thought about Rock. She really wanted to find out more about him, and specifically about the stuff that went on in the basement of the club.

Pam was putting her frozen dinner in the microwave when Tay arrived. Pam didn't have many female friends and she was so happy that she and Tay had become so close so fast.

Small talk occupied the first few minutes of their pick-up meal. As she took her plate out, Pam looked at Tay's sandwich, then down at her Healthy Choice Asiago Chicken

Portabello, which looked and smelled delicious, but she would have been just as happy with peanut butter. Just not as thin. Staying at a good weight was a constant struggle, one she lost as often as she won. "I hope you're grateful for your metabolism," she said as Tay settled on a kitchen stool.

Tay giggled. "No credit to me. I picked my parents right, that's all."

"Great way to look at things. Wine?"

With a little giggle, Tay nodded and said, "Okay, here's the question. Which is stranger: Wine and peanut butter or wine with a diet dinner?"

"I diet when and where it doesn't matter to me. Wine matters."

Pam poured two glasses of Pinot Grigio and sat down at the breakfast bar beside her friend. *Friend. How great is that?* They chatted while they ate and eventually, of course, the conversation turned to the business. "Tell me about some of the oddballs," Tay said, then shook her head. "Poor choice of words, but you get what I mean."

"Let me think. Several men haven't been what they purported to be, but this one was the ultimate. I remember him well." She gazed off into space. "He was not bad looking, although I don't know why that's the first thing everyone says when they describe someone. Brown curly hair, neat moustache, but hard eyes. Bright blue, I guess I might say icy. And his mouth was set with deep parentheses creases on either side, as though he wasn't expecting his needs to be met and in that he was always proven right."

She remembered the evening well. Robert. She remembered he told Marcy he never wanted to be called anything but Robert. That was what his mother named him and that was what he was to be called. Either Marcy or Pam should have realized that things wouldn't go smoothly right off, but he'd checked out and they had no reason right then not to take him at his word.

He'd wanted to use the Western room and had gone with the "sweet young thing saved from the evil gun fighter" scenario. He hadn't had too much to say about the woman he wanted to play with and Pam had been free that evening. Although she didn't often use the club's facilities, that evening had sounded pretty straightforward and she'd played that fantasy once before.

Robert walked in, pulling his fringed leather vest around his large chest and hiking up the low-riding gun belt. He was a substantially built man with a fringe of graying hair, wide shoulders and large hands. "These pants are quite a bit too tight," he said, obviously not yet into the fantasy.

"I'm so sorry," Pam said. She swung the apron that partially covered her full-skirted blue gingham dress. She untied the matching bonnet and put it onto the sheriff's large wooden desk.

Before she could begin to set the stage for his fantasy, he growled, "You folks must have gotten the wrong size."

Pam knew Marcy had gotten the outfit in the size he'd specified. She didn't make mistakes. Pam wanted to help him forget the small inconveniences and slip into the fantasy anyway. "I'm so sorry, Sheriff, but I want to thank you so much for saving me. I hope you'll let me make it all up to you."

"You're not concerned about whether I got hurt in the fight?" he bellowed.

Hurt? This was a fantasy and it always started after the encounter with the gunfighter. "Did you?" she asked softly.

"No, no thanks to you."

Right. "Well, I'm really grateful to you for helping me." She'd put a slight Western drawl into her speech.

He looked around. "This place is a little cheesy." He walked over to the wall, grabbing a Wanted poster. "You did this with clip art and it looks really phony." Pam said nothing as he prowled the room, criticizing several of the props.

Then he returned to stand in front of her. Her dress was quite low cut, and when she'd played this fantasy once before the guy had started things by looking down the bodice at her full breasts. He surprised her again. "Cheesy dress, too. And you're really short, aren't you?"

Oh God, how did she get herself into this? "I'm exactly five feet tall and you didn't specify anything about the woman in your story."

"Yeah, but you're also a little chunky for my taste."

There was no hope for it, she thought. No one could be a good enough actress to make this bloke happy. "I'm sorry, Robert, but I don't think this is working for you. If you're not satisfied I can arrange to have a refund put on your credit card."

He unzipped his pants and pulled out his fully erect cock. "Never mind. On your knees and suck this if you want to get paid."

The customer is always right. The customer is always right. And she was being paid top dollar. She got onto her knees and took his cock into her mouth. He cupped the back of her head and literally fucked her mouth for several minutes until, with a long, drawn-out sigh, he came into her throat. *No refunds for you*, she thought.

His knees shook for a moment, then, without another word, he left the room to change back into his street clothes. Pam would tell Marcy what happened and suggest that this guy not be allowed back. But then, she thought, why not? He'd gotten his rocks off and they'd get paid. Who cared what kind of scenario he wanted to play?

When she finished the story, Tay laughed and asked, "Did he ever come back?"

"Actually," Pam chuckled, "he did. Somehow playing the dissatisfied customer got him aroused. There's no accounting for taste and that's a great lesson to learn early on. I thought I knew what he wanted and he went in a completely different direction. It happens occasionally, and if you're fast on your feet, you can make most folks happy."

That evening was still a little difficult for Pam to shake. It was one of the only times she'd been made to feel like a whore rather than a courtesan. As she'd always done, she'd turned to Linc for comfort. She remembered what he'd said. "No one can make you feel something like that. It's the baggage you carry that brings the feelings. Are you sorry for what you do?"

"I guess when I wake up in the middle of the night, sometimes I feel a little down. It's difficult to get back to sleep."

Linc had looked surprised. "I don't remember any times you were awake in the middle of the night, and I'm a pretty light sleeper."

It had dawned on her at the time. "It doesn't happen when you're in bed with me. If I wake up with negative thoughts I just cuddle against you and go right back to sleep."

"I think there's a lesson there," he'd said, holding her.

Pam's thoughts returned to her kitchen and she watched Tay chew her peanut butter sandwich. Maybe Linc was right and there was a lesson in both the story and the realizations later. "That wasn't my best evening," she said, "but you asked about the strange ones."

"You look like it still bothers you."

"It's not my best memory of the club but every now and then you get a clinker. Fortunately they're a very small minority."

"Others?"

"A guy wanted to do it here in my bed and I drew the line at that. Guest rooms, yes, the bed that Linc and I sleep in, no. I remember a guy who wanted to cover my pussy with jelly and lick it off. Actually the sex with the jelly guy was great, but the cleanup afterward was a bitch. I did draw the line with another man at jalapeño peppers, however."

"You're kidding, of course."

Pam shook her head and Tay burst out laughing. Pam continued, "Fortunately most evenings go as well as yours did with Henry, and that's what to concentrate on. And, of course, your bank account."

"Right on all counts."

Chapter 17

Time to broach the subject Tay most wanted to talk to Pam about. "Ever been in the downstairs of the club? I hear there's quite a setup down there." Tay felt her face flame as she asked the question.

"You're blushing," Pam said.

"It's nothing."

"It's something and that's fine. Go with it. Interested in the bondage, discipline thing?"

"Perhaps."

"Hey, be proud of whatever turns you on. It's all normal and natural."

"Ever done it?"

"A few times, and it can be a real turn-on." Tay took a deep breath and let it out slowly, trying to slow her pounding heart as Pam continued. "Why don't you talk to Rock? He's really the one to give you all the guidelines. If playing either the dominant or the submissive turns out to be your thing there'll be no end of possibilities for you at the club. That sort of play is one of the most in demand."

"Really? It's that common?"

"Ever watch *CSI*?"

Tay was startled at the sudden change of topic. "Yeah, sometimes."

"Ever see the scenes in that house in Las Vegas, the one with the woman all in black with all the eye makeup? She's a really good-looking dominatrix. I don't remember any of the details, but they wouldn't put that stuff in one of the most watched TV shows if it didn't float a lot of boats in the audience."

"I guess." She wasn't sure how she felt about all of that.

"Don't let me skew anything for you. Spend some time with Rock. Let him explain, or even demonstrate. I gather he's really expert at that stuff." Pam studied her face. "I can tell that idea intrigues you. Go for it, despite all the little voices saying 'nice girls don't do this kind of thing.' After all, you only live once, and here you've got all the possibilities with none of the risks."

"If I mention it to him I'll never be able to look him in the face again."

"It's your decision, but I'd advise you to do what all our clients do. Let your fantasy be your guide."

"That's not as easy as you might think."

"Of course not, but when you get past your initial reluctance, it's all a gas."

Tay expelled a long breath. She'd have to think about it, and if she were being honest, the idea was so intriguing that she'd probably be unable to resist. She rose, rinsed out her wine glass and put it on the counter. "I've got to go to work tomorrow and I need my beauty sleep, so I'll be getting home."

"Think about what I said about Rock."

"I will." She could bet on it.

"Oh, one more thing before you go. I'm having a party here this Saturday evening and one of the women who'd agreed to be here has a family emergency. Now that I'm sure you're okay with the business end of all this, I feel comfortable asking. Can you fill in?"

Tay contemplated, hesitated, then said, "I guess. *That* kind of party?"

"Yeah. One of my regular clients is throwing a little gathering for several out-of-town sales leaders. He does it every Fourth of July weekend. His own personal fireworks, I guess. It's sort of an open secret that there will be willing women, although, to the best of my knowledge, no one has made it public that the women are paid. It's supposed to be just a group of lovely ladies, usually the same ones, who are supposedly all friends of the company's founder, a thirty-something dot-com guru. He knows, of course, as do a few of the other bigwigs, but I don't think the rest of the guys involved want to think about it any further."

"Sure. Sounds like fun. Will Linc be here to chaperone?"

"He's got other plans and these are regulars. No need for a bodyguard. Just to let you know, I'm going to be participating. We already know each other pretty well, but be sure you want to know me, or for me to know you, quite that well. I'll try to steer things so we're not in the same room but there's always the chance. . . ."

Tay gave it serious thought, then said, "It will take a little getting used to, but once I get over any initial hesitation, I think I'll be fine with it."

"Just be sure of that and if you want to bow out let me know with enough time to get someone else."

Tay thought for another few minutes, then said, "It's okay. I'm sure now. If I'm going to swim I might as well jump into the deep end of the pool." *Like with José,* she thought.

"Great. I'll talk to Frank and let him set up a cover story."

"Okay. I'll call you tomorrow or the next day and you can fill me in on the plans."

"I wouldn't do anything to jeopardize our friendship, including inviting you to this party. You've become very special to me, Tay."

Without conscious thought, Tay leaned over and kissed Pam on the cheek. "Thanks for being my friend, and don't worry."

"Back at you, lady."

Marcy called later in the week and again commented on Tay's success with Henry. She also asked whether Tay could entertain a client toward the end of July and Tay quickly agreed. However, she couldn't work up the courage to talk to either Marcy or Rock about the downstairs. *I'll wait until I'm there in a few weeks and sort of mention things casually. Sure,* she told herself. *Casually. Right.*

Tay spoke to Pam on Thursday evening. "You came in with a strange phone number and I almost didn't answer," Tay said.

"When I want to talk completely privately I use a disposable cell phone. You should get one, too. That way no one will know what goes on between you and the person on the other end. It's so much easier than trying to talk in code just in case anyone's listening."

"Healthy paranoia. I guess in our business that's a good idea." *Our business. Wow.*

Pam told her that the party would begin at around five on Saturday: cocktails followed by a lavish dinner, then dancing, maybe a dirty movie on her big-screen TV and hanky-panky later. "I didn't tell you that it might involve an orgy-type thing: making out in public, maybe more than one guy or woman at a time, toys. We often begin with games of strip poker or nude Twister."

"Twister? You mean that 'right hand blue, left hand red' game?"

"It's dumb, but especially if there are new guys it makes a great icebreaker."

Tay pictured all the possibilities, then said, "I don't have a problem with any of what you mentioned but to be perfectly honest I'm not sure about any lesbian stuff. I don't think girls are my thing."

"I'm glad you told me and I always, always, want you to be honest. I'll make sure that the other women know your preferences and we can steer things away from that. Actually I'd forgotten that one of the other women feels the same way. I'll be sure to point her out so you two can arrange to be out of any of that kind of action."

Tay sighed. "I was afraid I'd louse everything up by admitting my prejudices."

"Not at all," Pam said with a slight hesitation in her voice. "Just a final check with you. I can get along with one fewer woman if you want to back out. That's not an issue. Are you sure you're okay with everything and that you won't get squeamish when I'm part of the games? You're positive that you'll be okay with it?"

"Thanks for asking over and over but I've given it lots of thought and it's really okay. All of it."

"Wonderful. I'll be going in for a manicure and pedicure on Saturday afternoon. Want to join me?"

"Gentle hint?"

"Maybe not so gentle. Tay, this is the big time. Frank pays me four thousand per woman and he wants only the best. I know beneath your skin beats the heart of a true courtesan, but the outside could use a little sprucing up."

"If you think so," Tay said. She wasn't used to caring about her looks, and neither José nor Henry had.

"If you don't mind me saying it, I really do. In addition to toes and fingers, I'd suggest maybe some hairstyling and makeup tips."

Tay had never worn more than a little blush and lipstick. "You think that will make a difference?"

"Every woman wants to look her best and that goes double in our business. Can I set something up with a stylist I think you'll like and who does great work? If we're lucky she can squeeze you in Saturday afternoon after our mani and pedi. I'm a pretty good customer so I think she'll make room for you."

"I guess."

Justin showed up late Friday afternoon, back from his trip to Montana. "Fabulous state and all that space. I missed the city, though, and especially you."

Yeah, and especially me. Right. He's got girls everywhere, but I'm handy and he's good in bed, so what the hell. After dinner at a restaurant called Hernando's that served something called Mexican Fusion Cuisine they ended up in bed. Saturday morning Tay thought that she'd had more sex in the past week than she'd had any time in her life except her months with Steve. And she loved it all. "This was fabulous," Justin said as he walked downstairs. "I'm out of here. Don't expect me back for a few days. I'll be out on the Island with my folks for the rest of the weekend but I'll be back next week sometime."

"I have plans for the weekend myself," Tay said, noticing that he hadn't invited her to meet his folks. Just a casual, occasional friendly fuck. She thought of a term from *Sex and the City*. Fuck buddies. *Okay. Unlike with Steve, at least this time I know what kind of relationship this is.*

"What kind of plans?" he said, sounding a bit put out.

"Pam's having a party and I've been invited."

"You mean the woman you talked about with the house at the end of the street?"

Tay answered carefully. "Yeah. She does party planning

for a living and she's invited me to meet some of the people who will be there."

Justin didn't seem to notice Tay's slight hesitation. "That's great. I hope you'll have fun." His words were cheerful but there was an edge to his voice. In his mind, she guessed, dating others was okay for him, but not for her.

"I'm sure I will." The door closed behind him.

Pam picked Tay up later that morning. "Okay, what's first?" Tay asked.

"I thought nails, then lunch. I made a one-thirty appointment with Sarah, the gal who does my hair. You can discuss with her how far you're willing to go with your makeover."

"I don't know whether I want anyone to cut my hair," Tay said, fingering her French braid. "I've had it this way so long that it's part of me. And I gather that men like long hair."

"They do, and I'd suggest that you have it shortened just a little and shaped so it falls softly around your face."

"How come you don't let yours grow?" Tay asked.

"I'm so short that lots of hair will bury me." She smiled softly. "Anyway Linc likes it this way. He loves to run his fingers through my curls."

"Ah, the guy thing."

"Busted," Pam said, laughing. "By the way, I saw Justin's car in the driveway last evening. Did you two . . . ?"

"Of course. I'm not sure how much we really have in common, so we're both content to have dinner and then end up in bed. There's not too much conversation beyond the usual inane small talk."

"Just having someone to make love with is enough sometimes. Don't knock it."

"I'm not, believe me, and although he's pretty pedestrian in bed, I'm always satisfied."

"Nothing to sneeze at," Pam said. "Linc, on the other hand, is pretty creative."

Tay didn't want to go there, so she changed the subject.

At Queen Bee Nails the two women sat in adjoining chairs and had the special and pedicure, Pam in Parisian Red and Tay in I'm Not Really A Waitress. Pam suggested wraps to extend Tay's usually short nails. "I don't know whether I'll be able to use my computer," Tay said to Fran, the Asian manicurist.

"We can make them not too long," Fran said, and by one o'clock Tay had longer nails and both women were done and ready for lunch. They grabbed sandwiches at the diner and arrived at the hair salon just in time for Tay's appointment.

"Sarah," Pam said as they entered the Total Beauty Salon and greeted a tall slender woman with hair the color of overripe strawberries. She had tattoos all up and down each arm and over the parts of her chest visible above her smock. "This is my friend Tay. You two figure out how to organize her hair for a party tonight. Nothing too fancy, maybe just a cut and shaping."

Now that Tay had gotten past the color of Sarah's hair, she saw that the cut was beautiful, just brushing her shoulder and curving in beneath her jaw. "I like the way yours looks," she said to the beautician. "Can you do mine like that?"

Sarah looked shocked. "The color?"

"Sorry," Tay said, laughing. "Meaning no disrespect, I really like my color the way it is. I meant the style. It looks great on you."

Sarah looked Tay over carefully. "You're right. The shape would work well for you but I'll leave it a bit longer so you can keep your style if you want to. " She looked again, and said, "About the color. I certainly wouldn't make your hair this color," she said, flipping her bright red hair, "but a little highlighting would brighten it and accent your lovely eyes."

Tay stared at herself in the mirror. "You really think so?"

"She does," Pam said, "and so do I. Go for it. Have fun with your looks. How about one of those wash-out highlighters, Sarah? That way if Tay doesn't like it she can get rid of it in half a dozen washings."

"Perfect," Sarah and Tay said together.

"I like the way you've done your makeup, too," Tay said. "Can you give me a few tips? I seldom wear anything but a little blush and lipstick."

"Sure. As I said, you've got such great eyes it's a shame not to emphasize them."

"Okay, ladies," Pam said. "I've got a few errands to run for the party tonight. Tay, call my cell when you're done and I'll pick you up."

"Will do."

"See ya."

Chapter 18

The Tay Barwick who greeted Pam when she returned to Total Beauty was obviously the same woman, but she looked much more sophisticated. "You look like a well-retouched photo of yourself, Tay. It's wonderful."

Tay's grin was wide. "I was willing to go along and I thought I'd look very different. I like this even better because it's not too drastic. I love it."

Tay's blond hair was now lightly streaked with a slightly reddish highlighter and cut so it fell to her collarbones. Sarah had used a blow-dryer to curve it up in a slight flip that curled against her throat. Just a trace of wispy bangs fell to the tops of her eyebrows and accentuated her large, pale blue eyes. The stylist had assured her that her hair was long enough so that she could still French braid it if she wanted to. "Sarah suggested that I try some slightly deeper blue-colored contacts. What do you think of the idea, Pam?"

"That would look fabulous, but I certainly don't hate your eyes the way they are. And I have to say from experience," Pam said, remembering her afternoon with Logan, "that they take a little getting used to."

Sarah had showed Tay how to use blush properly, make

use of several shades of shadow and liner to bring out what color her pale eyes had, and use mascara to add color to her blond lashes. The makeup was not immediately noticeable but merely brought out the natural contours and colors of her face. She liked the look so much that she had bought several products from a display beside the register.

Again Tay gazed into the mirror, amazed at the subtle yet dramatic transformation. She didn't think she could smile any wider, yet she did. "It looks really good," she said.

"Amen to that," Pam said. "I always knew Sarah could work wonders."

Tay paid the bill and left a generous tip for the beautician.

In the car on the way back to Maple Court, Pam said, "You really look fabulous. Ready for the party?"

"I am psyched. You said around five? What should I wear?"

"Although it will be at my place, dress for a casual evening in the city. No slacks, no complicated shoes. Be accessible, but not obvious. That make sense to you?"

"It does."

"Why don't you get there a little early so I can introduce you to the other women I've invited."

When Tay was dropped off in her driveway she headed for Lissa's closet. She loved that she heard from her friend weekly and was amazed at how Lissa had blossomed. She seemed to be thriving in the life of a wildlife photographer. She'd sent Tay batches of pictures and videos and Tay had been blown away by the quality. Lissa had added very professional-sounding voice-overs to several five-minute segments and Tay really felt like she was watching a documentary on one of the nature channels. Lissa had even entered one film clip in a contest for new filmmakers.

Tay faced the e-mail she'd gotten earlier in the week with mixed emotions. Lissa had written that they would be staying for another three months. Tay was eager to see her friend again, but she was having such a great time living on Maple Court that she knew she'd be reluctant to leave.

Tay wrote back about Justin, the health of the menagerie, and bits and pieces of small talk. She told her friend about Pam and their blossoming relationship and even mentioned Marcy from time to time, but she didn't discuss her business arrangements with them. Would she when Lissa returned? She decided to cross that bridge when Lissa got back. The delay in her friend's return allowed Tay to put off a difficult issue. Where would she live when she had to leave Maple Court? Another bridge that would just have to wait.

She showered, then pawed through Lissa's closet trying on and rejecting several outfits before she selected a soft floral print skirt in shades of rose and gold. She paired it with a pale rose, short-sleeved blouse with a deep-scooped neck and small mother-of-pearl buttons. She had gotten enough of a light tan on her legs that she could go without stockings so she added only a pair of slip-on, gold, low-heeled sandals. She blow-dried her hair as Sarah had showed her, then carefully applied makeup, including a new lipstick in a soft coral shade. She dropped her cell phone and a handkerchief in a tiny gold purse, walked to Pam's and rang the doorbell.

Pam answered the door and led Tay into the living room. "This is Tay," she said. "She's from down county." They'd decided not to mention that Tay also lived on Maple Court.

Three other women sat in the living room. "This is Dorothy," Pam said, indicating a nice-looking brunette with large brown eyes, pale skin, rosy cheeks and great cheekbones that gave her face the kind of character that Tay had always admired in Katherine Hepburn. She shook the woman's hand, noticing on closer inspection that she was older than Tay had first thought, maybe closer to Pam's age.

"Hi, I'm Andi," another woman said. She was tall, very well endowed, with generous curves, short, curly, brown hair and a tiny, almost pouty mouth. She looked like the type Tay had first envisioned when she thought of a prostitute. "I'm delighted to meet you." Andi had a surprisingly cultured, British accent.

"This is Tina." She had the darkest ebony skin Tay had ever seen, and she showed it off with a white, two-piece, halter-top sundress. Her hair was short and tightly curled close to her skull. "I'm so glad to meet you." Like Rock, she had a slight bit of the South in her voice.

"I'm glad to meet you all," Tay said. "I hope you'll forgive my nervousness. I'm a real novice at this, so I'm a little uptight."

"I remember my first time," Andi said. "I pictured a scene from some porn flick, all naked cocks and breasts and I was ready for that. I was totally blown away, however, by the nature of the conversations leading up to the fun and games. So"—she floundered for a word—"upscale. All these guys are so well educated, not the type I anticipated, by far."

The other two women nodded their agreement. "That's what this is," Pam said. "Upscale entertainment." She was dressed in a full-shirted teal dress that zipped up the front, a decorative pull situated between her breasts.

"How many guys tonight?" Tina asked.

"Six. More of them than of us, but that never seems to slow us or them down."

Dorothy giggled softly. "I remember the last party I was at. There were only four of us and eight of them, but we held our own pretty well."

"Held our own, and theirs, too," Tina said, laughing as the doorbell rang.

"Well, ladies, the limo has arrived. Here goes nothing."

Six men trooped into Pam's living room. Pam put an arm

around one man's waist. "This is Frank. He runs the joint. And you two look familiar," she said, indicating two men standing together.

"We were here last year. I'm Brandon White and this is my brother, Greg." From a distance the two men looked very much alike. If Tay had to guess, both men were in their late thirties, with curling, deep brown hair and heavy eyebrows over deep-set hazel eyes. Brandon, slightly taller, had a small scar that cut through his right eyebrow, giving him a rakish look.

"That's why I remember you. St. Louis, right?"

"You remembered," Greg said, beaming. "I'm flattered."

"You should be," Pam said, a suggestive lilt in her voice. "For now, how about introducing everyone?"

Once introductions were made everyone got a drink. Some settled in the living room and three men, Andi and Tay walked out onto the patio. As often happened late on hot summer afternoons, the sky was filled with thunderheads, golden edges gleaming. In the distance, quick flashes of lightning occasionally brightened the sky, followed by faint grumbles. "That is so beautiful," Andi said, gazing at the panorama.

"I love evenings like this. In St. Louis, however, this might be followed by the tornado sirens," Brandon said. He was a big man and, like his brother, wore a bright red polo shirt with the company's blue and white logo on the pocket. When he got closer, Tay noticed that his hair was threaded with gray so she again revised an age estimate upward. Maybe forty-something. Not everyone was young and beautiful. Almost immediately, Brandon had latched on to her with a seemingly proprietary air and now he settled beside her on a two-seater swing as the group talked, one arm draped over her shoulders.

She discovered that Brandon was fond of card games and

spent many weekends in Atlantic City or Las Vegas. He also liked Indian food and classical music. "I'm particularly fond of Mozart's Horn Concertos," he said.

She also enjoyed Baroque music and hummed a few bars of one of her favorites. He looked bemused, then said, "I knew I loved you for a reason."

A uniformed server walked out onto the patio with a tray of tiny lobster patties, lamb riblets and little cream puffs filled with curried shrimp and another followed with glasses of champagne and white wine. They all helped themselves, setting their goodies on small tables carefully placed to make everything convenient. After about an hour of fascinating conversation, the couples heard Pam announce that dinner was served.

Brandon took her elbow lightly and guided her to a dining room chair and settled beside her. The table in the ivory and delft-blue dining room had had several leaves inserted so it easily seated the group of diners. The plates were a delft-blue and bone floral pattern and were paired with creamy ivory linen. Crystal and silver gleamed.

The talk was lively throughout the meal of cool melon and prosciutto or a cream seafood soup, rare rack of lamb with rosemary or thick slices of fillet of beef au jus, all accompanied by platters of perfectly cooked grilled vegetables, tiny broiled potatoes and a bowl of rice pilaf. Diners helped themselves from a large bowl of Caesar salad and a platter of cold, grilled fruit. By the time dessert arrived—a chocolate cake, an open apple tart and several flavors of ice cream and sorbet—everyone knew a lot about everyone else.

Tay had discovered that Brandon was a vice president of the company and the manager of its St. Louis office. He had been with the company since its inception in the late nineties and, thanks to Frank and Brandon, this dot-com had not gotten caught up in the bubble that destroyed so many others. The two of them, and several more of the men in the room, had become fabulously successful and very rich.

As she finished a portion of mango sorbet, Tay sat back for a moment marveling at how normal and ordinary this all seemed. Sometimes several conversations took place at once, and occasionally the entire table got involved in the same topic. The guests were all well informed and well educated. Everyone had attended college, and like her, many had completed their undergraduate studies. Dorothy and three of the men had master's degrees. Everyone seemed to be interested in everything and when any new subject was brought up several proved to be extremely knowledgeable about it. Topics ranged from her favorite, European history, to vintage film noir, from Nascar racing to the situation in North Korea. There was never a lull and from time to time she actually forgot what she was there for. She was getting paid very well for this. Well, maybe not this. She was getting paid for later.

Pam showed everyone the fully stocked bar in the sideboard, which included a dozen bottles of the best liquors, several bottles of wine and an excellent selection of after-dinner drinks and cordials. Brandon raised a questioning eyebrow and she asked for a white crème de menthe on the rocks. "Sounds good," he said, moving to the bar and splashing the clear liquid into two ice-filled glasses.

"I'm going to see to the kitchen staff," Pam said, moving toward the door to the kitchen. "They should be gone in less than half an hour." She gave a thumbs-up to her guests. "I'll be sure to let you know when."

"Then the fun begins," Brandon said into Tay's ear, his breath hot.

"It does indeed." Tay wasn't sexually aroused yet, having had too much normal fun at dinner, but she was sure that when the time came she'd be up for whatever everyone wanted to do. She was really getting into this courtesan thing.

The group wandered the main floor of Pam's house, some settling in the living room, others on the patio. Several, including Brandon and Tay, remained in the dining room. "You're quite a woman, Tay," he said. "I've been at Pam's parties before but I've never met anyone like you."

"I'm glad you approve," she said. "I really like you, too. I guess interesting people tend to like other interesting people."

"That statement can have many meanings."

Tay considered what she'd said, feeling her skin heat. "Originally I meant interested in the world, but I must admit that I could have meant it other ways. You can't be unaware that you're an interesting man on many levels."

He smiled. "No, I guess I can't, but it's not often I admit it. I might say the same to you."

She inclined her head but said nothing.

"You've very cleverly managed to find out a lot about me, but we haven't discussed you at all."

"I've got few secrets. What would you like to know?" she asked.

"Just give me the quick and dirty rundown, emphasis on the dirty."

She quickly filled him in on her background, her day job and the fact that she was new to Pam's operation, as she called it. She only omitted the fact that she was living on Maple Court. "Actually," she finished, "this is my first party."

"Mmm," he purred. "This should prove very interesting. Just so we're clear, what's not on your menu, sexually?"

How much should she tell him? She quickly decided to be honest. "I don't want to get into any same-sex stuff."

"No problem there. I'm a devout heterosexual." When she chuckled, he asked, "What else?"

"Nothing, well, let's just say too kinky."

"Kinky is a very personal judgment, but I think I understand. No problem with a little group activity? I'm not sure that I want to share you, but just in case it comes up."

She giggled at his unintended double entendre. "Not at all, so let's just see what happens."

Pam reentered the dining room twenty minutes later. "Kitchen staff is gone. Shall we start with Twister in the living room and/or poker in the TV room? Anyone who turns on the set, however, leaves." The group laughed, no one imagining that other entertainment would be needed.

"How about some music and slow dancing in the den?" Brandon asked.

"Sure, no problem." She hustled off to arrange a few CDs on the player.

Brandon took her hand and guided her to her feet. He stroked his palm down the silk of her blouse, causing tiny shivers to echo through her. She might not have been particularly aroused before, but she was rapidly climbing the ladder. "Want to dance with me?" he whispered, his lips nipping at her earlobe.

"I'd love to," she purred back.

"Hey," Greg called. "You've got to share this lovely lady."

"Buzz off, little bro."

"Okay, but only for a little while."

Tay wondered whether she should say anything. After all, she was being paid to entertain any of the men in the group, but Brandon quickly guided her into the den where a Michael Bolton CD was playing. He pulled his polo shirt from his slacks and took her in his arms. Knowing what he wanted, she slipped her fingers up under the fabric and skimmed his bare back with her nails. "I love the feel of a man's skin," she said.

Brandon pulled the back of Tay's blouse out of the waistband of her skirt and duplicated her movements. His hands were smooth and hot on her flesh as he stroked her. They moved their feet and slowly his hand pressed her body against his until there was no doubt about the state of his arousal.

His mouth found hers, and as they danced, they kissed, hot mouths fused. They moved, enjoying the feel of each other until Tay opened her eyes and saw that Tina and Greg had joined them.

As she looked over Brandon's shoulder she saw a bright red shirt fly across the room, landing on the chair where Tina had flung it. Greg, now stripped to the waist, removed Tina's white jersey top. Well proportioned, the statuesque woman needed no bra. Her breasts were truly beautiful, lacking any trace of silicone. Tay had never been particularly aware of the look of another woman's breasts but Tina's deep black skin and almost purple nipples stood out against her white skirt. No, she thought, she wasn't tempted tonight by the other woman's obvious sexuality, but for the future? She resolved not to make blanket decisions anymore. So much about her had changed in such a short time.

Chapter 19

After Brandon unbuttoned his shirt and Tay eased it off his shoulders he slowly unbuttoned her blouse and it followed the other pieces of clothing onto the chair. Brandon's fingertips whispered over the skin of her chest, teasing their way around the outline of her peach lace and satin bra. "Beautiful," he said, his voice hoarse and almost reverent. She'd never thought of herself as the person reflected in his expression but he seemed to think she was special. How wonderful.

A hand cupped the back of Tay's head and her face was turned toward Greg. His mouth covered hers and she felt Brandon lean over toward Tina. Quickly they'd switched partners and now her barely covered, erect nipples glided over Greg's furry chest, his groin steadily pressed against her pubic mound. "Only for you, bro," Brandon growled.

"I don't know who's getting the better of the deal," Greg said, his voice also hoarse.

For several minutes the two couples danced, then Tay's bra joined the growing pile of clothing. The couples exchanged partners several times as they danced, naked chest to naked chest. "I need more of you," Brandon said when Tay was in his arms yet again. Rapidly the two women removed their skirts and the men took off their slacks. When Greg started to pull off his boxers, Brandon said, "Think of the old bull." Greg left his shorts on, while Brandon pressed his brief-covered erection against Tay's tiny lace panties.

"What was that about the bull?" she asked.

Greg chuckled. Loud enough for Tina to hear as well, Brandon said, "Old joke. An old bull and a young bull were standing at the top of a hill looking down on a field filled with cows.

"'Let's run down the hill,' the young bull said, 'and nail us a cow.'

"The old bull replied, 'Let's walk down the hill and do them all.'"

Tina and Tay laughed. It was wonderful to be able to have fun in this sort of situation. "I've got an idea," Greg said, taking a moment to leave the room. During his absence Brandon wrapped an arm around each woman, filling his palms with breast flesh.

Greg returned with something in each hand. "Ladies, allow me to present your gifts." He extended his hands and Tay saw he'd gotten two large dildos. "I loved these last year when we were here. I gather Pam found these little beauties in a little boutique on the Net."

Greg made them sound special, but they looked like ordinary dildos to Tay. She must have looked a little puzzled. "They have special abilities. Kick your shoes off, but leave your panties on." The two woman obliged.

Greg then sat Tina on a chair and propped her heels on the seat. While the other two watched, Greg pulled the crotch of Tina's panties to one side and slowly inserted the dildo deep into her pussy. Then he replaced the panties so the silk held the dildo in place.

"Your turn," Brandon said to Tay as Tina rose.

"This feels really good," Tina purred at Greg, "but not as good as you'll feel later."

"You'll just have to wait," Greg said. "I'm the young bull, but my old bull brother just reminded me of the pleasures in the evening to come." He snorted. "Pardon the play on words. Or don't."

Tay dropped onto the chair, slid her bottom to the edge and bent her knees until her calves were against the backs of her thighs. As Greg had, Brandon slipped the dildo into her wet passage and moved her panties to hold it in place. He'd done things so easily and clinically that she hadn't come close to orgasm. She stood, enjoying the fullness. She became more curious when Greg brandished one small plastic box in each hand. Brandon took one and Greg kept the other. "I don't know which controller is which," Greg said. "Let's find out. Press yours first, bro, and let's see who reacts."

Brandon held Tay close as they began to move their feet again. With a grin he pressed the button on the controller. "Just keep dancing, ladies."

Tay felt a buzzing deep in her cunt. *Shit,* she thought, *that thing is dynamite.* She almost stumbled, but with great will power kept her steps even.

Brandon said, "The game is not to let either of us know who's doing what to whom."

Tay could barely keep her hips still as the dildo moved inside her. It was as though it were alive, bending slightly, then thickening, continually buzzing deep within her channel. With great difficulty she played the game and managed to look unaffected. She felt weak in the knees and her breathing quickened just a bit but she was pretty sure that Brandon couldn't tell that hers was the active dildo.

After a few moments, Greg said "I give" and pressed his finger on the controller he held and Tina squeaked.

"You win, Tay," he said. "Not a sign that I had turned your baby on."

A heavyset man in a brightly patterned Hawaiian shirt burst into the room. In a voice as loud as his shirt, he said, "Hey, guys, you're not allowed to hog these women." He reached for Tina's hand and gently pried her from Greg's arms. "I want a little fun, too." He leaned over and nipped at her dark nipple. Tay tensed. She didn't want any trouble.

"I suppose he has a point, bro," Brandon said, then caught his brother's eye. In a coordinated move, each brother grabbed the interloper by an arm and forcibly ushered him from the room. As the startled man looked back at them, they closed the door and pushed the heavy desk in front of it. Theatrically they brushed their hands together, high-fived each other, and said in unison, "Okay, where were we?"

Tay wasn't sure it was all fair, but Brandon was one of the big bosses and what he wanted, he got. It wasn't her problem, and she was sure that Pam and the others could handle anything that went on outside.

"Okay, ladies, now that we're alone, let's get back to fun and games." Brandon wiggled a lever on the side of his little box and the dildo inside Tay began to undulate deep within her.

"Shit," she hissed. "That thing is terrific."

"Need to come?"

"Yes," she moaned.

"Lie down on the desk," Brandon said, "on your back. You can be the goddess of the den and we will be your acolytes." As Tay climbed onto the flat surface, Brandon whispered, "If anything gets uncomfortable, just say the word and we'll stop. Agreed?"

"Agreed," she said, not sure whether she'd be able to say stop to a paying customer.

Theatrically Tay stretched out on the desk, lower legs hanging off the end, still wearing her panties with the dildo dancing inside her.

"This lady needs to come," Brandon said. "Greg, I'll give you the honor of the first." He turned to Tina. "You, my love, can just wait."

Silently, Tina held Brandon from behind and stroked his chest and belly with eager hands. Greg positioned himself at the end of the desk between Tay's legs and Brandon handed him the control unit. Greg quickly removed her panties, holding the dildo inside with his fingers. "Let's see what else this baby does." He played with the controls, driving Tay nearly mad with the variety of the dildo's movements.

Then she felt Greg's hot breath on her clit as he leaned over her. "How hot are you?" he asked. He blew a stream of cool air on her clit, and with a long moan she came. When she'd had a moment to cool down, Greg removed the dildo and helped her to a chair. It was Tina and Brandon's turn.

Tay had never watched a couple play in person before and she found herself fascinated by the sight of Brandon's head between the other woman's legs while Tina's body writhed in the throes of orgasm.

Then everyone was naked and Tay lay on the desk with a cock in each hand, Tina fondling first Greg's testicles then Brandon's. Tay prided herself on her skill and made every effort to bring each man off. Greg came first, spurting semen all over her hand. It wasn't long before Brandon climaxed as well.

The four talked together for a while but despite her previous orgasm, the sexually charged atmosphere kept her from cooling down totally. The sight of the two naked men and, she had to admit, Tina's nude body as well, was as erotic as any movie she'd ever seen. Oddly, she found her eyes straying more than once to the other woman's breasts and pubis.

"Do you trust me?" Brandon whispered in her ear after watching her for a few minutes. "I hope you know that I wouldn't do anything to hurt you."

Now where had that come from? "Of course," Tay said, not sure that trust could be that quickly given, but willing to agree.

"I am sure we're all still hot, and I, for one, am not willing for the evening to end just yet. There's a guessing game I'd like to play with you, Tay, but you will need to be blindfolded. Would you be willing to do that?" She took a breath, but he jumped in. "I know you're pretty new to this stuff, so I need you to understand this. There are two answers to that question, yes and no, and no one will think less of you if you said you'd rather not."

"That's comforting, and yes, I'd love to play."

He kissed her. "Great. Lie back down on the desk. I'll tell you when and what you have to guess." When she had complied, Brandon draped a shirt over her face. "This is merely so you can't see, but you can remove it any time if you like. Now spread your legs." She complied. "See whether you can guess which of us is doing what. I'll ask you later."

The fabric over her eyes didn't totally shut out light, but images were impossible to make out. Then a mouth was on her breast, licking and nibbling at her flesh. Shards of pleasure knifed through her. It stopped and was followed by a breath of cool air that made her nipple tighten. A mouth was between her legs, a tongue flicking over her clit, not firm enough to help her toward orgasm, just enough to keep her flying.

An erect cock rubbed over her belly. She hadn't been asked to say anything yet so she merely enjoyed all the sensations. Someone was nibbling on her toes. She wriggled and pulled her foot away, the tickling irritating. "Okay, no toes." From the sound of the voices she knew that Greg was the one currently at her feet. "Then how about here?"

She felt a tongue lick her instep. Erotic. She never realized how many erogenous places she had. When she had time to think about it, she'd have to catalog all this for future reference. But not now. She was panting, her pulse was pounding and her pussy was twitching, aching for relief. Again a tongue flicked over her clit. Brandon? Greg? Who cared.

"Oh God, please," she moaned.

"Need to come?" Brandon asked.

"Yes, please."

A mouth fastened on her clit and sucked, teeth lightly squeezing. A finger slowly entered her channel, and as she was about to come, she felt the finger replaced with a cock, the mouth still licking, sucking, driving her upward.

"Yes," she groaned. "Yes."

As she was about to climax a hand turned her face to the side, moved the cloth up slightly and another cock filled her mouth. She came, screaming the word *Yes* over and over.

The cock in her pussy pulsed and came as well. The one in her mouth took a few moments longer but soon her lips were covered with the semen she couldn't swallow. She went totally limp.

Later, as Brandon removed the condom from his cock, Greg pulled the cloth from Tay's eyes. "Okay, now the question," Brandon said. "Whose mouth brought you off?"

Suddenly it dawned on her. A cock in her pussy and one in her mouth. "Shit," she said, grinning.

"Yeah," Tina said. "I hope you don't mind. I love doing that."

"You're not angry?" Brandon asked. "I know you're a woman with an open mind and I saw an opportunity to show you something you'd never been aware of before. Not mad?"

What a lesson, she thought. "Not at all. Not at all." She'd have to think about all this. Later.

Eventually Greg pushed the furniture back where it belonged, left and returned with a tray containing four glasses of champagne, a plate of chocolate-covered strawberries and a bowl of chips. "Fucking always makes me hungry," he said with a snort of laughter. They all agreed and munched, relaxing and talking easily. All too soon a car horn sounded in the driveway.

"Guys," Pam yelled, "the limo's here!"

"I don't want to go yet," Brandon and Greg said together.

"Okay, guys, we agreed on two AM," Pam said from the hallway.

Brandon looked at his watch. "Shit. It is two and we've got a client group meeting us at nine in the morning for golf."

The group dressed and, arm in arm, walked into the living room. From the flushed, grinning faces and empty glasses, Tay gathered that everyone had had a fabulous time.

"If you'll wait a few minutes, I've got a limo coming for you ladies," Pam said as she escorted two men to the door.

"Tay," Brandon whispered in her ear, "can I see you when I'm in town next?"

Tay smiled. She'd obviously done well. "I'd love to. You can always reach me through Pam."

"Wonderful. I'll be in touch."

Finally all the men were gone and only the women remained. Pam made a phone call, then said, "Sorry, ladies. The limo's been a little delayed. It won't be here for about half an hour."

"No problem," Tina said. "Got any more champagne?"

When those who wanted had a drink, they sat around the living room. "We all know each other rather intimately," Pam said, causing a titter among the women, "but since Tay's new here I'm sure she'd like to know a little more about you. Maybe she'll start."

"For me," Tay said, "I'm going to be thirty soon, recently in and gladly out of a lousy relationship with a guy who was more interested in my bank account than in me. When I stopped buying him the stuff he wanted, he split."

"Men," Tina said. "I'm twenty-six and originally from Atlanta. I moved here ten years ago when my dad got transferred. I've got a wonderful little girl who's two and a half and is staying with my folks tonight. Your guy decamped when you ran out of money, mine split when I got pregnant. At least I have Olivia and she's the best." Tina beamed when she talked about her daughter. "I've gone back to school to finish my bachelor's degree in accounting, heading for my CPA."

"Good luck with that," Pam said. "Andi?"

"Well," Andi said and as she sipped her champagne, her accent became thicker, "I guess you figured I'm not a native. I moved here from London five years ago, sure I could make it in movies or TV. Sadly, that didn't work out, but I'm not really bummed about it. I met Pam through Linc when we did a catalog shoot together and now I work through her and Marcy. You know Marcy, Tay?"

"I do indeed. She's a wonderful woman."

"She is that," Dorothy said. "I'm a little older than the rest of you, almost forty now, with two great kids heading for college. I don't work too often, but my husband, who sells computer services, enjoys his occasional night without me and paying for college is a bitch."

"He knows what you do?" Tay asked.

"He does, and he's okay with it, as long as I tell him all about it and fuck him senseless when I get home."

"How did this first evening go for you, Tay?" Andi asked.

"I enjoyed it thoroughly. What could be better? Great conversation with nice people, lots of hot sex and I get paid for it, too."

"True enough," Pam said. At that moment her cell phone rang and she glanced at the screen. "Great. The limo's here."

As they started for the door, Tina moved to Tay's side. "I hope you've forgiven me for that prank we played on you," she said, sotto voce.

"No problem," Tay whispered. "I certainly learned something."

"Good." Then she asked, loudly, "Do you need a ride, Tay?"

"No thanks," Tay said, remembering the story to avoid saying she was staying on Maple Court. "I'll make my own way home."

"Well, I just want you to know that it's been a pleasure and I hope to work"—Tina grinned—"and play with you again." The other two dittoed her comment.

"Me too," Tay said to the three women.

The women put down their glasses and rose. There were a few hugs and then the three women from the city were gone. "Did you really have a good evening?" Pam asked a few minutes later as she walked Tay to the door.

"I had a great time and I'd love to do it again whenever you need another courtesan."

"I'm glad. Night, babe." Pam bussed her cheek.

Tay walked down Pam's driveway, unable to remove the grin from her face.

Chapter 20

Throughout the remainder of July, Tay was kept delightfully busy. Her day job kept her occupied for most of the weekdays, but not too busy to have lunch with Pam at least once a week. Evenings and weekends found her working in the club more and more frequently and on one memorable Saturday evening she entertained a gentleman at another of Pam's parties. She'd made love with several wonderful men who, she was sure, could have gotten dates any time but probably preferred the stressless non-dating and creative sexual atmosphere that Pam and the club provided. She'd gotten along well with a New York Ranger hockey player and a rock singer whose name had been familiar.

She'd played scenarios in several of the rooms at the club. She'd been a bride on her wedding night, complete with white dress, a doctor examining a very embarrassed patient with a huge erection, and the worldly older woman to the client's new-to-sex young man. With this one she found it difficult to stay in character since the guy was at least fifty, with a large belly, thick glasses and bad breath. She chalked it all up to experience and enjoyed watching her bank account increase. Although there had not been a repeat of the girl-on-girl lovemaking she'd experienced on her first evening at Pam's, she'd decided not to rule out any scenario without at least some serious thought.

During the first week of August, Marcy called and asked her to play the prisoner to a client's prison guard, utilizing the dungeon in the basement of the club. Tay reminded her that she'd never played a dominant/submissive fantasy. "I've read lots of stories on the Net that involve that sort of thing, but I've never done anything like that for real."

"I knew that you'd never done it here, but I thought you might have played games like that in your personal life. However, if you're not into it," Marcy said easily, "I can certainly find someone else. I try to keep every one of the women who work for me within their comfort zone and this sort of thing isn't for everyone. If you never play, that's fine, too, and I can certainly find partners for you who aren't interested, either."

"I'd like to try it, but I'm a little reluctant to do something so new to me when I'm not sure I can pull it off." Tay found the idea of being a totally submissive prisoner made her juices flow, but it scared her as well. Why? It wasn't much further beyond the pale than she'd already gone. She was a prostitute, after all.

"I wouldn't worry about your acting ability," Marcy said. "I know you well enough by now to be pretty sure that you can get into most situations, but why don't you talk to Rock about it? He's really the expert on dom/sub and bondage/discipline setups. He can tell you what to expect, and if it doesn't curl your toes I'll give the job to someone else. Anyway, if it's not this guy, you might decide to play in the future, and there's quite a bit you'd need to know, from safe words to the trust issue."

Tay took a deep breath. The idea of bondage and all that went with it, including mild pain for pleasure, titillated her, but also frightened her a bit. Was it too kinky for her? She'd always thought so, but then she'd thought that having a woman bring her to orgasm with her tongue would turn her off until she'd experienced it. This was another experience, and with Rock she'd feel safe.

"I'd like to learn."

"Good. You've got a date here on Wednesday." Marcy knew everyone's schedule. "Why don't you get here early and I'll ask Rock to show you the ropes downstairs? From what I've learned about you, I think you'd really enjoy that phase of our club. I'll make a tentative date with the prison-guard guy for Saturday and if you're amenable I'll firm it up with him. If not, I'll get someone else. I want you to be totally familiar with everything before you play. That work for you?"

"Sounds like a plan," she said.

Tay could hear Marcy clicking computer keys. "You're scheduled for eight-thirty on Wednesday and there won't be anything I need Rock for before that. Why don't you come over between seven-thirty and eight and I'll tell him to expect you?"

Tay took another deep breath and let it out slowly. "Okay, I'll be there." It was scary, but deliciously so.

Although she worked efficiently at her job through the week, her mind kept flashing to Rock and their learning session. Somehow she thought of this as a big step forward in her life as a courtesan. Was she like Darth Vader turning to the dark side? Nonsense.

On Wednesday, Tay grabbed a bite of dinner near work, then took the subway to the station nearest the club. She was playing a simple scenario, pretending to be a schoolgirl being "educated" by her professor. Nothing painful, no corporal punishment, but she thought that a spanking would be a delicious addition to this scenario for the future.

A few minutes before eight she used her key, unlocked the door to the brownstone and entered the appropriate security code. Rock was waiting for her in the living room. He sat on the sofa watching a cooking show on the Food Channel on which a man in a tall chef's hat was demonstrating the proper technique for deboning a duck. He turned as he heard her at the door. "Right on time," he said, using the remote to turn off the TV.

"I guess Marcy told you that I'd like you to help me understand about some of the heavier things that go on in the basement." She'd rehearsed that sentence all the way uptown on the subway.

"Nervous about all this?" he asked.

She let out a long breath and decided to be honest. "You bet. It's different and really scary to me."

"Do I scare you?"

"That, too."

"Good. That adds spice to the lesson." He took her purse and put it into a closet, then he grasped her cold, clammy hand in his huge, warm one and led her to the door to the basement. "I'll give you all the good info in a few minutes. First, though, I want to tell you that I'd really like to initiate you into the world that this room represents. I have a sixth sense about people and this sort of thing, and I know that you'll blossom in the forbidden world we play in down here. It is always up to you what and whether you play and I'll tell you about safe words and the like. My sense tells me, though, that you're intrigued, but frightened about playing the submissive. In only a few minutes you'll understand that the submissive really has all the control in these situations."

She couldn't swallow and her breath caught in her throat. She gave a slight nod, not quite sure what he meant by the submissive having control but content to let things evolve. God, she was hot. The guy she'd be with tonight better be a good lover.

"I won't ask you whether you want to play with me here," he said, his hand on the light switch, "because I know you'll tell me in one way or another. What Marcy wants you for and Jace is very lightweight and that's all well and good. It will be easy for you and a great way to begin. What you and I will explore here, that is if you're as eager as I am, will be the more advanced ideas that dwell deep inside dominant-submissive behavior.

"Intrigued?"

She nodded just a fraction of an inch, and his face lit up. "I knew it." He grabbed the bottom of her braid, pulled it lightly so she looked up at his face, then lowered his mouth onto hers. The kiss was deep, powerful, yet asking, not demanding. She let her arms hang at her sides and just melted into what he was proposing.

He moved back and flipped on the light to the downstairs. "We've redone it several times and I think it's just about perfect now," Rock said. "Oh, and it's totally soundproof."

Tay stared at the room with new eyes. She'd seen it briefly on her first visit to the club, but now that it was getting personal, everything took on a deliciously sinister air. Since three of the walls and the ceiling were mirrored she and Rock were reflected over and over.

"That's new," she croaked, staring at the table in the center of the room. The one she'd seen when she was here weeks before was relatively plain, like the exam table upstairs. This one was upholstered in black leather and thickly padded, covered with a collection of straps and chains. Hooks and rings studded the legs and sides of the table at various intervals. She'd read enough stories on the Net to know that a person could be fastened to the table in various ways. She stood frozen on the top step, unable to move.

"It is, and it was specially made to my specifications. As you'll see if and when we play, it's got a lot of special features." Rock let her stare in silence until finally saying, "It's quite something, isn't it?"

She swallowed hard, amazed that she could around the lump in her throat, and said, "It certainly is."

"If you decide to play with the client Marcy told you

about you and he will be down here. We'll arrange it so that the more advanced toys will be out of sight. He's not interested in heavy stuff anyway, just subservience on your part. Maybe a little light bondage. He'll be the guard and you'll have to do whatever he wants, no exceptions. He's played this fantasy with several other women and never given us any trouble. Each of the women has said that she would play with him again, but he likes a new prisoner each time.

"I'll be right upstairs. The room is miked, but the system is activated only by loud noises. I don't want him, or you for that matter, to think I'm eavesdropping, but it's for everyone's protection. Like upstairs, there are panic buttons in several spots, too." He showed her buttons hidden in three different locations. "Just be assured that, if you yell or signal, I'll be down here in a flash. I don't expect you'll need me, but I want you to feel totally secure."

"That's good," she croaked, then cleared her throat and added, "thanks."

"If you decide to do it, before your date with Jace I'll change the room so it will appear to be a cell, with barred windows, straw-covered floor, and like that. The mirrored walls and ceiling will be covered and we'll make it feel cool and dank."

Tay knew how carefully they arranged for each fantasy, so she didn't doubt that Jace would be delighted.

"Let me explain the rules for playing any bondage games. Jace knows them inside and out and has agreed to abide by all of them. The penalty for him if he violates any is immediate revocation of all the privileges of the club."

"Okay," she said.

"First. No means no, and a safe word means stop. Always and without exception."

"Safe word?"

"I'll get to that." He crossed the room, hoisted his large, muscular body onto the edge of the table and patted the leather beside him. She perched next to his thigh. "Trust is the basis of everything that goes on in here. We vet all our clients as you know, but you might decide to play this kind of game with someone you know outside of the club. You must trust him, or her, completely in order to do that. If you can't trust your partner to stop when you tell him to, don't play."

"Sounds logical."

"It does, but you'd be amazed at how many people let their hormones carry them away, and get hurt. The second element to all of this is your ability to say stop."

"I don't get that."

"This kind of game isn't an endurance contest. It's supposed to be pleasure for both participants. If you're merely doing things to please your partner, even a paying one, it won't work. You can push your own limits, of course, but you must be able to 'holler uncle,' as I call it, at any time, regardless of your partner's desires. We can always give the person his or her money back. That's not an issue. So if you can't trust yourself to do that, don't play. Clear?"

She thought for a moment and then said, "I never thought of it that way, but it does make sense."

"Good. To play this kind of game you need two consenting adults. No drugs, no alcohol—at least no drinking to excess. Both of you need your wits about you, whether you're the dominant or the submissive. Also, as with everything else, condoms at all times, even if it breaks the mood."

"Okay. You spoke about safe words."

"It can enhance things if the submissive can yell stop or help and know that the partner won't listen. Pleading can be delicious to listen to and to do. However, you then need a way to say stop and really mean it. Here at the club we use the words red and yellow for that. Red means 'stop now,' no questions asked. After the game has ceased you can talk about the whys and wherefores, but only afterward. First, everything stops. Immediately.

"Yellow means I need to stop for a moment without totally breaking the mood. I've got a foot cramp or my arm's asleep. Or maybe one partner just needs a moment to catch a breath. Like that. A small adjustment will be able to fix things. Everyone who plays any kind of power game knows and agrees to the rules, including the safe words. No exceptions. Got all that?"

"Got it. It sounds like you've given this a lot of thought."

"Tay, I've been part of the BDSM scene for a lot of years. You have one bad experience and you learn. Very quickly."

"You had something bad?"

"I'm not going to go into details. Suffice it to say that I played with someone I shouldn't have trusted and learned a hard lesson."

"Why did you say before that the submissive has all the power?"

"Most doms don't completely understand this, but the subs do have all the control. The sub's the one who can stop anything at any time."

She considered, then said, "I see. What's so attractive about playing games like this?"

"You know the answer to that yourself. You feel it and it excites you. It's a power thing. I find power a strong aphrodisiac. I love to be in control, to be able to do anything I want with my partner having no say in the matter, except for the safe words. Oral sex, anal sex, a spanking or some other kind of pain." He turned and smiled at her with real pleasure. "But I've been the submissive, too, and that can be really freeing. When I'm being controlled by someone else I don't have to think about anything, just do as I'm told. You might like both sides of it, I think, but most people prefer one or the other. I think you'll prefer being controlled. We'll have to experiment with all of it." He cleared his throat and squared his shoulders. "Kiss me," he snapped.

Startled, she hesitated.

"I said kiss me!"

She leaned toward him and pressed her mouth against his. He sat, unmoving. Then his hands were on her breasts, pinching her nipples. She was immediately hotter and wetter. He pulled on her braid to move her away. Then a smile slowly crossed his face. "Point made?" he asked, his voice now soft.

She sighed and smiled. "Okay. Point made."

"Got all the rules memorized?"

"Got it, boss."

"Boss. I like that," he said, his grin showing his white teeth. "Are you going to play with Jace on Saturday?"

"Sounds intriguing. As long as I'm not supposed to know anything about all of this and he'll lead."

"That's what he wants. You'll call Marcy?"

"Sure."

"Good. And shall we make a date for Monday evening, just the two of us, say around seven-thirty to explore the depths of our mutual fantasies? Since the club is closed we can have the whole place to ourselves. I would invite you for dinner, but that wouldn't set the right tone for your first time."

Should she do it? With Rock? God, she wanted to, but it was still a little embarrassing. Who was she kidding—admitting that she wanted to be under Rock's control was very embarrassing. But she did want it. She nodded.

"Not good enough. I know how awkward you must feel this moment, but I need to hear you say, 'I want to play down here with you. I will be yours to do with as you see fit.'"

She took a deep breath, trying to concentrate over the sound of the blood pounding in her hears. "I want to play down here with you. I will be yours to do with as you see fit."

He hugged her shoulders. "Oh God, you're fabulous. We'll explore so much and we'll both enjoy it to the fullest. You might even want to control me some time."

She considered, then said, "I might at that."

Rock slid from the table. He took her hand and helped her down from the table, then bowed his head and extended his hands, palms up, changing his attitude with a single gesture. "I would love to be your slave sometime, mistress." He raised his head and winked at her, then looked at his watch. "You've got a client coming in a few minutes and I've got things I need to do. Someone is using this room later tonight."

"Oh." In her mind she pictured what might go on here. "This has been quite an education," she said. "I never realized this sort of thing was so popular."

"I think there are a lot of things you never realized."

She thought about Tina. "That's an understatement."

"I love a quick learner. " He kissed her again, his hands cupping her buttocks, pressing her groin against his erection. "I'll see you Saturday, but I'm looking forward to Monday."

Chapter 21

The following Saturday Tay arrived at the club and changed her clothes. Rock opened the door to the dungeon and, as she started down the stairs, placed a light kiss on the back of her neck.

True to his word, Rock had transformed the room. Fake walls had been added so the remaining space was tiny, with a small barred false window high on one side. The floor was covered with straw and a small wooden bench stood in one corner. A metal plate and cup were stacked on a small shelf.

As she settled onto the bench she realized that she, too, had been transformed. She wore a shapeless many-times-washed gray sack-dress and gray cloth slippers. Underneath she wore only white cotton underpants, also shapeless from hundreds of washings. She'd removed any trace of makeup and used dark powder to dust deep hollows beneath her cheekbones and eyes. She'd unbraided her hair and mussed it thoroughly, shaking on some of the same dark powder to dirty up both her hair and her body.

She'd also changed her posture. Thinking what it must be like to be locked up like this, never allowed company or the sight of the outdoors, she let her shoulders droop and her body go slack. Then she waited for Jace.

He came down the stairs wearing a dark blue uniform, a pistol on his hip with thin leather gloves covering his hands, one of which was holding a swagger stick. He was of average height and weight with long medium brown hair that he wore tied with a strip of leather at the back of his neck. He was an ordinary-looking man with a weak chin hidden behind heavy five o'clock shadow. Except for the uniform he could have been anyone who passed you on the street.

He had been smiling when she first saw him at the top of the stairs, but now his face changed quickly to an expression both harsh and unforgiving. She'd acted in a few plays in middle and high school but these acting jobs here at the club brought out all her skills. Although she knew this scenario called for his attitude, she could imagine how she might feel if this were real. She gathered that feeling into her, slumped, and cast her gaze downward.

"Good morning, prisoner 2573," he said, his voice low pitched and loud. "It's time for your exercise period." He banged his swagger stick on the wall. "Up, up. You need your daily workout."

She almost smiled. Daily workout indeed. But she stayed in character and slowly got to her feet.

"Now walk around," he ordered. "Get your blood flowing in your veins. It's necessary for your continued health."

"I'm glad my health concerns you, sir," she said, keeping her voice soft and weak.

"Oh, it does. It does indeed."

"Well, sir," she continued softly, "I'm very hungry. Could I have something more to eat?"

"You would have to have something to give me in return. What do you have to offer?"

She'd given the scenario a lot of thought and had read a few notes left by his partners. She thought she might do things just a little differently, play the frightened virgin. She felt that her radar was good enough to shift gears quickly if it appeared that she wasn't giving him what he wanted. She made her voice shake with fear. "As you well know, I have nothing. The guards took everything I owned when I arrived. I don't even know why I'm here."

"You're here because you're an enemy of the state, and you seem to be a very interesting little lady. Very interesting." He paused and a smile crept across his face. "You can't mean that you don't know what kind of payment makes things happen around here."

"Oh, sir, no. I'm just a poor country girl and I'm not accustomed to such things. I've never . . ." Her voice trailed off.

"You can't mean . . ."

She merely stared at the floor, hands clasped in front of her. His genuine smile told her she'd guessed right. He liked the idea she injected into his drama.

"Oh, how fabulous. A virgin. Someone for me to play with and be the first." He grabbed the front of her well-worn–looking dress and yanked until she stood dressed only in her white underpants. Marcy had loosened the seams so the garment came apart easily. "Stand up straight," he barked. "I want to see what my options are."

She straightened slightly, still rounding her shoulders, and her chin dropped to her chest. He grabbed one breast and squeezed, then ran his gloved fingertips down her ribs. The feel and smell of the leather was very erotic. "Bony thing, aren't you." Never before had Tay been glad she was thin. When she didn't answer, he growled, "Speak when you're spoken to."

"Yes, sir," she said, her voice barely above a whisper.

"Louder."

"Yes, sir," she said.

"Good. You're learning. You answer when I ask you a question. Are you truly a virgin?"

"Yes, sir."

"Didn't you have a boyfriend? Before?"

A little smile lit her eyes. "Oh, yes, sir."

"So, how far did you go with him?"

She knew full well what he was asking, but she decided to play dumb. "I don't know what you want to know, sir."

"Did you let him put his tongue in your mouth, grab your titties, play with his fingers in your cunt? Answer me!"

"No, sir—I mean, yes, sir. That's too many questions, sir."

He looped his index finger over the waistband of her panties and pulled her close. "Did you let him put his tongue in your mouth like this?" He grabbed the back of her neck and pressed her lips against his, trying to force his tongue into her mouth. She kept her teeth tightly shut. "Open, bitch!" he snapped. He gathered her hair into a hank in his hand and pulled.

She allowed her teeth to part, and as his tongue finally entered her mouth she heard his breathing quicken. He plundered, then he moved away and a small smirk curved his mouth. Tay was amazed that she found all this very arousing. Power. As Rock had said, it was a strong aphrodisiac. Without needing any acting, she shivered.

"Did you let him play with your titties like this?" He leaned over, cupped one breast, lifted it to his lips and tongued the tip. "Well, if you didn't, he missed something. Your little nippies get all hard when I do this." He licked, suckled and teethed her flesh. "You must be a real slut to get all hot like this."

"Oh, no, sir," she said, a begging tone creeping into her voice. "I never—"

"Not likely. I know sluts like you enjoy teasing." For long moments he contented himself with her breasts and nipples, biting enough to cause her slight but exciting pain. "Yes, you're a real cock tease." He grabbed her hand and pressed it to his crotch. "Feel how bad women like you arouse men."

True to her character she tried to pull her hand back, but

he was very strong. "Feel it, bitch! Feel what bad women can do."

She loved how erect he was. Obviously this fantasy had great potency for him. She went with it all. "Please, sir, no. Don't make me do bad things."

"I can make you do whatever I want. You said you were hungry. What if I put you on half of what you're getting now? I can do it, you know."

She remained silent.

"Now feel what you do," he roared, pressing her hand more tightly against his cock. She moved her fingers and heard him gasp. She fondled and squeezed until he flung her hand away and moved backward. "I knew it. Slut! Harlot! Whore!"

Tay dropped to her knees. "Please, sir. No more. I'm a good girl. I'm promised to a man in my village. Don't shame me."

"I'll do whatever I please. Pull off those panties." She complied. "Now stand there, naked, and spread your legs."

She moved until her feet were about a foot apart. "Wider." She widened her stance. She jumped from the momentary sting when he pulled her pubic hair. The safe word was *red*, she told herself. Just in case.

She was starting to understand. He knew that she was aware of the safe words so he could pull and grab and even cause her a little pain, secure with the fact that she would tell him to stop if she needed to. "Understand, bitch?" he said, releasing his hold on her.

She let out a long breath of resignation. "Yes, sir."

He stepped back. "Good. You're starting to really get it. Now stay that way and stand still while I see what I've got." Slowly he walked around her, squeezing, pinching, tweaking, poking. Despite the slight pain he was causing, she didn't move.

He parted her ass cheeks and prodded her anus with the end of his swagger stick. He wet the handle with her juices and inserted it just a fraction. She had had anal sex a few times so she wasn't shocked or upset. Rather the feel of the hard leather in her ass was undeniably erotic. "No," he snapped, withdrawing the instrument and slapping her firmly on her buttocks. "Your virgin pussy is too much of a temptation to be distracted by your lovely ass."

Again in front of her, still fully clothed, he rubbed his gloved fingers through her folds, then rubbed them together. "You're very wet, my little whore. You really are a bitch in heat."

She knew she was drenched in her own juices.

"Remove my jacket." He said it in a low voice, assured she would do whatever he wanted. With trembling hands she complied. "Now my pants." With a few more commands he stood before her, naked except for his gloves. She'd learned from Marcy that the gloves were important to the illusion.

"Now, my beautiful little bitch, we'll see about your virginity." Of course, he must know that she was no virgin, but she'd play the part as best she could. He pushed her down on her back on the bench and put one of her legs on the floor on either side so she was wide open for him. He quickly put on a condom, straddled the narrow seat, slid up between her thighs and lifted her hips. Holding her by her ass cheeks he rammed his fully erect cock into her. Although she really didn't remember her own first time, she tightened her vaginal muscles as much as she could and screamed as she thought a virgin might.

He plunged in, then pulled back, becoming so aroused that his thrusts almost pushed her headfirst off the bench. She grabbed him behind his knees and held on.

He came, throwing his head back. He came hard and long. And loudly. Rock had said he'd be able to hear her if she called for assistance. She didn't know how the sound system worked but she thought everyone in the house could have heard his climax, soundproofing or not.

He remained on the end of the bench until his breathing returned to near normal. "That was the best it's ever been. What's your name?"

"Tay," she said.

"Can I ask for you again so we can play the same scenario?"

"I thought you liked to have a different woman each time."

"I used to, but this was so perfect that I'm sure no one could play it as well as you did this evening."

She blushed. "Wow, that's quite a compliment." She hesitated, then looked at the floor of her cell. "Sir."

Jace slipped on his pants, gathered the rest of his uniform and climbed the stairs. As he opened the door she heard him say, "Delightful. Just delightful."

Chapter 22

For the first time in all the years she'd been working in the city, Tay played hooky. She called in first thing Monday morning and told the powers that be that she was ill. She'd get some work done at home both that day and the next, she told them, and she'd be in the office bright and early Wednesday morning.

Work today? There was no way. Her mind had been in turmoil all the previous day, anticipating her evening with Rock. Her experience with Jace had showed her what power games had to offer and now she was going to taste the ultimate, with Rock as her teacher.

Her hands shook and her vaginal tissues swelled just thinking about it. She had masturbated to relieve the stress twice on Sunday and once before she got out of bed on Monday morning. She was a wreck.

She spent the day trying to stay calm. She exercised the dogs, cleaned the snake, rabbit and ferret cages, swam fifty laps both morning and afternoon and did what work she couldn't avoid.

What was all the agitation about? she wondered. She was a prostitute and had played a power game with Jace. She considered herself a sophisticate, so why was this evening with Rock giving her such a difficult time?

This kind of game isn't an endurance contest. It's supposed to be pleasure for both participants. She heard his words and realized that that was the crux of it all. She wanted to give Rock pleasure. She admitted to herself that she had a bit of a grown-up crush on Rock. Oh, she understood that he wasn't a relationship guy, and right now, she wasn't a relationship woman. Despite all that rationality she also knew that she wanted to please him, impress him with her sensuality and ability to play his games. She wanted to give as good as she got, and more.

Could she do that being submissive to him? What did a good little slave do that was different from any other warm body? She'd have to figure it out as she went along.

Skies were leaden and a storm threatened as she drove to the east fifties and parked in the lot she had used several times before. It was only six-fifteen, but she hadn't been able to sit still in Westchester any longer. She thought she'd find someplace near the club to have some dinner, but she knew she wouldn't be able to eat a bite.

She walked south on Second Avenue and tried to play out the scene. What would he do? What should she do? Finally she took a deep breath and stopped banging her head against that particular wall. She wouldn't have to do anything. He'd be in charge. *Stop worrying! He'll be giving all the orders.*

She looked up at a street sign and discovered that she was at Twenty-first Street. She'd walked more than a mile. She turned and began the walk north.

It was almost exactly seven-thirty when she opened the door to the brownstone. As before, Rock was waiting for her in the living room dressed in his standard costume: tight black T-shirt, black jeans and black motorcycle boots. The large diamond studs winked in his ears and a large diamond ring almost covered the lower joint of his right pinky. He looked up from a copy of the previous day's *New York Times Book Review,* which lay on his lap. Again Tay marveled at the contradictions that were Rock. "Good evening," he said, his face breaking into a smile. "I'm glad you didn't change your mind."

"Hi." Her voice was small. "I almost did."

He stood, looking suddenly very big and very tall. Powerful. "Nervous?"

"Very."

"Good. Leave your purse here and come on downstairs."

Everything was starting slowly. He could just as well be asking her into the kitchen for a snack. Her mind was reeling, not knowing what to expect. What should she do? How should she act? He opened the basement door, and as she started to precede him down the steps, he grabbed her by her braid. "Once you pass through this door you belong to me, and as such, I go first. You follow. Always, in all things."

She stopped and let him pass.

As they descended he said, "I would assume that you're worried about how to behave. Don't. That's the beauty of all this. You do nothing except exactly what I tell you. Don't think, don't worry, don't plan. Got that?"

"Yes," she whispered.

They reached the lower level. The room was back the way it had been before it was altered to fit Jace's fantasy. The lights were almost blindingly bright, reflecting off the mirrored walls and ceiling. Dark velvet draped large pieces of equipment arrayed around the periphery of the room. What were they for? She mentally shook herself. *Stop thinking. It's all up to Rock. You don't need to know anything, or do anything for that matter.*

"You're thinking much too much. Leave it all to me."

She merely nodded.

"I don't usually tell my partners what to expect but I will

give you a few bits of information. Things get very fluid and will change according to our mutual reactions. I will probably tie you down and play with you with various implements."

Implements? She thought he probably meant sex toys. Or something kinkier. She shuddered slightly.

"I will feel free to use any orifice in your body for my pleasure. I usually know my partners very well in advance, but tonight I will do you the courtesy of asking. Anything off limits?"

Oral, anal, it was all right with her. She wanted to give him pleasure. "No," she said, unable to keep the quaver out of her voice. So many emotions were swirling inside her that it was impossible to know what she was feeling.

"We might find that a little pain is a turn-on for you, and we might not. Do you remember the safe words?"

"Red and yellow."

"Good. Then we can experiment." His demeanor suddenly changed. His expression became harder, his spine straighter, his shoulders more rigid. Instead of the friendly, accommodating man he usually was, he was now forceful, masterful. And she loved it. "Strip!"

She felt very small and it took her a moment to react. A moment too long.

"When I tell you to do something, you do it immediately. Now, strip!"

She nodded, and with a pounding heart and a dry mouth, she slowly unbuttoned her blouse. She'd chosen her clothing carefully. Just because she was his property this evening was no reason she couldn't tease him a little. Without being obvious, she intentionally pushed each button of her Kelly green cotton shirt slowly through its buttonhole. Although she didn't look at him directly she knew from his almost inaudible chuckle that he was watching her and that he knew she was doing things a little more slowly than she might. He didn't order her to speed things up. She let her blouse slip to the floor.

Her bra was lacy, off white with a rose on the front of each cup hiding her nipples. She slipped off her shoes and unzipped her white jeans, letting them drop, and stepped out of them. Her panties matched her bra and the flower over her pubis teased the viewer with visions of what was beneath.

His laugh was full and rich. "Okay," he said, "enough, woman. This is my party. I'll tell you when to tease, and now isn't the time."

"Okay."

"Wrong answer!" The powerful Rock was back. "Yes, sir."

"Yes, sir." She unhooked her bra and let it fall beside the rest of her clothing.

When she took her time hooking her thumbs in the waistband of her panties he grabbed her arm, spun her around and slapped her ass cheeks. There was little pain, but the noise echoed in the large room and made her jump. "Point made?"

"Yes, sir," she said, not intimidated, just enjoying herself.

"Lie down on the table, head at this end." He patted the leather. "Feet there."

When she stretched out he fastened her wrists to the sides with fur-lined manacles then moved to the foot of the table. As he fussed, attaching her ankles into preset positions, he did something she couldn't see that made a loud clack. Then she realized that the table had split up the center between her legs. He parted the sides until her legs were spread apart.

"Look up," he said, and she moved her eyes to the ceiling. There she was, reflected in the mirror, legs wide, body displayed. As she watched she saw that her wrists weren't fastened to the table but to padded armrests. He pulled her arms straight out from her shoulders and locked the mechanism in place. "Try to sit up," he said, his voice gruff.

She did and realized quickly that she was held fast. The only thing she could move was her head, and he took care of that with a band across her forehead. "Shit," she hissed, not sure exactly what her comment meant.

"Watch." He sat on a rolling chair similar to those in a doctor's office and pushed himself until his head was near her pussy.

She could feel his heated breath on her soaked flesh and see the top of his shaved pate in the mirrored ceiling. Then his tongue touched her and she flew. "Yes," she hissed. "Yes." She came with almost no provocation, waves of pleasure burning through her, causing her hips to buck. The spasms continued rocketing through her until he finally moved away. She hadn't realized how close she'd been and now she was disappointed. She'd come and all this might be over. Maybe she wasn't disciplined enough for this kind of play.

As she tried to catch her breath, she heard his chuckle. "You're too easy, love. Now that you've got some breathing room, let's play."

"Breathing room?" Let's play? It wasn't over?

"After your first climax you'll be able to proceed more slowly. The edge is off."

She let out a long, shuddering sigh. First climax. He seemed sure that there would be more. And if he said so, she didn't doubt it.

He circled her anus with his finger. He paused, giving her a chance to say no, but she didn't think she'd say no to much he wanted to do. She heard the sound of a drawer being opened and from his movements she guessed it was in the foot of the table. Then he rearranged the panels to which her legs were attached until her knees were bent, her heels almost touching her buttocks.

She heard some rattling. Not knowing what he was doing

was both scary and incredibly exciting. When he moved to her side, he had a pair of latex gloves in his hand. Slowly he put them on, making a show of smoothing the plastic over each finger. Then he showed her a slender dildo with a wide flange at the end. He withdrew a bottle from a drawer in the side of the table and proceeded to pour lubricant in his palm. While she watched, transfixed, he smoothed the liquid over his fingers and the dildo. "Let's see how this feels."

He moved to the end of the table and rubbed his gloved finger around her anus, getting closer to her hole with each pass. Then he slowly inserted one slender finger into her. "Now," he said, as if he were giving a student a lesson, "there are lots of nerve endings around your anus that are pretty much tied into the ones in your pussy." He looked at her. "Would you like to know the names?" He moved his finger a little deeper and they both knew that she couldn't have cared less.

"Oh well," he said. Deeper and deeper his finger pressed until it was as far inside of her as it could go. He withdrew, then pushed in again, simulating fucking her ass. He leaned over and again touched his tongue to her clit and she came once more. "God, you taste so good," he said as waves of pleasure filled her. He finger-fucked her ass, then pulled out and inserted the dildo he'd shown her.

He slapped the side of each ass cheek several times. Hard. The pain should have brought her down but, in contrast, it pushed her still higher. Then he inserted another dildo into her pussy and licked her clit.

It was as though one orgasm blended into the next as she lay, writhing, on the table. Part of her wanted it to continue forever, but eventually she was exhausted. "Enough," she said softly. If that didn't stop him, she'd say *yellow*. She didn't have to.

He pulled the toys out, removed his gloves and unfastened her bindings. She curled onto her side and concentrated on trying to breathe. "My God, you're so responsive. It's fabulous," he said.

She'd pleased him. Wonderful. Finally, when she could speak, she asked, "What about you?" She glanced at the bulge in his jeans. "I could . . ."

"No, you couldn't. Not right now, at least. However . . ." He pulled his T-shirt off over his head, then removed the remainder of his clothing. He grasped his fully engorged cock and stroked it. "I particularly love it when a woman watches me. I can't do it with my clients, but . . ."

She licked her lips at the sight of his erection, clear fluid oozing from the tip. "Beautiful," she whispered as he fondled himself. She reached out and covered his hand with hers, and he slipped his hand from beneath hers and used her hand to manipulate his cock. It took only moments until he threw his head back and semen erupted, squirting onto her arm and side.

"Woman, you're terrific. Next time I want to introduce you to a little more pain. We'll explore the edges of your desires. I know you'll be as responsive to that as you have been to everything else."

He rummaged in another drawer and pulled out a thin gold chain. "I want you to have this. It goes around your waist and when you feel it occasionally, think about what we'll do next time."

As she lay in bed hours later she thought about two things: Rock and pain. After they'd quieted, he'd laughed, long and rich, and she'd joined him. Sex was such fun and they admitted to each other that they'd just had about the best sex ever. "I'm starving," he'd said, and they'd shared peanut butter sandwiches in the kitchen. They'd talked for an hour, but, as though these were two different people, nothing more had been said about the evening. What could be said? They didn't need or want any declarations of affection, certainly not love. She realized that her "crush" on him was partly the acceptance that sex, for recreation, was fabulous. And this was sex for fun and games, and nothing more, and they both knew it. She cared a lot about him, and she was sure the feeling was mutual.

Love was something quite different, and as she looked back at her relationship with Steve, she realized that, for her, it had been good, lusty sex and not much more. She wasn't sure she'd even liked him much.

She'd learned so much about herself and about sexuality in general since then. She loved what she was doing and she was also earning big bucks. Life didn't get much better than this. Oh, sure, she admitted, eventually she wanted a full-time relationship like Marcy and Pam each had, and maybe kids, too, but for now, she was completely satisfied, in more ways than one.

Then she thought about the pain she'd experienced, both with Jace and with Rock. To many, she knew, pain was anathema. It had nothing to do with sexuality. For others, now including herself, a little painful stimulation was erotic, exciting and arousing. She thought about some sites she'd visited on the Net, with pictures and videos depicting whippings, severe spankings and other forms of what she still viewed as torture. That kind of heavy stuff wasn't for her. Yet. She knew now though not to rule anything out too firmly.

She fell asleep content with her life and delighted with the people in it.

Chapter 23

"You seem very distant today," Pam said at lunch on the Saturday of Labor Day weekend. She had just come back from a two-week vacation in France with Linc, and it was the first opportunity the two women had had to see each other since Pam's return. They'd spent the first half hour sharing all the events of the past few weeks—Tay's adventures at the club and Pam's immediate love of Paris. "It felt like I'd lived there before, like I'd come home."

"Linc liked it, too, I gather?"

"He was in heaven. Of course it was August so the city was all but deserted, but it even smelled good. And Notre Dame is not to be believed."

When Tay merely nodded, Pam said, suddenly serious, "Something's bothering you."

"It's nothing. Tell me more about France."

"I know you well enough to know that it's not nothing. If you don't want to talk about it, that's fine, just say so. Before we change the subject, though, let me ask just one thing. Is there anything I can help you with?"

So typical of Pam. She'd be willing to help with most things, and although Tay could use her help, she didn't want to ask. "I'm really sorry and I don't mean to throw a wet blanket on the stories of your trip." When Pam didn't say anything more, Tay huffed a quick breath. "I got an e-mail from Lissa yesterday."

"She's not sick or anything," Pam said, looking genuinely concerned. "Dave's okay?"

"No. Nothing like that. They are both great and excited to be coming home. In a week and a half."

"Oh," Pam said, quickly assessing the situation. "What will you do about where to live? Can you stay on after they come home? I'm sure they'd be delighted to keep you around."

Tay sighed. "I need my privacy, especially with the business I've gotten into. Lissa knows nothing about this part of my life and I want to keep it private. I'll tell her what I decide to tell her when I'm ready. Meanwhile, I'm going to look for a place in the city, maybe near the club."

"How about the guesthouse? Couldn't you stay there?"

"In the short run that will work, but it isn't a long-term solution by any means."

Pam looked teary. "I guess. I want you nearby, that's all." She sniffled. "I'm sure Marcy and Rock could help you find someplace in the city."

Tay realized that her eyes were beginning to mist over, too. "Summer's over, Pam. Lissa's coming back and it seems like something's ending. It's been so idyllic and letting it go truly bums me out."

"Nothing's gotten started that can't continue. Something has begun, too. Your new life, in so many ways."

Tay smiled a watery smile. "Yeah. That's for sure."

"What are you going to tell them about your desire for privacy? It's your decision, of course, but from what you have told me about Lissa I think she'll get it." Pam reached over and squeezed Tay's hand.

"A few other things have happened since you've been gone. I've decided to cut my job back to half time, about twenty hours a week, for appropriate pay. I'm making so much at the club that I don't need the everyday stuff anymore. I try not to make plans for the evenings before work days, but I want to be able to take whatever's offered. For a while I'll keep my day job part-time, however. It's give me a safety margin, someplace I can always go back to if things at the club go downhill."

"I think working only three days a week is a great idea. Will they let you cut back?"

"I don't think it will be a problem for them. I can do the publication and grant editing in those three days and they can easily hand off my Web stuff to someone else or farm it out."

"Have you spoken to them about it?"

"Not yet, but I think they'll be happy to pay me as a consultant, on an hourly basis. I did some figuring and I'll set my rates so that my hourly pay will pretty much cover my expenses and the equivalent of half my salary. I'll have to pay for my own medical insurance and there will be no vacation pay, but it should even out for all of us. Then they can do the rest more cheaply in-house or out."

"Will you do most of your work from home or go into the office?"

"That's the best part. I figure I can even work two ten-hour days, or four five-hour ones from wherever works out best for them and for me. I'll go into the office when I need to and work from home for the rest as long as the job gets done."

"You're making a lot of changes in your life. Nervous about all this?"

"I guess. Yeah. Terrified, actually. I haven't told anyone else yet and saying it out loud makes it true. My mother always warned me not to throw away my dirty dishwater until I had clean, but I can't burn my candle at both ends. I love working with Marcy and she's got all the clients for me that I can handle. But what if—"

Pam interrupted. "What if you are hit by a bus crossing the street tomorrow morning? If this seems like what you want, go for it. With your resume I'm sure you can either go back to full time or get another job if you want or need to."

Tay considered, then took in a deep breath and let it out. "Yeah. I guess."

"Well, I think it's all fabulous, and perfect for you. Have you started looking for an apartment?"

Tay's rueful gaze was her answer. "I guess I've been hoping Dave and Lissa would stay in China forever."

"Well, they aren't going to. So move into the guesthouse until you find a place."

Tay remained silent. "I don't want anything to change, especially between us." She felt like she did when Lissa first called her. Again she was changing her life. Again, it would be like taking a leap of faith. Moving to Maple Court had been the beginning of so much and now she'd be leaving it.

Pam reached across the table and again squeezed Tay's hand. "Listen, babe, you're the best and most sincere friend I think I've ever had. I can't imagine any circumstance under which I wouldn't want you in my life. The thought of you living in the city, so far away, totally messes with my head, but we both know it's time." She smiled ruefully. "Somewhere in the back of my brain, however, I'm hoping you won't find an apartment for months."

"You're the best."

"So are you, Tay, and I need these lunches to keep me sane." Pam sat back in her chair. "By the way, Linc asked me to marry him again while we were in Notre Dame, of all places."

"And you said no as usual?"

"I haven't said yes or no. Yet. But I'm seriously thinking about it."

"That's fabulous, Pam," Tay said, leaning over and kissing her friend's cheek. "You and Linc belong together and I knew you'd figure it out eventually. Hell, I want to be the one to throw you the biggest engagement party ever."

"Not so fast. I have been saying no for so long that I'm not sure I know how to say anything else."

"Of course it's all up to you, but—well, you know how I feel about you two."

"I keep asking myself, why get married? Things are fine the way they are. Maybe if we make it official something will change."

"Maybe it will change for the better. It's too bad that your first marriage made you so wary of the institution."

"Who wants to live in an institution?" Pam said, eyebrow raised. "Sorry, old joke."

"Okay. I realize you don't want to think about it seriously yet so let's change the subject."

"Good. Let's talk about how to decorate your new apartment when you find it."

"Don't make me think about not having you next door," Tay said, tearing up again. "If I do, I'll cry for sure."

Impulsively Pam leaned forward and kissed Tay on both cheeks. Tay did cry.

Justin arrived back in the middle of the following week, and as usual took up residence in the guesthouse. The first night he was back he was exhausted, but the following evening he and Tay went out to dinner and followed it with a bout of hot sex. When their labored breathing slowed, Justin asked what she'd been doing for entertainment since he'd been gone. She almost laughed but knew he'd wonder what the joke was and she was reluctant to tell him about her "other life."

The following evening he found out. Tay was on the phone with Marcy, discussing plans for an evening at the club when Justin burst into the bedroom looking like he could murder someone. Her. "Call you back, Marcy," Tay said, then snapped her cell phone closed, annoyed at herself for leaving the bedroom door open.

"What the hell was that all about?" Justin said, banging the door open so hard the knob slammed into the wall.

Tay replayed the last few moments of her conversation and realized she'd been discussing whether a client might want to use the dungeon. She'd said that, since her evening with Rock she'd be able to play the dominant as part of a bondage session. She had said that she was interested in trying her hand at the dominant side as well and she'd discussed how much she'd learned from Rock.

Shit, shit, shit. She'd forgotten that they had dinner plans. "Were you eavesdropping?"

"I couldn't help but overhear that you were talking about tying someone up."

"I guess I was," she said calmly.

"Bondage? I don't get it." Justin's face changed from angry to curious and back again.

"What don't you get?"

"I thought you were a pretty ordinary woman, Tay. Sexually that is."

Tay was getting annoyed at his assumptions. "Does the idea that I'd be willing to participate in a bondage session frighten you?"

"It surprises me. You're not that kind of woman."

"Well, you're wrong about that. I'm whatever kind of woman I want to be."

"Come on, Tay. You don't have to do that sort of thing to attract a man. You're a great girl."

As much as his assumptions, his use of the diminutive word *girl* pissed her off. "Justin, forget it. Let it drop."

"No! I don't want to see you getting mixed up with kinky people. It's ugly, nasty and certainly not up to your standards."

She was becoming furious. "Shows what you know about me. It's too late, Justin. I already am."

Justin stood in the bedroom doorway. "What about me?"

"What about you?"

"I thought we had a good thing going here."

"Bullshit. I'm convenient, easy and fun in bed. That's what we have going here, and nothing about that has changed. You want to fuck me whenever it's convenient, then waltz off to be with someone else, fine. Casual fucking is great. You can pay me with a really good dinner."

Justin was baffled. "Pay you? Is that what it is?"

Her voice now several decibels above its normal level, Tay continued. "Of course. You pay me with a little good conversation—actually it isn't that all-fired good—and we end up in bed. Others pay me with good old cash."

"Pay you?"

Tay realized she'd said too much, but right now she was too angry to care. "You heard me. I get well paid by really great guys for things you get for only the price of a good meal."

Totally nonplused, Justin walked slowly into the room and plopped on the edge of the bed. "Are you trying to tell me you're a hooker in your spare time?"

"Not only in my spare time."

"Is that what you're cutting back on your day job for?"

"I'm earning enough doing whatever I please with the rest of my time."

"You mean doing kinky stuff on street corners."

She'd gone this far and she knew she was taking a risk, but she couldn't seem to stop her mouth. "I don't do anything on street corners. I'm high priced and very, very good at what I do."

He slapped her across the face. "Shut up. You're not a whore. I would know if you were."

His slap had caused more sound than pain, but she cupped

her cheek. She was suddenly very calm. "Justin," she said, her voice more weary than anything else, "get out before I throw you out. No one hits me. Ever."

"You mean without paying for it first."

"Justin, get out."

She watched his shoulders slump. "I'm so very sorry about hitting you, Tay," he said, seeming genuinely contrite. "It happened before I thought about it."

"Well, think about it on your way down the stairs. Out. Now."

Chapter 24

Justin packed up and left the following morning, leaving Tay with a bad taste in her mouth and doubts about how Lissa would react. She was pretty sure that her friend would understand, but how well did anyone really know anyone?

She called Pam around ten and invited herself over. In the kitchen she told Pam about her encounter with Justin. "The slap was unforgivable," Pam said, getting the coffee pot from the warmer. "I'm so sorry it had to happen." She poured them each some coffee, probably considering what she'd say. "Tay, you've made some choices," she said as she put mugs on the table, "and you have to live with them. I wish I could tell you that everyone you meet will be understanding about what you're doing, but that's not going to be the case. I don't tell too many people outside the business what I do for just that reason. If you'll remember, it took weeks before I told you."

"And I understood."

"Of course you did, but I knew you would before I said anything. From what I know of the Bonners, I think Lissa will, too, but there's always a risk. Only you can decide how much you want to tell her."

Tay wasn't really looking forward to Lissa and Dave's return, now scheduled for the following Tuesday. She'd already asked Lissa whether she could use the guesthouse while she looked for an apartment, and as she'd expected she'd gotten an immediate yes.

"Why not just stay where you are?" Lissa's note had asked.

"I've gotten used to privacy and being alone," she'd replied. "I hope you understand."

"Of course. Whatever you want."

If she decided to tell her friend, she'd have to consider the possibility of a negative reaction. She might have to move in with Pam for a short time if Lissa decided she didn't want a prostitute living on the property.

Of course, part of her reason for wanting to be out of the Bonner house was that she was keeping strange hours and engaging in intimate phone calls on her new disposable cell phone. She couldn't risk the Bonners, or anyone else, hearing what went on.

"Hi, Tay," Marcy said as Tay settled the phone between her ear and her shoulder.

"What's up?"

They talked for a few minutes and Marcy told her that she'd already been poring over the real estate ads for some suitable apartments. They talked about Tay's requirements. "When Zack and I were looking, a real estate agent suggested that we make a 'need' list and a 'want' list. It made us think seriously about the difference between what we could and couldn't do without if push came to shove. That goes for rooms, location, closets, like that. You need to consider whether you want something furnished or not, too."

"That list thing is a great idea. I'll do that. And I also have to think about furniture. I have nothing, but maybe I want to buy my own stuff."

She and Marcy discussed her new job status and Marcy was delighted. "More time for the club. You're becoming one of my most popular ladies."

"I will definitely need high-speed Internet access at my new place for my day job," she said, using the term "day job" as a joke.

"For other things, too," Marcy said, sounding serious, but she quickly changed the subject. "On the business side of things, I've been asked to find someone to hold a phone-sex conversation with the friend of a long-time client."

"Why in the world would someone want phone sex when he could have the real thing? The club's set up for almost anything."

"First of all, the guy's currently toward the end of a four-month stint on a research station on the edge of the Arctic ice."

"Ahh," Tay said, understanding.

"There are several women in the group, but he wants to keep them as friends, not bedmates. He's also got a wife. He's read just about every bit of porn on the Web and seen lots of videos—and probably jerked off a zillion times—but that's not enough anymore. And his wife isn't interested in anything more. He complained to this friend who then called me."

"I guess phone sex is the best he can get. He doesn't consider phone sex cheating?"

"He and his wife have decided that as long as he comes home to her, it's not. So, are you interested?"

"Why me?"

"Because you're flexible, articulate and quick on your feet, and you've got a great voice for it. You can sound incredibly sexy."

Tay had never thought her slightly husky voice an asset, but obviously Marcy did. She tuned back in to the conversation. "Why us? Don't we charge quite a bit for stuff like that? Can't he get it for a lot less with one of those outfits that advertise in the skin magazines?"

"He can, but his friend told him about us. He wants a fantasy, similar to ones he's dreamed about for years. The friend he discussed it with—who's a client and has indulged in phone sex himself on occasion—has more money than he can spend, so he gave this guy an hour of phone sex as a gift."

"Ahh. So he'll be new at this, too. What fantasy does he want?"

"He wants to have a medical exam with a lovely woman doctor and . . . well, you can figure out the rest."

"Sounds like fun. Sure, I'll do it."

"I'll set it up for, let's say Friday evening. I'll get his phone number and a specific time. And be sure to use your disposable cell phone. You don't want anyone getting your phone number and calling you back."

"I know, like the drug dealers use. Will do."

"Hello."

"This is Dr. Wallace's office," Tay said to the guy who answered the phone. "Is Mr. Smith there?"

"Er, this, er, this is Joe Smith." He had a nice, gentle voice with a thick Texas drawl.

"Good," Tay said. She'd thought about an easy way to slip into the fantasy without sounding totally phony. "The doctor suggested that I call and let you know about your exam. You know, how it will go, what will happen."

"Er, yeah."

"I'll tell you as much as I can." She softened the official tone she'd used when placing the call. "When you get to the office you'll be shown into an exam room. You know how they look, right?"

"Tell me."

Tay smiled. This was going to work out fine. She could already hear the sound of his heavy breathing. She thought about the exam room at the club. She had played with a client there several weeks before and had a pretty good idea of what he'd enjoyed. "The room is pretty small, with pale green walls and lots of cabinets. There's a desk on one side with a computer console on it and an exam table in the center with a white paper sheet covering the leather. A chair with little wheels allows the doctor to move from her desk to the exam table should she need it. There's one of those blood-pressure machines on the wall."

Tay thought quickly. What else would he want to know? She thought back to her most recent doctor's visit. What would add to the picture she was painting? "The temperature in the room is low and it smells slightly of disinfectant and alcohol. It's very quiet and private and all you can hear is the rustle of the paper as I straighten the table drape for you. I'll ask you to strip down to your shorts, put on a little blue cloth cover-up, with the opening in the front, and tell you that the doctor will be right with you."

"Ohhh." It was almost a sigh.

"You'll get undressed, everything but your shorts, and put on the gown. Then you sit on the edge of the table."

Another long, pleasure-filled sigh was his only response.

"You've never met her, so I must tell you that the doctor's really pretty. She's got a small waist and generous hips, long legs and large breasts. She's wearing a V-neck sweater so you can see just a hint of shadowy cleavage. She's also got on a slender black skirt with a long slit up the side, with a white lab coat over it all."

"What does she look like? I mean, does she have long hair, and does she wear it loose?"

That was more than he's said during the entire phone call so far, so this must be important. "Why, yes, how did you guess? Let's see whether you can guess the color."

"It's black. Raven black, and she's got blue eyes and full lips."

"Right again. Her hair is down almost to her waist and she wears it held back with two small combs." She could hear his heavy breathing. "She comes into the room. 'I'm Dr. Wallace,' she says, 'and I promise this won't hurt a bit.'"

More raspy breaths. Good. She paused momentarily, realizing that she was having fun with this guy and she was sure he was enjoying it as well. "She washes and dries her hands, and you know that she needs to put on latex gloves. She pulls a pair from a box on one counter and puts them on, very slowly and carefully. You can see each finger as it fills the glove. She snaps the cuff as she completes the job." She remembered her excitement when Rock put on gloves, and she used that for this fantasy.

"First she'll have to take your blood pressure and listen to your heart and breathing. It's all pretty easy. However, when she bends over to tap your knees with her little hammer you can smell her light perfume and get a look down the front of her sweater. You can see that, beneath her black bra, she's got beautiful breasts."

She listened carefully and heard him pant. Wonderful. "Next she'll have you lie on the table on your back. She's got to check your belly. You stretch out and she presses her fingers on your abdomen. It's very erotic and you can feel your penis getting hard. It's very embarrassing, so you want to hide it from her, but you know she'll see."

"Oh God," he whispered.

"As she presses on your belly your erection gets harder and harder. She looks at it and says, 'Don't be embarrassed.

Getting aroused is really quite normal.' Her smile of encouragement pleases you.

"'Now I have to check for hernias. Turn your head away and cough for me.' You do and she presses deep into you, just above your root. Your cock is so hard it almost hurts.

"'Okay, now for the slightly difficult part,' she says. 'I need to check your testicles.' She reaches down the waistband of your briefs and cups your sac, squeezing and probing. It makes you really hot and you almost erupt in her hand."

"Yes," he whispers over the sound of his hard breaths.

"'One last thing,' she says. 'I need to do a rectal.'" Tay hadn't been sure about this part so she listened very carefully to the sounds at the other end of the phone. His tiny "Oh no" told her that he didn't mean it.

"She takes out a tube of lubricant," she told Joe, again remembering her session with Rock, "and squeezes a big dollop of it into her hand, making it all slippery. You know what's going to happen, don't you, Joe?"

"Yes." The word was hardly more than a breath.

"All right. Put your knees up against your chest so she can do her job." She paused as if he were really doing it. "Good. Now you can feel her finger ever so slowly penetrate your anus. Your cock is twitching, needing to come. She knows that, so she grasps your hard cock and gives it a gentle squeeze."

There was a gasp at the other end of the phone. Had he climaxed? Tay hoped so. "Semen squirts from your penis and gets all over her hands, running down her gloves. It's really embarrassing, but you couldn't help it, could you, Joe?"

"No, ma'am." His voice was louder now, more in control. "Thanks for talking to me like this."

"You're so welcome, Joe. I hope you enjoyed our visit."

"Oh, I did, ma'am. Very much. Can you call me again sometime?"

"I might just do that."

"Thank you again."

Chapter 25

Tay called Marcy to let her know how well the call with Joe went. "I assume his name isn't really Joe Smith," she said.

Chuckling, Marcy replied, "According to his friend, it really is." Then she heaved a big sigh.

"Problems?" Tay asked.

"I'm feeling like a whale. I'm hot all the time, my back hurts, I'm hungry morning, noon and night and the kids are driving me nuts. Other than that, I'm fine." Another deep breath. "Sorry, bad day."

"Oh, Marcy, I'm so sorry. I wish I could help. You haven't got too much more time left, though."

"Two more months, and I'm starting to remember how much I hated the last few months of my last two pregnancies. At least this one isn't twins."

"I can't really imagine what it's like, but you have my sympathy."

"Thanks. I'll think about that when I feel like a cow and can't turn over in bed."

"How's Zack?" Tay and Zack had become quite friendly and she loved Marcy's kids. She'd visited several times and the children had begun to call her Aunt Tay. Several weeks ago she'd gone to dinner with Rock, Marcy and Zack, and Pam and Linc. It amazed her that this group of professional courtesans of both genders sat like any other group in a trendy Indian restaurant, critiquing the cooking and talking politics.

"Zack's in his element. He loves the idea of another baby, especially since he doesn't have to give up wine, coffee and other fun stuff."

"Fun stuff. You don't mean that you have to give up sex, do you?"

"Well, I wouldn't go that far." Laughter united the two women.

"I didn't think so."

"Zack loves to put his cheek against my belly and feel the kicks. Of course, that's always right at bedtime and sleep is getting more and more difficult."

"Poor Marcy."

"You just said the exact right thing. How about a few more poor baby's?"

"Poor baby," Tay said, then echoed it three more times.

After a few more minutes of pleasantries, Marcy said, "There's a reason I'm calling, and I want you to feel free to say no."

"Okay. With that warning, it must be something really unusual. Someone want something way out there?"

"Sort of. We've got a prospective client who wants something a little outside of what we usually do and it's off premises. I know how far you've come with all this, but . . ."

"Why don't you stop beating around this gigantic bush and spit it out?"

"Okay. You're right. This guy and several of his friends are going to a sex club this Saturday evening. He's not sure why he agreed to go but he's been making up a story about a fictional, really hot girlfriend and the guys have informed him that they don't believe him. He's a sweet, sort of nerdy type and I think the taunts of his friends about his lack of kinky sex finally got to him, so he invented a hottie named Cindy. They dared him to bring her and he finally said yes."

"Good lord. You mean he actually agreed to bring this Cindy to their little party at this sex club?"

"In a moment of craziness, yeah. Now he's backed himself into a corner. He finally told his tale to his brother last evening, the only one it seems he can really talk to, and, after trying to talk this guy out of the whole thing, the brother finally suggested us."

"The brother is a client?"

"No, but a friend is and he knows about us. We've got quite a network and very good PR. So anyway, the guy in question calls, we meet and now I'm trying to find someone for him for this Saturday."

"Short notice."

"Right. I've got just about everyone but you booked. I know your friend and her father are getting back this weekend, so I've pretty much left you off the radar. However, when I got in a jam I thought of you for my new guy. You know that any time you're presented with an opportunity you can always say no. This guy's really nice and I feel for him, but I can always turn him down."

"What's involved?" She was glad for the opportunity to take her mind off Lissa's imminent arrival, but she wasn't sure how she felt about leaving the relative safety of either the brownstone or Pam's house.

"I know the club he's talking about. It's a little seedy and a little wild, but both reputable and safe. They have sex shows with live fucking on stage, not totally legal but tolerated by the local cops. You'd go as his girlfriend. You'd have to be willing to do almost anything and help him build his reputation in any way you can. Think you're up to that?"

She thought a moment. She might be asked to do things she didn't want to do, but she'd be free to demur. Most of her thoughts were of some poor guy who'd never been anything. "Sure. I've got the picture. Nerdy guy rates hot, sexy slut and ends all the bad PR he's been getting from his friends—if you can call them friends."

"Oh, he knows they're not friends, but he'd still like to stick it to them, if you know what I mean."

A chuckle slipped out. "Yeah. Sounds like something I'd love to do. Count me in."

"Tay, you're a lifesaver. Why don't you come down here? I'll leave Zack with the kids and we can grab a bite of dinner. I can give you a hand if you like, finding anything you'll need—clothes, slutty makeup, whorehouse shoes, like that. We've probably got everything you'll need here."

"Sounds great."

The two women met at six-thirty at an Italian restaurant they'd eaten at a few times. "Between my closet and Lissa's I think I've found everything I need," she told Marcy as they bussed cheeks, then she twirled for her friend's inspection. "What do you think?" She'd discovered a burgundy sweater in the back of Lissa's closet, a size smaller than usual and its deep V-neck and a black push-up bra left over from her clubbing days with Steve created cleavage where she usually had little. Back then she'd also bought a short, tight black skirt, slashed up the side and a pair of black-mesh stockings to show off her long, shapely legs. Steve had loved the outfit and had stripped it off her when he first saw it.

Despite the fact that Marcy had told her that the guy wasn't very tall, Tay was wearing stiletto heels. She'd downplayed her makeup so as not to look too way out, but she must have looked like quite a piece of work. As the two women turned toward the small, local restaurant, she grinned. "We make quite a pair," she whispered to Marcy. "Slutty-looking woman with large, pregnant friend."

Through her laughter, Marcy said, "You look terrific." Then she added, sotto voce, "Just slutty enough."

When they were seated, Tay asked, "What's this guy's name, anyway? I keep thinking of him as 'the nerd.'"

"Brent. Somehow the name Brent conjures up a tall, brawny, sexy guy with a granite chin and deep blue eyes. This Brent is short, maybe an inch shorter than you are, even without the heels, balding with a thick waist and matching thick glasses."

"I can change into the flats I brought if you think it will be better."

"I think the statuesque look will do fine for him. He told me he's managed not to tell any of the guys involved what his secret lover looks like."

They continued to make small talk for several minutes. Finally Marcy looked at Tay seriously. "Actually," Marcy said, "there's something else I want to talk to you about, but let's order first. Brent is arriving at eight-thirty."

Tay's attention ramped up a notch. Something was up.

After the waiter brought their salads, Marcy picked up the conversation where she'd left off. "I have a favor to ask of you, beyond tonight, and I hope you'll understand that I make it with all good intentions. Any luck with any of the apartments?"

Tay had been making phone calls and setting up visits to see those that seemed promising. "Some. I've got a few visits lined up for next week, after Lissa and Dave get back. I've got most of my stuff in the guesthouse already and that will do fine until I find a place. And many, many thanks to both you and Zack for all the efforts on that front. You've been great, lining up places for me to see and all. It shouldn't be long before I can get settled."

"That works out fabulously well for me."

"You lost me. In what way?"

"Tay, I have to stop working. Zack's been suggesting it

for more than a month and I finally have to admit that he's right. My pregnancy is so obvious that I'm afraid it's causing new clients to reconsider when I do interviews. I'm also really tired and I need some time off before this baby comes. I want you to take over my end of the business for at least six months."

Tay was flabbergasted. "Take over?"

"I can't do it anymore. I need time with my kids and with Zack. I need to get off the treadmill I'm on and get out from under all this stress. It's not good for me or for the baby."

"The baby's not having problems, is it?" Tay asked, suddenly worried. She hated calling the new addition "it" but Marcy and Zack had decided not to find out the baby's gender.

Marcy patted Tay's hand. "No, no, nothing like that. Everything's fine on that front, for now, but I have to slow down."

"Okay, I can understand that. But why me? What about Pam or one of your other employees?"

"Pam's doing her thing in Westchester and she has her house and all. I need someone here, in the city. There are probably others who could do a good job, but you're my first choice. I can still handle the bookings and keep the records until you're ready for that part, and I have an accountant who does all the tax and insurance stuff. It's the personal touch I need—interviewing new clients, finding out what they want, setting up the fantasies, matching the men to our employees, like that."

Tay's mind was whirling. "That sounds like a lot of careful handling. I don't know whether I'm right for it."

"Tay, I know you better than you know yourself, and you're the best. You've got great people skills and that's most of what's needed."

"Okay, but . . ."

"Please consider it. I'm sure you'll have an apartment in no time, so interviews in Manhattan won't become a transportation problem. When I had Eliza more than five years ago I had Chloe to take over. And I was younger then."

Tay laughed. "Right. You're old and decrepit now."

"Okay, maybe it's just that I feel older, and much, much more exhausted. I can't keep up the pace I've been living at. Then there will be a new baby in my life, and although all the other children will be in school, at least part time, and I do have a nanny, I need a little peace and quiet." She snorted. "Did I say 'quiet' and 'new baby' in the same sentence?"

Tay's answering smile said it all. "You did."

"Okay, but you get the message. I really need your help."

"I'll ask again, why me?"

"Why not you? You're bright and very quick, a real people person who I'd trust totally with my clients. You did a wonderful job of finding the exact right balance with that phone-sex guy."

"How do you know that?"

"His friend called, raving about you. You not only gave him a wonderful experience that evening, but he said he'll be using it as a basis of his dreams until he comes home."

"It was fun and not difficult at all."

"Been there, done that, and it's not difficult for some, very difficult for others. You have the ability to know what people are thinking and dreaming about. I want someone for the interviews who can react quickly on her feet and who will be able to explore a guy's—or a woman's—fantasy without prejudice, without making him or her feel in any way less of himself. Almost everything is possible at the club, and that's our strength."

Marcy reached across the table and took Tay's hands in hers. "Look, Tay, let's be serious here. I want you for this because I think you'll do as good a job as I do, and that's the bottom line for me. Of course, we'll make some financial arrangement that will enable you to quit your job if you want to. Please." She squeezed her friend's hands. "Think about it."

"Give me a few days?"

"Of course. But this is a busy time for the business and I really want out. I'd really like it if you'd decide soon. If you don't want to do it, I'll have to think of someone else."

She knew that Marcy was being manipulative, but Tay understood. She loved the work and she really liked the men she'd dealt with. She could see herself cutting through a guy's nervousness and natural reluctance to find out about what he wanted most. "It might work."

Marcy's eyes brightened. "I don't want to push you, nudge, nudge. Say that you'll think about it."

Tay couldn't see a downside. If Marcy trusted her enough to let her take over, why not? "I don't have to. I'll be glad to do it."

"Oh God, Tay. You're the best. I can't thank you enough."

Tay thought back to the phone call from Lissa six months before asking for her help and how that had led to the monumental and wonderful changes in her life. Now more changes, wonderful ones here, too, she hoped. No, she knew. "Don't thank me. I'm grateful to you and Pam for all of this." She felt her eyes tearing. "I'm going to miss Pam so much when I don't live next door to her anymore."

"You've seen a lot of me and the club from Westchester. Trains run both ways, you know."

Tay watched Marcy through watery eyes and tried to smile. *Yeah*, she thought. *Trains do run both ways*. Maybe she'd even get a car.

She was sitting in the living room of the club when Brent arrived. He was just as Marcy had described him, wearing a light blue polo shirt and jeans, with his bare feet stuffed into deck shoes. His face as she stood up was priceless. He looked both pleased and terrified. "Uh, hello. You're going to be Cindy?"

"I sure am. Come on in, Brent," Tay said, "and let's take some time and get our stories straight. First, what shall I call you? Brent's sort of formal and we should have nicknames for each other."

"Could you call me Boo? That's what my little brother always called me."

Little brother indeed. God, how had this guy survived? "It's a little cutesy, but okay," Tay said. "Call me Cyn. It's *C-y-n*, but it will sound like the word *sin*. They'll love the double entendre. Call me that from now on, just to get used to it."

"I don't even know your real name."

"Good. That way you won't slip up."

She took him to one of the bedrooms upstairs so they could have total privacy, and so the clients of Club Fantasy who came and went through the downstairs could remain relatively anonymous.

For almost an hour, with Brent in a chair and Tay stretched out on the bedspread, they compared notes about favorite foods, drinks, movies, TV shows, the dates they'd been on and the places they'd gone. She asked him about his job as a salesman for a large insurance firm, and they decided that she would be a receptionist for a medical practice. He told her about the guys they would be meeting. "If something comes up that we're not sure of," Tay suggested, "let's just giggle and say that we don't want to talk about it, or something similar."

Brent had calmed significantly. "Okay. That should work as long as we don't do it too much. I'm afraid my friends might ask lots of questions. They don't believe you exist, you know."

"Well, I do exist and they'll know it immediately. By now I think we know enough to pull this off."

Brent beamed. "You know, this might work after all. You've thought of so much that I hadn't even considered." He looked down. "And you're really nice."

"Thanks, Boo. We have one last topic. Sex."

"Oh, I couldn't talk about that," he said, winking at her. "At least that's what I can tell anyone who asks."

"Good job," she said, grinning. "You've got the idea. What position do you like best?"

"Why do you need to know that?"

"If I can slip that into a sentence it will add to the reality. But if it's too personal . . ."

"You're right, of course. I haven't been with a lot of women, but usually I'm on top. I'm pretty big and it's been difficult to get comfortable."

Pretty big. *Sounds promising,* Tay thought, ideas for making his reputation whirling in her head. "Okay, let's not go any further with that part. I think we're ready. What time are we meeting your friends?"

"Around ten. The Pussy Cat Club is down in the Wall Street area and they tell me that things don't get going until at least ten-thirty. We planned to all get there by ten so we'll be sure to get a table right down front."

"Okay, let's get going." She dropped her feet to the floor and pulled Brent from his chair. She wrapped her arms around his neck and pressed her lips against his. He was a little awkward at first, but quickly got into the swing of things. He turned out to be a pretty good kisser.

When they parted, he asked, "What was that for?"

"Fun. Can you look on this evening as fun?"

"No," he confessed. "I'm scared to death that something will go wrong."

"At which point you'll be no worse off than you are. Do you trust me?"

He hesitated, then said, "Yes."

"Good. Just follow my lead and I can almost guarantee you that things will be great. Oh, and I like the way you kiss."

Chapter 26

They'd stopped in the living room for a quick beer before leaving, so it was a bit after ten when Brent and Tay arrived at the club. "I thought it would be a good idea to be a little late," Tay suggested, "like we'd had better things to do than rush out. It will also keep them guessing and make our entrance more spectacular."

As the cab pulled up in front of a nondescript storefront in lower Manhattan, Tay cupped Brent's face and kissed him, deliberately smearing a bit of lipstick on the corner of his mouth. Then she mussed his hair a little and stepped out of the taxi. "You're one lucky guy," the cab driver muttered.

Brent was grinning while he paid the fare. "This just might work out."

"It will work out, and don't you doubt it for a moment. Together, we can get around anything."

Still smirking, Brent led Tay into the club. The room was large and probably seated more than fifty at small tables. Waiters in thongs and waitresses in not much more wiggled between the closely packed drinkers, taking orders and bringing drinks and snacks. Although tobacco had been banned in all such establishments, the room still smelled slightly of stale smoke and sweat. Marcy had said it was reputable and Tay noticed that several burly men in tight navy T-shirts and jeans, who resembled Rock and probably served the same function, stood on the periphery of the room.

Tay spotted a group seated at a table near the stage. They waved as they obviously recognized her partner so she took his arm and hugged it to the side of her breast. "That's them?" she whispered.

He gave a slight nod. There were three couples already seated around a tiny table, drinks in front of each person, several plates of nachos scattered around. "This is Cyn," Brent said as they reached them.

"Hello," Tay said, lowering her voice so they had to strain to hear her over the loud music. "Boo has told me so much about you." She held on to Brent's arm and looked back at him, obviously totally disinterested in the other guys and their dates.

"Boo?" One man, a guy with large, whitened teeth and curly brown hair, laughed loudly.

"Sorry, baby," Cyn said quickly to Brent, then turned to the table. "I forgot." She leaned over, showing her cleavage, and said, conspiratorially, "He hates it when I call him that in public. But you guys aren't public, are you?"

"Not at all," the same man said with a leer. "Actually we'd be happy to become much more 'private.'" Tay saw him wince. From the look on his face and the glare from the woman sitting beside him, his lady must have squished the hand she was holding.

The two newcomers settled in the remaining chairs, with Brent on her right. When the waiter arrived, Tay jumped in and said, "A Long Island Iced Tea for each of us." She'd learned that was his favorite drink and a little verisimilitude always helped.

The eight people made insipid conversation, about nothing more substantive than TV shows, movies and the baseball standings. These people weren't her type, Tay thought. Lightweights. She hadn't realized how used she'd become to spirited, intelligent conversation. At one point she asked, "Do you all work with Boo?"

The men all nodded. "And you?" a guy she'd learned was named Pete asked. He was sitting on her left and kept moving his chair closer to hers.

"She works in a doctor's office," Brent said.

"Actually it's a large medical practice with more than a dozen doctors."

"That sounds like a lot of work," Pete said.

She learned that two of the other women worked in the garment industry and the third was a secretary to a company treasurer. "How nice," Tay said brightly.

"How did you and"—Pete raised his eyebrows—"Boo meet?"

They hadn't covered that question and Brent squeezed her hand tightly, obviously nervous. Unflapped, Tay looked at her lap. "It was my fault, really. We had a little accident. We were at a local Starbucks near where we live. Did I tell you we live only a few blocks apart? Anyway, I turned and spilled my coffee all over his shirt, and, well, the rest is history."

The group of them continued to chat and dance on the handkerchief-sized dance floor. Although several of the men asked her to dance she staunchly refused, dancing only with Brent. At the beginning of the evening she knew the men in the group suspected that she was a ringer, but as time passed she was pretty sure they believed the stories Brent and Tay told about their relationship.

At about eleven, the music stopped and the master of ceremonies brought out a microphone and tapped on it to get everyone's attention. "Ladies and gentlemen, and whoever else is in the room"—he paused for the resulting titter to subside, then continued—"it's time for the show." He told a few bad jokes, then said, "Now for our performers."

The lights in the room dimmed as the stage lights brightened. Curtains parted to reveal a small stage, and two scantily dressed, silicone-enhanced women began an undulating dance. "Why can't you do that for me once in a while?" a guy named Manny hissed to his date, a woman named Darla. She merely glared at him.

Two muscular men with washboard abs and well-developed arms and shoulders, wearing just pouches to cover their obviously large packages, joined them. "And why don't you look like that?" Darla asked, loudly enough for the entire table to hear, and laughter erupted from everyone.

The action on the stage had gotten seductive, with the men trying to entice the women into removing their tops. After much hooting and whistling from the audience, the women pulled off their bras, leaving their large breasts poking out for all to see. The men got on their knees and nuzzled their tits and bellies as they danced. Sweat began to form on the tanned skin of the dancers.

Tay had had little to drink beyond the beer she'd consumed at the club. She'd been pouring bits of her alcohol into Brent's glass when no one was looking. She knew she needed a clear head to take advantage of whatever presented itself, any opportunity to give Brent's reputation a boost, but she wanted him a little looser. Brent was definitely getting a little buzzed.

She reached over and insinuated her hand into his crotch and found his cock semierect. He really was large, she realized. He glanced at her as he felt her fondle him and she whispered "Trust me" so only he could hear. He nodded and returned his gaze to the stage.

"Something going on over there?" Pete asked.

"None of your snoopy snoot," Tay said, not stopping her manipulation of Brent's cock.

As the action on the stage got raunchier, with hands roaming everywhere, Tay felt Brent's rather large cock grow beneath her fingers. With no warning, Tay slipped from her chair and knelt between Brent's legs. He was obviously too shocked to move, but as she unzipped his fly, Pete grabbed her shoulder. "Cut that out."

"Why? Boo needs a little tender loving care."

The MC of the show, who had been standing at the side of the stage, moved to the table. "Hey, you two, want to entertain us all?"

"Us?" Brent asked, looking like a deer in the headlights.

Tay knew this was her chance. "My Boo's a little shy," she said.

"That's not a problem," the MC said. "We love to have amateurs perform for us."

Tay looked up. "Really? Do you think people would like to see us?" She indicated her small breasts. "I'm obviously not built like your lovely ladies."

"We'd love to see what you two have got."

Tay looked up at Brent. "Come on, Boo, we'll have a little fun."

The MC clicked on his microphone. "Ladies and gentlemen," he said, and the people on stage stopped their playing, "we have another couple who would love to join our show." The reaction of the four performers was so automatic that Tay reasoned this happened frequently. They said, in unison, to the audience, "Let's give them a big hand."

There was much applause, especially from the three couples at their table. "Come on, Boo." "Go get 'em, Boo." "Is this our Brent?"

Again, Tay asked Brent to trust her and he slowly stood up. She was taking advantage of his inebriation. She knew that, if he hadn't been a little drunk, he never would have agreed. She pulled his shirt off over his head and then removed hers. She was wearing a tiny black lace push-up bra with tiny pink bows at the front of each cup. Brent had a hairy chest and a belly. Holding hands they made their way onto the stage.

"Hi," she said into the microphone the MC held. "He's Boo and I'm Cyn."

"Oh, I love sin," he said.

"It's short for Cindy," she giggled, "but we love that kind of sin, too."

"Well," the MC said, "let's see what you two can show us."

Brent stood frozen. "Come on, Boo, wiggle your hips for everyone," she said as she danced around him, rubbing her body against his. She grabbed his hips and moved them against her groin, rubbing his bulge against her pubic bone.

Slowly he began to move just a bit. "That's my Boo." Then she knelt and unbuckled his belt, pulling it off through the loops and tossing it on their table.

"I don't know about this," he said, his voice a little shaky.

"I do, Boo, baby," she said, knowing she could be heard throughout the room. "Come on, let's show them how it's done." His jeans were already unzipped so when she unbuttoned the waist it took only a little tug to pull them down. His groin was still covered by the fabric of his white briefs, but it was all too obvious that he was well endowed.

She deftly removed his shoes and threw his jeans to the guys at the table, who sat, staring in rapt attention. Then, with Brent standing, shuffling his feet, she began to strip. She took the mike from the MC. "Although I haven't got too much up here," she said to the audience, cupping her small breasts, "my Boo loves it when I dance for him. Is that okay with you folks out there?"

Cheers and applause answered her question. Then she

began to undulate around the stage with Brent following each move with his eyes. Soon her skirt had joined his jeans on the table. The matching lace panties also had a bright pink bow, right over her pubic hair. Her hands roamed both her body and his. Then she unclasped her bra and tossed it to Pete.

Louder applause filled the room and soon her panties joined the rest of their clothing. Now she wore only her thigh-high black stockings and black heels. She sidled over to Brent and pulled down his briefs, revealing his prodigious, fully erect cock. She took a quick glance at their table and saw that his buddies and their dates sat with their mouths agape. "Would someone hand me a chair?" she said to the guys at the table.

They lifted a chair to the stage and she pushed Brent into it so he sat with his erection sticking straight upward from his crotch. "I don't play without protection," she said into the mike. "Anyone able to help?"

As she'd expected she was pelted with condoms. "Oooh," she said as she picked up a black and gold foil packet, "this is my favorite." She'd seen enough types of condoms in her time to know this one. She tore open the foil and pulled out the black latex. "Really sexy." She slowly unrolled it over Brent's dick as he sat totally immobile.

She straddled him and arched her back until one nipple was almost in his mouth. As she'd anticipated, he took it into his mouth. She let her head fall backward and lowered her body onto him. Then she levered herself up and down until she knew he was ready to climax. She looked at him and clenched her vaginal muscles. Then she quickly rose and pulled off the condom so the entire audience was treated to the sight of semen spurting from his cock. Then she thrust her pubis into his face, took his hand and rubbed her pussy with it and feigned her own climax.

With exaggerated panting, she sank onto the floor beside Brent's chair.

"Let's thank our amateurs of the evening with lots of applause," the MC said and again the room was filled with the sounds of whistles, hoots and clapping.

Tay took Brent's hand, led him down to the table and pulled on her panties. Almost in a trance, Brent dressed, and when they were both clothed, Tay said, "I'm going to take Boo home. I hope you don't mind, but I didn't really get enough up there so I'm eager to get back to bed."

Without another word from anyone, they left. She knew his address, so she hailed a taxi and they drove to his building. By the time the cab was fully under way, he seemed more aware. "I don't believe I did that," he said, looking both bemused and delighted. "I don't believe it."

A grin covered Tay's face. "Yeah, it was very out-there, but you did. I got a little carried away with the dumb-date routine, but I think they bought it. Your buddies won't ever forget it. Oh, and in a few weeks you'd better tell them we had a big fight and broke up. That way they won't wonder why you never bring me to any future gatherings."

"That should do it." He leaned over and kissed her. "You're a genius. I can't believe what happened."

"It all worked out. Now you've got the reputation you wanted. I hope it turns out well for you."

"Me too. What's your real name?" he asked.

"Tay."

"Thanks. I want to remember you as Tay, not Cyn." The taxi pulled to the curb and Brent climbed out and paid the driver to take her to the club, where she'd spend the night. "Good night, Tay."

"Good night, Brent. I hope you had as much fun as I did."

"Oh, you can bet on that."

Chapter 27

Lissa and Dave arrived back on Maple Court the following Tuesday afternoon just as they'd left: with little in the way of real luggage but a dozen camera cases and two laptop computers. Tay remembered the look of Lissa's new, crisp bags when they left. Now everything looked like it had been dragged all over China behind a Jeep.

Dave said all the right things to Tay, thanking her for doing such a great job keeping the house, grounds and animals in tip-top shape. He and Lissa had purchased several gifts for Tay, including several pieces of native clothing, a hand-carved wooden statuette of a local god and a beautifully intricate bracelet, necklace and earring set. After half an hour of storytelling, Dave disappeared to work on his computer. Lissa, on the other hand, spent several hours regaling her friend with more tales of her adventures in "the wilds," as she called it.

"And the best news of all," she burbled, "is that I got a certificate of merit for the video clip I sent to that contest I told you about." They discussed the prestige of the magazine, one Tay had never heard of. When Tay nodded, something she'd done a lot of in the past hour, Lissa continued, "Imagine. Me. A certificate of merit."

"I'm delighted for you," Tay said with genuine appreciation. "That's really fabulous."

When Lissa finally wound down and had patted and caressed each of her animals, she said, "You've been a gem here, Tay. I'm so glad you came. I hope you weren't too bored."

Bored. What a joke. "Not at all. I had a great time."

"From your e-mails I gather you got to be friends with our neighbor. What's Pam like?"

What to say? "She's a wonderful woman and her boyfriend, Linc, is quite a hunk."

"She does some kind of party planning. You never told me in your e-mails. Did you get to go to any? Did you see anyone famous?"

Tay told Lissa about a few parties, leaving out any sexual details, and about several famous faces she'd encountered. She figured she'd eventually have to tell her something more, but how much? The opportunity presented itself a few minutes later. "Did you meet any guys while you were here? I hope you found someone to push Steve completely out of your brain. Justin?"

"Justin's a bit of a prig," she said. "Very straightlaced."

"Funny, he didn't seem that way to me. Was it a problem?"

Tay took a deep breath. If she didn't tell her friend, Justin probably would. "It was. You see, he found out that I'd taken on a second job."

"Right. You wrote that you were cutting back your days at work. Is that why?"

"Yeah."

"So what else are you doing?"

Another deep breath. "I've become a courtesan."

"A what?"

"I entertain men. For money."

Lissa had been pacing across the living room but now

dropped into a chair, hand theatrically over her heart. "You're shitting me."

What the hell. "No. I'm not."

"Okay, best friend, tell me everything."

"I will, but I want you to continue to be my friend. No snap judgments. No recriminations. Just listen."

Eyes wide, she said, "Tay, you know I love you like a sister. Now give!"

It took half an hour to tell the entire story. Tay withheld nothing, except Pam's part in it, the name of the club and the identity of any of her clients. She told Lissa that she'd met Marcy through someone she'd met at one of Pam's parties and let it go at that.

"Holy shit. I don't believe it. A courtesan. You make it all sound so logical."

"It really is just that. Logical and more damn fun than I could have imagined."

Over the next hour Lissa asked all the same questions Tay had asked Pam when she first learned about the business, and Tay answered them in the same way.

"Wow! No wonder you needed the privacy of the guesthouse. Are you going to do any stuff there?"

Tay looked horrified. "Of course not, and I haven't done anything here, either. I would never compromise your home or your privacy."

"Sorry, that was thoughtless of me. Of course you wouldn't. Wow. A high-class call girl, like the ones I read about occasionally in the papers. How the hell about that. Tay, do you think they might need anyone else to do that? I could use the money and I'm pretty good in bed. God, I think I'd love that."

Tay joined her friend's laughter. Lissa was Lissa and thankfully everything was great. She had told her about Marcy's pregnancy and told her friend that she'd introduce them after the baby was born. The two women could decide where to go from there. The conversation couldn't have gone any better.

In early October, with the help of Marcy and Zack, Tay found the perfect apartment. It was a one-year furnished sublet in a rent-controlled building on West End Avenue, with two bedrooms, a tiny kitchen and a living room with a fifty-inch plasma TV Tay thought she'd never watch. However, one evening, very bored, she discovered the joy of both the History Channel and History International on the gigantic screen.

Her new apartment was a quick cab ride to the brownstone, where she found she was working two or three evenings a week, and a short subway trip to her day job. Marcy had shown her the club's computer system, and although Marcy was still able to input data, Tay found she was taking over more and more as Marcy got bigger and bigger. She'd joined Marcy on a few interviews with perspective clients and now she'd actually done a few herself. She had a knack for helping a dreamer realize his deepest desires.

Just after Halloween, Pam came down to the city and asked both Marcy and Tay to meet her for a very late lunch. They gathered at a small business-lunch spot with a wonderful assortment of thick sandwiches and daily specials with homemade pies for dessert.

After the women ordered and caught up on Marcy's pregnancy and Tay's adventures at the club, Tay asked, "What's new with you, Pam?"

She looked uncharacteristically reticent to speak. Finally she said, "I do have a little news. Linc asked me to marry him again, and this time I said yes."

Girlish squeals attracted the attention and glares of business diners in their vicinity, but the women ignored everyone else and hugged. "That's so great," Tay said. "I'm so happy for both of you. I knew it would happen eventually."

"We knew you would do it. Congratulations, and we can decide on the details of the shower later," Marcy continued, trying to sit back down gracefully.

"We're both delighted," Pam said, "and I want to ask you two to be my bridesmaids. Oh, and you get to pick the dresses. The wedding will be during the week right after Christmas, so, Marcy, you'll be able to wear real clothes. No matching ugly dresses that you'll never wear again, I promise."

Tay felt tears spring into her eyes. "God, I'm so happy."

"Me too," Marcy said, also tearing up. "Oh God. Real clothes. I don't know which makes me happier. You getting married or me in real clothes." She looked down at her huge forest green maternity shirt.

"There's more," Pam said.

"What more could there be?" Tay asked.

"Well, Marcy, save some of those clothes for me."

"You're"— Marcy sputtered—"pregnant?"

Pam actually blushed. "It seems I am."

"I thought . . ." This time it was Tay's turn to struggle for words.

"So did I," Pam said. "I was sure I couldn't have kids, and I haven't conceived in all these years."

She sipped her herbal tea and continued, "So I missed a period, but I've never been particularly regular, so I ignored it and the nausea I felt occasionally. But when Linc asked me again to marry him I burst into tears. That just isn't me. I'd decided to say yes, but I wondered at the totally overwhelming emotions. I don't live in a vacuum, so I got suspicious and I got one of those kits. I didn't really think that the results would be positive, but I'll be honest and say that

I hoped a little. Needless to say, I didn't tell anyone. Well, one pee and I knew. I'm almost forty, so I found a doctor who specializes in later-in-life pregnancies."

"Didn't your husband tell you that the tests proved you couldn't have kids?" Marcy asked.

"He did. I asked the doctor about it and he said that the test could have been wrong, or Vin could have lied to me. It might have been his sperm that was the problem all along. He wouldn't have enjoyed owning up to that."

"I hate to be a wet blanket, but are you sure it's Linc's?" Marcy asked, her voice low.

"Thankfully, yes. I've used protection with all my clients and I haven't gotten pregnant up to now. I counted back and I wasn't with anyone but Linc in the month before and the one after the date the doctor says I conceived. Needless to say, Linc and I haven't used protection since soon after we met. I didn't think we had to."

"Oh my God," Tay said, all but bouncing in her chair, "you're going to have a baby. " She looked at Marcy's belly. "And you're almost due." She crossed all her fingers on the table. "I hope to hell it isn't catching. I've got everything crossed." She crossed her eyes. "And I mean everything."

The three women cracked up. "Just wait, Tay, your time will come," Pam said. "Eventually. Marcy and I will save the fat-lady clothes for that moment, and we'll all have another good cry."

"What does Linc have to say?" Marcy asked.

Pam sobered and let out a long breath. "One of the reasons I've been reluctant to marry him is that I knew he wanted kids and I thought I couldn't give them to him. Needless to say, he's blissful."

"Holy shit," Tay said, still breathless. "I'm almost as flabbergasted as you must have been."

"Are you sure you want to wait to get married if you're pregnant?" Marcy asked.

"Very sure. We've been together all this time, and we've no qualms about letting folks know we're going to have a baby. Catch that 'we' part? Anyway, there are a few good reasons to wait.

"First, I'm having some problems with really bad morning sickness."

"Ah, so that's why you made this lunch so late," Tay said.

"Right. Afternoons seem to be okay. Anyway, my doctor tells me that there's a good chance that will be gone by Christmas. I really don't want to throw up on my wedding guests. Second, the idea that you'll have had your baby, Marcy, is an incentive, too. I want you to bring the new baby and the other kids, too. They'll be off from school, which is another reason for picking that week. And Zack will be there, of course, and Rock. Tay, I'd like to invite Lissa and Dave, too. God, there's so much to plan. I'll have to make lists of everything."

"Pam, you're a professional party planner. You could do this with both hands tied behind your back," Marcy said.

"I know, and you're right. Anyway, I won't have to decorate if we have the wedding Christmas week. We want to be married on Maple Court and the house will look sensational with all the Christmas stuff around."

With that, Pam burst into tears. Marcy found a pack of tissues in her purse, passed one to Pam and pulled out one for herself. Tay extended a hand, and Marcy put a third tissue into it. For several minutes there was much eye mopping and watery grinning.

Tay thought about the two couples, Marcy and Zack and Pam and Linc. Did she regret that she didn't have a full-time significant other? She had lots of friends; the two best ones were seated at the table with her, and Lissa wasn't far away. Several of her friends were male, like Rock, but there was no love interest. Not yet. Eventually. Maybe. But right now she was so happy with her life that she didn't need any other relationship to make her feel whole. She and Rock got together from time to time and kept exploring new and intriguing avenues of sensuality.

Thanks to fate, or whatever, she was a lucky woman. What lucky women they all were, each in her own way. She lifted her water glass. "Here's to us, three happy women who have what they want and are lucky enough to know it."

"Bravo," Marcy said, touching the rim of her glass to Tay's.

"Hear, hear," Pam said, adding her glass.

A week later, Tay met with a new client, a man named Mark. "I'm not sure I want to talk about this to you. Sorry, no offense."

"None taken," she said.

"Maybe a man might understand a little better than a woman," he said.

"There aren't many fantasies I haven't heard about, and for most the club has proven the ideal spot for realization."

"Really?"

"I've talked to foot fetishists who wanted nothing more than to polish a woman's toes, a man who wanted to eat oysters from his lady's body, a man who wanted to watch his lady pee and more than a few who want to taste the exotic world of whips and such. Those are really scary and I'm difficult to shock. Please, relax and take your time. Then let's see what the club can help you enjoy."

"Well, if you really think it's okay. . . ."

Dear Reader,

I know you've enjoyed your visit to the world of Club Fantasy and Maple Court. When I finish writing a novel, I miss my characters—like Pam and Marcy—who appear in some of my previous books. I will also miss Tay, a newcomer to this world. You never know what future books they might appear in.

Many of you have read my previous books, but if you haven't, let me list all the books in the series, in the order I wrote them: *The Price of Pleasure*, *Night After Night*, *Club Fantasy*, *Hot Summer Nights*, and *The Madam of Maple Court*. I've written freestanding erotic novels as well. You will enjoy *Never Enough* and *The Secret Lives of Housewives*.

When I first started writing erotic novels I wrote six of them for another publisher. Kensington has rereleased them in 2-for-1 volumes. *Made for Sex* contains *Black Satin* and *The Love Flower*; *Take Me to Bed* is made up of *The Pleasures of Jessica Lynn* and *Velvet Whispers*. The third, as yet untitled, has *Slow Dancing* and *Midnight Butterfly* and is due out in November. Phew, a collection that will give you many hours of delicious fun. And that list doesn't include my short stories and nonfiction. For more information check my Web site at *www.joanelloyd.com*.

Please drop me a note at *joan@joanelloyd.com* and let me know how you liked this volume and which character you'd like me to bring back. I make no guarantees, but you never know.